"A deep, passionate romance that transcends time and age. Readers will appreciate this highly intense coming-of-age story that shows how much some are willing to risk for love. *One Step to You* has been aptly compared to the novels of Nicholas Sparks and John Green and will appeal to readers of those highly emotional tales."
　　　　—*Booklist*, starred review, on *One Step to You*

"Capture[s] the turbulent passion of teen love."
　　　　—*Publishers Weekly* on *One Step to You*

"Federico Moccia has touched the romantic heart of a whole generation."　　　—*Il Giornale* (Italian newspaper)

"Federico Moccia is the romance king of the Mediterranean bestseller."　　　　—*Woman* (Spain)

"Federico Moccia knows how to get straight to the heart of all young readers. His words always hit the right spot."
　　　　—*TTL* (Italian newspaper)

"With his novels, the writer Federico Moccia has revolutionized young people."　　　—*Glamour*

three times you

three
times
you

FEDERICO MOCCIA

TRANSLATED BY ANTONY SHUGAAR

GRAND CENTRAL

New York Boston

Copyright © 2017 by Federico Moccia
By agreement with Pontas Literary & Film Agency.

Cover design by Kathleen Lynch/Black Kat Design
Cover photos of couple on bridge from Getty images and sky from Shutterstock
Cover copyright © 2023 by Hachette Book Group, Inc.

Grand Central Publishing
Hachette Book Group
1290 Avenue of the Americas, New York, NY 10104
grandcentralpublishing.com
twitter.com/grandcentralpub

Originally published in 2017 as -Tre Volte Te by Nord in Italy
First U.S. Edition: June 2023

Grand Central Publishing is a division of Hachette Book Group, Inc. The Grand Central Publishing name and logo is a trademark of Hachette Book Group, Inc.

The publisher is not responsible for websites (or their content) that are not owned by the publisher.

Grand Central Publishing books may be purchased in bulk for business, educational, or promotional use. For information, please contact your local bookseller or the Hachette Book Group Special Markets Department at special.markets@hbgusa.com.

Library of Congress Cataloging-in-Publication Data
Names: Moccia, Federico, author. | Shugaar, Antony, translator.
Title: Three times you / Federico Moccia ; translated by Antony Shugaar. Other titles: Tre volte te. English
Description: First edition. | New York : GCP, 2023. | Series: The Rome novels ; 3
Identifiers: LCCN 2022057933 | ISBN 9781538732830 (trade paperback) | ISBN 9781538732816 (ebook)
Subjects: LCGFT: Romance fiction. | Novels.
Classification: LCC PQ4913.O23 T7513 2023 | DDC 853/.92—dc23/eng/20221213
LC record available at https://lccn.loc.gov/2022057933

ISBN: 9781538732830 (trade paperback), 9781538732816 (ebook)

Printed in the United States of America

LSC-C

Printing 1, 2023

*To my son, the friend of my heart, who
every day gives me all the memories I
could no longer recall for myself.*

*To my daughter, so very beautiful,
who makes me laugh with delight.*

three times you

Love is when the other person's happiness
is more important than your own.

H. Jackson Brown Jr.

Chapter 1

I am hopelessly in love with Hope. The understated graffiti gleams in all its tough disenchantment on a slat in the gate. I smile to myself, thinking that maybe Hope had given him some reason for hope, but I have no way of knowing whether or not that's true so, with my heart in my mouth, I walk into the villa.

I walk in silence until I reach that room, and looking out of that window, I take in the sight of the sea. It all belongs to me now, the terrace that gently drops down to the rocky shore, the outdoor showers with their yellow and blue tiles featuring hand-painted lemons, the marble table by the large window looking out onto the horizon. The sun is setting—exactly like that day nine years ago.

"Are you changing your mind? If you don't want the place anymore, you'll have to pay double the deposit in indemnity. Or else trigger a lawsuit I won't live to see the end of."

I glance at him, amused. This spry old gent has a young man's energy.

He frowns and coughs. "But you want this house, don't you?"

I sit down next to him and start signing the pages without so much as a glance. My lawyers checked them all.

"So you're buying the house, right?"

"Absolutely, it's exactly what I want..."

The old man collects the documents and hands them to his assistant.

"Let me tell you the truth, youngster. I'd have taken a smaller offer."

"And let me tell you the truth, sir. I'd have been willing to pay twice as much."

"I don't believe that. You're just trying to get my goat."

"That's as may be." I smile at him.

At last, the owner stands up, walks over to an antique wooden cabinet, and opens the door. Inside is a fridge, and he pulls out a bottle of champagne. He pops the cork with genuine delight and fills two flutes with ice-cold bubbly.

The owner raises his glass in my direction. "I told my lawyer we could have asked for more..."

I shrug and say nothing. Especially about the ten thousand euros that I slipped his lawyer to help grease the wheels.

I sense his eyes focusing on me in concern. I wonder what he's thinking. He shakes his head with a smile. "I hope you'll be happy here. Let's drink to that." And he raises his glass and drains it in a single gulp.

"Tell me something though. How did you manage to get your offer in the second I put it up for sale?"

"Do you know Vinicio Foods, the grocery store at the bottom of the hill?"

"Of course."

"Well, let's just say I've known the owner for years."

"So you were looking for a house around here?"

"No, I was waiting to find out when you'd be ready to sell yours."

"Just this house? No other house would do?"

"That's right. I was determined to make this villa mine."

And in a flash, I am hurtled back in time.

⌒

Babi and I were in love. I still remember that day. *She was on a field trip, and I pulled up on my motorcycle. She walked over, lighting up all my shadows with her smile. I blindfolded her with the dark blue bandanna I'd stolen from her, and she climbed on the motorcycle behind me, holding tight. We rode up the Via Aurelia all the way to Feniglia. The silvery sea, the yellow broom plants, the dark green bushes, and then that villa overlooking the rocks. I pulled over and turned off my motorcycle. We got off, and in a flash, I found a way in. There we were, walking through Babi's dream house.*

I pinch myself because it seems so incredible, as if I were back there right now, holding her hand as she stands, still blindfolded in the silence of that day, at sunset, as we listen to the regular breathing of the sea below and our words echo through those empty rooms.

"Step? Where are you? Don't leave me here alone! I'm afraid..." I took her hands, and she jerked in surprise.

"It's only me."

She recognized me and relaxed, smiling again. "The crazy thing is that, when I'm with you, I'd let you do anything."

"That sounds good!"

"Idiot!" She flailed out blindly but finally made contact with my shoulder and let loose with a good hard punch.

"Ouch! You pack a mean set of knuckles!"

"Serves you right! All I meant is that it's crazy to think I'm here. We broke a window to get in, and I didn't say a thing. Obviously, I trust you."

"Isn't that a wonderful thing? To put yourself into someone else's hands, ignore your doubts? I think it's the finest thing on earth."

"What about you? Do you trust me?"

For a moment, I said nothing, gazing at her face, half-hidden behind that bandanna. Then I watched as she drew herself erect, perhaps disappointed at my silence. Strong, in-dependent, alone.

So I made up my mind to open my heart to her. "Yes, it's the same for me. I've given myself to you, body and soul.

"And it's a beautiful thing."

⌒

"So, may I ask? What are you thinking about? Come back to earth. Cheer up. After all, you just bought the house you wanted, didn't you?"

"You're right. I was just falling back in time. I was thinking about the things you say when you're swept away by emotion. It's crazy, but I feel as if I've been here before, lived this moment at some previous time. Absurd, I know."

"Oh, sure, a déjà vu! The same thing happens to me."

He locks arms with me and leads me to the window.

"Just look at how beautiful the sea is from up here."

I breathe a tentative "yes," even as a wave of sickly sweet scent washes over me from his weirdly puffy, teased-out hair. Is this what I'll look like someday? Will I have that uncertain, hesitant gait? Will my hand tremble as I gesture, like his does now, as he prepares to impart who knows what mysterious information?

"So, let me tell you. You've already purchased the villa, but you might as well know. You see these steps that lead down to the water?"

"Yes."

"Well, a long time ago, intruders came up that way. They can arrive by boat, so you'll need to be careful if you come and live here," he says, with the cunning of someone who's knowingly kept his lips zipped until it's too late.

"Who came up the steps?"

"I think a couple of young people, or maybe a whole gang. They broke a window, walked all around the house, broke whatever they felt like, and even defiled my bed. Bloodstains on my sheets. Either an animal sacrifice or the girl was a virgin!"

He snickers as he says it, choking as he laughs too hard.

"I found wet bathrobes, so they had their fun. They even stole a bottle of champagne I left in the fridge. But worst of all, they stole my jewelry, fine silver, and other precious possessions worth fifty thousand euros...Luckily, I was insured!" He glares at me, proud of this string of astonishing facts.

"Well, Signor Marinelli, you might have spared me that information. It might have been better."

"Why? Are you afraid now?"

"No, but now I know you're a liar. They didn't come up

the steps, they brought their own champagne, they stole absolutely nothing, and the only thing they broke was that window right there..." I point. "By the door."

"How dare you? Who do you think you are?"

"Me? No one, just a boy in love. I entered this house, more than nine years ago, I drank some of my own champagne, and I made love with my girlfriend. But I'm no thief, and I stole nothing from you. Oh, well, I did borrow two bathrobes..."

I remember how Babi and I played at dreaming up names to match the initials embroidered on those bathrobes, an *A* and an *S*. After running through a list of weird names, we opted for Amaryllis and Siegfried and left them lying on the rocks.

"Ah...so you know the truth, do you?"

"Yes, but you and I are the only ones who know it. And you've already sold me the house."

Chapter 2

An anything but ordinary day, not long ago.

My secretary Giuliana follows me, as always, with the desk diary she uses to make notes of all our important appointments and deadlines.

"Let me remind you that you have an appointment in Prati, at the Network, to close the deal on your program, and then lunch with De Girolami."

Seeing my puzzled expression, she helpfully adds, "The writer who works for Greek television."

"Oh, right. Cancel it, please. We've got a better offer from a Polish network."

"What should I say? He's sure to ask."

"Don't say anything." I wait for her to move to the next item.

"So, we're done with lunch. What else for today?"

"Well, an appointment at Dear studios. Then at six p.m., you're supposed to go to this art opening. It must be important because you told me to make sure you didn't miss it." Giuliana hands me the invitation, and I turn it over in my hands. *Balthus at Villa Medici.*

"Who sent this invitation?"

"It was delivered by hand, addressed to you."

Typical art event meant for business networking. I draw a blank.

"I told you it was important? You're certain?"

"Absolutely. I asked if I should make a note, and you said, 'Yes, I can't miss it.'"

I slip the invitation into my pocket and grab the black briefcase with my various format presentations for the Network meeting. "If you need anything, call my cell phone."

Chapter 3

Villa Medici is imposing, elegantly and geometrically spare and beautiful, with its lovely Room of Birds and its enchanting, diamond-shaped gardens. Well-tended hedges guide my footsteps until I reach the front gate, where a hostess smiles and takes my ticket. I follow the line of well-dressed people down the red carpet, the soft music coming from first-rate speakers hidden in the greenery. Soon we're inside, admiring the paintings. The first one is dated 1955: *Nude Before a Mirror*. Below that, the lender: *Pierre Matisse Gallery*. Then the artist's name: *Balthasar Klossowski de Rola, French painter, Polish born. Working as Balthus.* I wander over to the window and gaze out at the dome of St. Peter's Basilica. From behind, I hear someone say my name.

"Step...?"

That voice suddenly transforms everything that surrounds me, pulverizes my every iota of certainty, erases any and all thoughts. My mind is empty.

"Step?"

I must be dreaming.

"Step? Isn't that you?"

So I wasn't dreaming after all.

Chapter 4

Babi is behind me, waiting patiently, fingers knit around the handle of her Michael Kors purse, resting gently against her stomach. Her hair is shorter than in my faded memories, although her blue eyes are as intense as ever, her smile as lovely as it had always been. There we stand, in silence, staring at each other in this Medici villa. Behind me stretches out the immense panorama of all the roofs of Rome, and in front of me, Babi, bathed in the red sunlight I see reflected in her eyes and splashed across the vintage sideboard behind her. We're alone in this room, with no one to interrupt this magical, special, unique moment.

How many years have passed since the last time we saw each other? Five? Six? Yes, maybe six. She's beautiful, terribly, terribly beautiful, I'm afraid. Then Babi makes a strange face, tilts her head to one side, and smiles with that pout all her own, the pout that won my heart.

"You know that you look even better? You men, I swear, it's not fair—you get better as you get older, the opposite of what happens to us women."

She smiles. Her voice is different. She's a woman now,

slender, her hair darker, her makeup restrained. She's even prettier. But I keep that to myself.

She's still looking at me. Delightedly, she drops her Michael Kors bag and throws her arms around me, leaning in and resting her head on my chest.

"I'm so happy to see you again!"

At those words, I take her in my arms.

Chapter 5

Now Babi and I are strolling through a perfectly mani-
cured garden. The sun peeks down over the far-flung
roofs. The air is still. It's May 4, and it's already hot out.
We're sitting across from each other at a table. We've just
placed our orders. Yes, something to drink, perhaps a bite
to eat. I don't remember what, maybe a cold cappuccino
for me.

She takes a sip of her Crodino and eats a potato
chip and wipes her mouth. There was a chill in the
air, even six years later, about her decision to move on
without me.

"Step?"

She's looking at me, seeking my approval, trying to
come to terms, perhaps angling for me to forgive her in
a way. Yes, she's in search of clemency, but I don't know
what to say to her.

So she lays her hand on mine again and smiles. "I know
what you're thinking, I know why you're mad..."

I'm tempted to tell her that she doesn't know a thing.
She strokes my hand and goes on staring at me, and her
eyes start to glisten, as if she is on the verge of tears,

and her lower lip begins to quiver. She's either become a talented actress over the years or she really is struggling with controlling her emotions. What can this be about though? Has she found out about me and Gin? So what if she has? I have nothing to hide. Then the expression on her face snaps back into shape, her eyes open wide as if to make me laugh, and then, suddenly cheerful, she exclaims: "I brought you a gift!"

She digs in her purse and pulls out a dark blue gift wrapped package with a sky-blue bow. She knows my tastes so, of course, there's a card. It's fastened to the bow with a length of twine, sealed in place with a slug of wax. I look at it and, I admit, I'm stunned and confused. I start to open it, but she slips it swiftly out of my hands.

"No! Wait…"

I glance at her, baffled. "What's wrong?"

"There's something else you have to see first or else you won't understand."

"In fact, I can promise you that I don't understand…"

"Just a second, you'll understand and then it will all be so much simpler."

Then she exclaims: "There he is!" And her face lights up. She raises her hand high and waves, shouting in delight: "I'm right here! Right here!"

Now I see a little boy running right toward us, and a woman dressed in white is standing in the distance, holding a small bicycle. Babi throws her arms wide, and he leaps into her lap, knocking her back in her chair.

They hug lovingly. Babi's eyes seek out mine through

the boy's tousled hair, and she nods, as if trying to tell me something. Suddenly, the boy pulls away from Babi.

"I'm a champion, Mamma! Right? Aren't I a champion?"

"Yes, sweetheart. Can I introduce you to my friend? His name is Stefano, but everyone calls him Step."

The little boy turns and sees me. Then he hesitates, unsure about what to do next. But he quickly smiles. "Can I call you Step too?"

"Sure." I smile at him.

"Then I'll call you Step! I like that name. It reminds me of Stitch!" And he runs away. He's a good-looking boy. His lips are full, his teeth are straight and white, and his eyes are dark. He has a striped T-shirt, white, dark blue, and light blue. "He's a beautiful boy."

"Yes, thanks. He is."

Babi watches as the boy reaches his nanny, takes his bicycle, climbs onto it, tries to pedal and, finally, succeeds. He rides a certain distance without falling.

"Bravo!" Babi claps her hands.

She's filled with delight at his achievement. Then she turns and hands me my gift.

"Here. Now you can open it."

So I unwrap it. I find a T-shirt, XL, which is my size, with a white collar. I take another look. I can't believe my eyes. It's striped—white, dark blue, and light blue—identical to the one her little boy is wearing. I look up and meet her gaze, level and serious now.

"Yes. That's right. And maybe that's why I've never really missed you." Suddenly, I'm having trouble breathing, and my head is spinning. I stand there, my jaw hanging open, stunned, excited, surprised, angry, confused, and, yes, at a loss.

Then Babi touches my hand again. "Aren't you going to say anything? Don't you think your son is handsome and wonderful?"

Chapter 6

A lightning bolt has split my life in two. I have a son.
And to think that it's exactly what I've always longed for.
To have an unshakable bond with a woman, not a promise
of love or a wedding vow but a living, breathing child.
The union of two people in the form of creation, that almost divine instant that manifests itself in the encounter
between two human beings, in a dizzying mixture that
spins, choosing details, nuances, and pigments, that daubs
at a tiny painting destined to bloom in the future. She
and I. Me and you, Babi. And this child. I try to string
together a few coherent words.

"What did you name him?"

"Massimo. Like a warrior on a prancing steed, even if
he's only managed to ride a bicycle so far. Still, that's a
victory of sorts." She laughs lightly and tosses her hair in
the wind.

And I think back to that party, six years ago, that my
friend Guido took me to. That splendid villa, the cheerful
crowd, the glass of rum—Pampero, the finest. Then another glass, and yet another. The sound of that laughter
in my memory matches up with another peal of laughter

from a nearby room at that long-ago party. No doubt even then: Babi's laughter.

The rest is history.

Babi ... Babi ... Champagne for both of us, on top of the rum. And then we danced, and then she grabbed my hand and pulled me out the door of that villa, across the lawn, down the drive, out the gate, into her car, and out into the night. And we made love as if this were a new beginning, as if nothing could ever change from that day on. Like a message from destiny, a fork in the road.

It started to rain, and she dragged me out of the car, her blouse unbuttoned, because she wanted to make love in the pouring rain. She let the water embrace her, along with my kisses on her rain-drenched nipples. Under her skirt, she was naked, sensuous, daring, and lustful. I let myself go. Babi straddled me, wrapped her arms around me, and I lost all control. She whispered, "Come on, come on, come on." And she pulled away only at the end, when I was already coming. She collapsed on top of me, and as she planted a light kiss on my lips, only then did I sense my guilt. Gin.

And then, back in the car, the first words Babi spoke cut like a knife. "In a few months, I'm getting married." That's what Babi told me, still warm with the heat of the two of us, of my kisses, of our sex, of our sighs.

"In a few months, I'm getting married." Like a song on an endless loop.

"In a few months, I'm getting married."

And it was all over in a flash. There was a knot in my stomach. I could barely breathe.

"In a few months, I'm getting married."

It all ended that night. I felt dirty, stupid, and guilty, so I

*decided to tell Gin the truth. I begged her to forgive me because I
wanted to delete Babi from my life, and also that Step, the one
drunk on rum and her. But can love be forgiven?*

"Are you trying to figure out when it was?" Babi's voice
brings me back to the present.

"There can't be any doubt about it. The last time we
were together. When we met at that party."

She glances at me mischievously. She seems to have
turned back into the girl of six years ago. It almost hurts
to wrench my eyes away from her, but I have to do it.

"I had a lot to drink."

"Yes, that's true. Your kisses were all the more passionate. You were out of control." Then she falls silent.

"It was that night."

She sighs. "So the next day, I had sex with him. It was
a sacrifice, I could still taste you on my skin, but I had
to make it look credible. Afterwards, I wept. I felt empty,
sad, and meaningless."

"So why do you think he's my son?"

But no sooner do I finish that question than I see
him coming toward us on his bike. He's pumping wildly,
standing on the pedals, and he swerves as he brakes, fish-
tailing, but the bike goes over and he manages to land on
both feet. He looks up, slightly embarrassed.

"Mamma, that other boy did it." He turns his head,
gesturing vaguely behind him. Then "Step, will you teach
me?" And with that, he gets back on the bike and rides
off, happily.

Babi watches him go. "How can you even ask if he's
yours? He's like you in every way, every single thing he
does. There's only one thing that's a little different."

As if startled out of a trance, I turn around to look at her, more curious than I've ever been. "What's that?"

"He's better looking!" And she bursts into laughter, delighted to have tricked me, tossing her head back and extending her legs. She's beautiful, just gorgeous, a woman in full, more sensuous but also a mother. Does that make her more desirable?

I think about what she said. "I had to make it look credible…" Those words stir up a sludge of guilt.

Suddenly, Babi stops laughing and lays a hand on my arm. "You were there, every time I held him in my arms. And that's why I didn't really miss you. I had you the whole time."

I'm lost. I was born to be with Babi. It goes beyond mere reason; she's everything I could never understand. And as I watch her leave now, I tell her in my mind, that walk that is all you, and even though it's been six years, I've never forgotten a single detail of that gait. Your back, your hips, your tanned legs, those high-heeled navy-blue shoes that swing with every stride you take. And you don't turn around, but that little boy turns instead, raising his hand and waving goodbye, hurting me more deeply than anything I've felt yet.

Chapter 7

I head back to my car. Stunned on this ordinary day, a day like any other. Out of the blue, my life is changed forever. I have a son. Not some theoretical, future development. No, my son is right there, handsome, smiling, funny, and smart. And suddenly, I'm jealous, more jealous than I've ever been in my life. Jealous of a man I've never met, the father he's always known, even if he's no father of his at all. A father who hugs him, kisses him, whispers fond words, and even yells at him, scolds him, and berates him. Things he has no right to do, things only I should be able to do from now on. How dare he? My thoughts, my imaginings of him scolding *my* son, my recent memory of that boy. It all goes black.

"Would you fucking watch where you're going, asshole!"

I have slammed into some guy walking in the opposite direction. I see his face in front of me, eyes big, hair dark, a beard, a jacket, a grown man, big and strong, with a snarling voice. Instinctively, both my hands lunge for his throat, and I slam him against the wall, throttling him and lifting him until his feet dangle helplessly, unable to touch the ground.

I shove him and choke him and bear down harder, and then I imagine Massimo riding up on his bike and smiling. He shakes his head. *"Step... no, don't. He has nothing to do with this."*

He's right. I realize what's happening. I'm choking the life out of another man. He must be forty or so, his eyes are half-shut, squinting, as if struggling to breathe. I let him go, and he slowly sinks down, hunched over, coughing. And I look down at my hands, red and swollen. I gaze at them in horror as if they were bloodstained, and only then do I realize how my rage has blinded me. I just thought... I thought that this man was hurting my son. My *son*.

Then I turn around, and Massimo is gone. I'm all alone.

I help the man to his feet. "Excuse me..." I don't know what else to say. "I didn't mean to bump into you... I don't know what came over me."

But he looks at me with fear, and I realize the best thing to do is leave without saying anything else. I'd only make things worse.

Chapter 8

I walk into work and go into my private office and shut the door without a word to anyone. I open my navy-blue mini-fridge and pull out a Coke. I tip it up and guzzle it down, thirstily.

Someone knocks at the door, and I swallow the last gulp. I launch the bottle into my trash can, hitting dead center for once.

"Who is it?"

"It's me."

I recognize the voice and its confident assurance. Yes, maybe it will do me good to talk to someone. "Come in."

Giorgio Renzi enters, takes a Coke out of the mini-fridge in his turn, and looks up, asking an entirely rhetorical question: "Mother, may I?"

"Asshole..." I reply.

He smiles, opens the can, and sits down in the large leather armchair next to the window. "Well, that 'asshole' makes me think things aren't all that bad."

I look at Giorgio, and he laughs, confident he knows more about things than anyone else. He's fifteen years older than me. His physique is still youthful, his hair is long, he surfs, kitesurfs, and has a shelfful of trophies, and I've seen him fight. I wouldn't want to take him on. His specialty is money. He knows how to get it, grow it, and pay it back with dividends for both lender and himself. He's the reason I'm sitting in this office.

And I trust him. He's no Pollo, but he makes me feel better when I miss my dead best friend.

"Well? Tell Uncle Giorgio all about it."

"All about what?"

"Whatever it is. You're in here with the door closed, guzzling Coke like you wish it was rum or whiskey."

"Okay."

"Then things aren't right." He crosses his legs and takes a sip.

"I have a son."

He comes close to choking. A drop of Coca-Cola lands on his sweater, and he wipes it off with his sleeve. He leaps to his feet, landing on his powerful legs. "Fuck! That's great news! We need to celebrate! I'm happy for the two of you! It's fantastic. Did Gin just tell you today?"

"I have a son, and he's six years old."

"Ah." He flops back down in the chair. "Right. You *have* a son, you're not *going to have* a son. That's a little complicated. Who's the mother? Anyone I know?"

"Babi."

"Babi? How can that be? You've mentioned her, but I didn't think you were still seeing her. How did it happen? How did you find out?"

"I ran into her yesterday at Villa Medici. By pure chance..." And the instant I say it, everything becomes blindingly clear. "Giuliana..."

"What does Giuliana have to do with it?"

As Giorgio looks puzzled, I lean forward and call her on the intercom.

"Could you come in here for a moment? Thank you."

A few seconds later, there's a knock on the door. "Come in."

Giuliana is dressed professionally and seems calm. She's carrying a folder. "I brought these in. They're checks to deposit for the two new television formats Antonello wrote up on your specifications."

"Okay, thanks, just leave them on my side table. Could you close the door? Thanks."

She turns to go.

"No, no, you stay here. Just shut the door. Are you in a hurry to leave?"

I see her blush, and Giorgio sees it too. His expression changes as if to say, *Whoa, whatever this is, you're clearly right about it.*

"Have a seat. Make yourself comfortable."

Giuliana sits down in the middle of the room, facing my desk. I start pacing, with my back to her. "You never asked me whether I enjoyed the Balthus exhibition..."

"True. But I saw you rush into your office and shut the door. I just thought you wouldn't want to be disturbed."

"Fair enough, but now that you're here, you can inquire." I turn and stare at her.

She looks at me, and then Giorgio, hoping for a lifeline. But none is forthcoming. So she takes a deep breath and speaks. "Did you go to the show? Did you like it?"

I look at her hands, neatly folded in her lap. I look at her neck, and I can almost see her pulse race in a throbbing artery. I smile. "I did, a lot, but I just wonder how much that ticket must have cost."

She looks at me, raises an eyebrow, smiles, and shakes her head in surprise. "Oh, no. The ticket was free. That was an invitation."

Suddenly my voice grows cold and cutting. "I know that. I mean how much it cost that woman to get you to make sure I accepted the invitation."

"No, really..."

I raise my hand to halt her before she says anything more. I say nothing. She's clearly starting to sense the risk I might lose control. I speak quietly, enunciating clearly. "You have one last chance. I'll ask you again. How much did she pay you?"

Then Giorgio speaks, calmly but firmly. "Maybe you should tell him."

Silence falls, heavy and grim. Giuliana toys with her left forefinger, picking nervously at a cuticle. Then she confesses, "She gave me five hundred euros."

I look at Giorgio with a smile and a shrug. I sit down and lay my hands flat on the table. "Five hundred euros. How much do we pay you?"

Giorgio sighs. "Fifteen hundred a week, after taxes."

"So five hundred euros nowadays will buy what thirty pieces of silver used to be worth," I comment sarcastically.

Giuliana looks up, pleadingly.

"Tell me what happened."

Chapter 9

Giuliana is starting to realize that she's wandered into something much bigger than her. "I used to see her every day in the café where I'd go for coffee and a breakfast pastry. She was always there before me. Sitting in a corner with her newspaper, *Repubblica*, I think, but looking as if she had other things on her mind.

"So one morning, I was at the counter ordering my usual whole-grain and honey pastry when I was told they'd run out. So she came over and offered me hers. We sat and ate together, and before long, we were breakfast buddies, I guess you could say."

Giorgio listens intently and then gestures as if to say, *Whoa, buddy, this woman was planning things out.* I have to agree.

"Okay, and what details did you share with this new friend of yours?" I ask. Giuliana sits silently.

I persist. "What did you tell her about me?"

Giuliana looks up and shakes her head. "I didn't tell her anything." But I don't believe her.

"Just get to the point."

She goes on. "She asked the kind of things you'd ask,

where I worked, what I did. Nothing more..." What else was she supposed to ask, I thought to myself, but I refrained from interrupting. "Another time, she told me about the work she did. She said she was an illustrator, and she did children's books. She showed me one of her books. Then she said, 'Maybe they need someone at your company. I could do a really artistic logo.' And then she asked me my boss's name. I told her, that's not a company secret. She was shocked. 'I can't believe it. He's a dear, dear friend.' So I said: 'So much the better! You won't need me to show him your work.'"

I look at Giorgio. Neither of us knows what to say.

"But now she looked sad. I asked why, and she told me the two of you had quarreled, and through no choice of her own, you weren't friends anymore."

I'm more confused than ever, but Giorgio comes to my aid. "And then what, excuse me? She offers you five hundred euros to help her run into Stefano by chance? Help me out here, your story just doesn't add up."

"Well, actually, nothing else happened that day. I didn't see her again for another month or so. One morning, she sat down at my table, where I was already eating. And then something really did happen. As sweet as could be, she said, 'You need to know the truth. Otherwise you can't make up your mind whether or not to help me.'"

Then Giuliana says nothing, as if trying to build up the suspense. "I was uncomfortable, so I went to the restroom. When I got back, there was a folder on the table. I thought it was just more of her work, but I was wrong."

This time, Giuliana has managed to build up tension.

"She says, 'Open it.' So I did, and I saw it was a page from an old copy of the Rome newspaper *Il Messaggero*."

Giorgio cocks an eyebrow in bafflement, but I understand immediately.

"It was a picture of the two of you, on a motorcycle, running from the cops, or at least that's what the caption said. I was stumped. I asked her 'What's this all about?'" Giuliana falls silent, as if reliving that scene.

Giorgio and I lean forward, consumed with curiosity. In unison, without a glance at each other, we both exclaim, "And then what happened?"

"Not a word of explanation. She just looked at me and said, 'I lost my chance at happiness.'"

Chapter 10

The ancient Greeks said that fate is the unexpected bursting in on life, a momentary variable that has the power of a hurricane. In one day, more has happened to me than in the past six years. And that's why the ancient Greeks went to their oracles, to find out how to turn destiny into character.

Luckily, I have Giorgio to take the situation in hand, even if he's not exactly the Delphic oracle. "Okay, give us the room, please."

Giuliana stands up and walks to the door. Before leaving, she turns and glances at me. "I don't know, something about what she said really hit me. I thought she might be telling the truth. Yes, in a certain sense, I did it for her happiness," she says with a faint smile, as if she knows she really put her foot in it this time. Then she turns and leaves, shutting the door behind her.

Giorgio stands up, walks over to the fridge, and opens it. He looks inside. "You know, I'd restock the fridge. No more Coca-Cola and green tea. Just beer, vodka, and rum. Strong drink, in other words. I mean, we're on new ground. This is a 'search for happiness' now."

"Shut up and give me another Coke."

"Well? If nothing else, we might have a format for a series."

"Not bad. This could be the pilot," I say.

"Sure, but what happens next?"

I find myself forced to peer at the situation through a new prism. "Right, so I went to the Balthus show because she wanted to talk to me. That's one solid fact. The second is that Babi has no interest in working for us."

"Are you sure?"

"Absolutely. Babi would never do anything of the sort." As I utter those words, I realize I have no idea what she would or wouldn't do. Who is Babi, anyway? What's happened in all this time? How much has she changed? I find myself staring at the Coca-Cola. Giorgio is right. We need strong liquor in this office. It would help at times like this.

"Well, Babi isn't looking for a job interview. She was there to introduce me to my son." As I say it, I feel a knot in the pit of my stomach and a pang in my heart. Giorgio must notice, because he leaves me alone and stops peppering me with questions.

"Do you need some time to yourself?"

"No, don't worry. But what I don't understand is why it took her so long. Why did she wait? Why did she decide to tell me now, of all times?"

"Because she knows you. She knows you'd have kicked up a ruckus. She knows you would have wanted a different kind of life for her."

"Yes." I'm stunned. A different kind of life for her. A different kind of life *with* her.

But she didn't give me that chance. And now it is too late.

"So what are you going to do?"

I look at Giorgio in surprise.

"Do you think that she's trying to get you to pay child support?"

"Look, I have no idea what's happening. I've just been catapulted into the past, and I'm discovering that the past is not only my present, but actually my future. I thought I'd forgotten Babi, and now I found out that something still ties me to her, and forever. We have a son."

"Okay. Well, one thing is clear…" He gets up and strides resolutely toward the door. I finally glimpse a flash of light. When you're as confused as I am, you need someone who can think clearly.

I look at him with profound curiosity. "What's that?"

"I'm firing Giuliana right now."

Chapter 11

*G*in remembered the night it all happened. She'd been ignoring all of Step's pleas to reconcile, his silent vigil outside her apartment building. But then, one day, her mother gave her an invitation from her friend Eleonora to meet her at a chic restaurant for a night out, just girls. What a relief, what a break from all that tedium and grim, unrelenting heartache.

As Gin parked her car, she felt her cell phone buzz. Someone had just texted her. She looked at the time. It was nine p.m. Could Ele have become so remarkably punctual? She never had been before. And now she wants me to be punctual? That's just crazy. *That's when she realized how wrong you can be. The text was from Nicola. Absurd, what a coincidence. She'd just been thinking about him. He asked her out for the next night.*

Well, Gin thought to herself, he might not be Step, but at least he's likable. Sure, she replied. See you tomorrow.

Gin went in the front door of the hotel and followed the instructions. She stepped into the elevator and pushed seven. The doors slid shut, and the elevator cab took her up to the top floor of the splendid building. When the doors opened, her jaw dropped. Dim lights, flowers everywhere, vitrines glittering with crystal, blown-glass vases and antique porcelain items, perfect. The big picture windows of the restaurant overlooked a breathtaking vista, ranging from the turn-of-the-century buildings that dated from the reign of King Umberto I on the Pincian Hill all the way down to the historical city center and even farther, where the last roofs of Rome faded into infinity. The dining room was completely empty of customers. There was just one waiter, about fifty years old with a slightly receding hairline, smiling at her. At his side stood the chef, a man with a goatee and an attentive look, dressed in a perfect chef's uniform, right up to the toque on his head.

"Buonasera. You must be Ginevra," said the waiter courteously. Gin could do nothing but nod. "We've been awaiting your arrival. This way please. Your table awaits."

Gin followed both men without a word.

"Please, be seated." The waiter pulled back the chair and helped her to sit down.

The chef turned and gave her a handwritten menu. "I've taken the liberty of preparing these dishes, but if they're not to your liking, just tell me what else you'd like."

Gin took the menu, on a handsome cream-colored, fine laid paper, and started to read. She gulped. She couldn't believe her eyes.

Spaghetti with clam sauce and bottarga. Sea bass baked in salt with a side dish of asparagus and purple potatoes. For dessert, pineapple and pistachio gelato.

All her favorite dishes. She could barely stammer, "No-no, this will do fine." The chef smiled, but Gin knew that something didn't add up. This couldn't be Ele's doing. She could barely remember whether or not to sugar her coffee. She'd never come up with such a detailed menu.

"With your permission, I'll just head back to the kitchen," the waiter said. And both men walked politely away.

And then Step appeared out of the shadows.

"Hello, Gin. Seeing you in this state of misery is devastating for me. I look at you now, and I'm even more ashamed. I wish I'd never done what I did. I'd go back in time and erase that moment if I could, but I can't. They haven't invented a time machine to make it possible. Only you can do it, if you choose to, with a simple smile and by putting all this pain behind you. I beg of you, do it. Give me this new opportunity, and I swear to you, it will never happen again."

Step threw both arms wide, shut his eyes, and waited for his fate to be sealed, one way or another. He heard Gin's chair push back, and he squeezed his eyes shut even tighter, took a deep breath, and hoped against hope. At last, he felt her embrace him, fully and passionately.

Step opened his eyes. Gin was pressed against his chest. She pulled back a little and smiled at him. "Will you marry me, Gin?" She nodded, smiling through her tears.

They kissed. From the back of the restaurant, through the glass window of the kitchen door, the waiter and the chef watched the scene. "At last," the chef sighed, "dinner can begin."

Chapter 12

In the dim light of the bedroom, Gin undresses me. She unbuttons my shirt and quickly untucks it from my trousers, popping the last button off. We laugh. My belt has a snap buckle so I help her undo it, and then she goes for my trousers' fly and pulls it down. She gets to her feet and, in the blink of an eye, lets her dress fall to the floor.

She removes her panties and bra and stands there naked, walking toward me and putting her arms around me while our bodies quiver with desire and she unabashedly takes my penis in her hand. "It's his fault, but I love him. He's made me the happiest woman on this earth…" And she adds, "So I want to give him a special thank-you…" She drops down, squats in front of me, and starts kissing my penis. Every so often, she looks up and gives me a mischievous smile, sexier than ever before, or is it just the way she looks to me right now?

Gin takes a drink of champagne and kneels down again, just like before, and I feel an incredible shiver, cold liquid and carbonation, and her mouth, her tongue, and the champagne pouring over it. She hands me the bottle and leaves the room and turns off all the lights in

the house. Then I can hear her rummaging around somewhere, drawers being opened, a match being struck. She
comes back to the bedroom and hands me a glass, and I
lean forward and sniff at it. Rum.

"I know how much you like it. I bought the Zacapa
Centenario, the best one, the most delicious... I'd better
not have any, I'm not supposed to drink alcohol."

And she smiles. I taste it, and then I take a long sip.

Then she takes my hand. "Come with me. There's
something I've been wanting to do."

She leads me through the dark, empty house. Nearly
everything is shrouded in shadow now. In the living room,
in the study, and in the dining room, I see candles, one in
every room. And she continues to pull me forward until
we arrive in my office. She pushes a few things aside atop
the desk and then sits down on it.

"There, you have no idea how many times I've dreamed
of doing this, as if I were your secretary and I'd been
coming on to you."

And I laugh at the boldness of that phrasing. "Yes, come
on to me..." And I kiss her. And she spreads her legs and
places one foot on the armrest of my chair, the other on the
office drawers next to the desk, and relaxes there, sweetly
akimbo, looking me in the eyes. Then she takes my cock
in her hand and delicately guides it inside her. And she
starts moving back and forth, thrusting her pelvis.

"Hey... what's come over you?"

"Why?"

"You're always incredibly sexy, but you've never been
like this before."

"It's just that you've never noticed." And Gin frees her

legs and then wraps them tightly around me, clinging like a vine. She moves her hand on the desk, bumping against the mouse on the little pad, and the movement is enough to turn on the computer screen.

Gin notices. "Hey, people are going to see us through the window."

And for a moment, behind her back, I glimpse the open Safari page, the command line on top, the chronology, and then below it, my searches, everything I saw before, the pictures of Babi, her life, and her wedding. Then the computer screen goes dark again. And Gin laughs.

"That's a relief. They didn't see us, did they?"

"No, I don't think they did."

"Let's hope not." I can hear that Gin's breathless because she's liking this, and that excites me even more. She lies down on her stomach on top of the desk, her legs extended, slightly splayed, and once again she guides me inside of her. She holds tight to the desk and tries to anchor herself as I move faster and faster inside of her.

"Wait. Take your time." She pulls away and picks up the glass of rum. "I want him to have a taste of it too." She takes a long drink, but then she doesn't swallow. She kneels over, and with a mouthful of rum, she takes me in her mouth.

It drives me crazy. It burns, but it's incredibly pleasurable. "I can't take it. It's unbelievable."

Then she stands, pulls me up, and drops me on the sofa, climbing on top of me, and in a second, I'm inside her. She moves back and forth on top of me, fast and then faster, until she whispers in my ear, "I'm coming, my love."

And then I come with her. We remain there, arms

wrapped around each other, our mouths close to each other, reeking of rum and sex. I can hear our hearts pumping frantically. We breathe in silence while our heartbeats gradually begin to slow down. Gin's hair is hanging over her face but I can see her eyes and her satisfied smile.

"You sent me straight to Omega."

"You're wild. You've never been like this before," I say.

"I've never been this happy before."

She throws her arms around me, and I feel guilty. Then I embrace her, holding her tight, ever tighter.

"Hey, you're hurting me!"

"Sorry, you're right." And I loosen my grip. "We have to be careful now." I smile at her.

"You know, it was beautiful to feel you come inside me, to know that everything's already happened…"

"Yes." I don't know what else to say. And at that exact same instant, I'm reminded of that night with Babi, six years earlier, having sex with her after the party, both of us drunk. She wouldn't let me go, thrilling to the experience and riding me wildly as if I were a horse. And she wanted me again, and again, and again. And she would only let go of me after I'd come. That's when it must have happened.

"My love? What are you thinking about? Where are you? You seem so far away…"

"No, I'm right here."

"But are you happy that we're going to have a baby?"

"Certainly, I'm overjoyed. But how did it even happen?"

"Well, I have some ideas, you big dummy. Would you tell me what's going through your head?"

I try to come up with something plausible. "I was

thinking that, this evening, you really filled me with surprises. You left me speechless."

"Yes...but you didn't seem all that upset about it, after all."

"No, actually, I guess I wasn't. But I don't understand how all these fantasies popped into your mind."

"You're the one who gave me the book! In *The Dream Merchants* by Harold Robbins, there was a scene where she did exactly the same things that I did to you this evening."

"Seriously? I didn't remember that..."

"I thought it was a subliminal message and that you wanted to teach me new sex techniques..."

"I have to be a little more careful about the books I give you."

"You're right. I'm going to have to start behaving now that I'm going to become a mother."

And so we go on chatting, laughing, and joking light-heartedly, eating the leftover berries with whipped cream from last night's dessert. Gin puts on my shirt, and I grab a T-shirt and a pair of pajama bottoms, and we wind up in bed. Gin starts to fantasize about the gender and names for our baby. "If it's a baby girl, we'll name her after my mother, Francesca. But if it's a little boy, I was thinking about Massimo. It's a name I've always loved. What do you think?"

I can't believe it. It's as if life is doing it on purpose, two children, from two different mothers, but with the same name.

"Yes, why not, maybe so...It's a name for a great general." That comes spontaneously to me, paraphrasing

Babi. And I drink some more rum, and by now I feel as if I might have drunk too much rum, and I wonder if I shouldn't stop drinking and tell her the truth.

"My love, I have a surprise for you too. Today I saw Babi..."

"Oh, really, and that's the way you tell me?"

"And that's not all, just think of what a remarkable coincidence: turns out I have a son with her, and his name just happens to be Massimo."

But I don't say a word. Gin goes on chatting, cheerful and contented, and I feel tremendously guilty because I understand that her joy is hanging by a thread, a thread that I could snap easily, forever shattering her beautiful smile.

"Just think about my folks when they find out. They're going to be overwhelmed, but with happiness. Anyway, I'll tell them after the wedding. You know, they're kind of old-fashioned that way, if they find out that I'm already expecting...I know my father. He'd tell me I'm a hussy, that I could have waited. No, not really, my father adores me. He dotes on me..."

And I pour myself another dollop of rum and toss it back at a single gulp, as if that could somehow help me. And as I listen to her chatter away about which of her girlfriends to choose as her maid of honor, the readings to do in church, and the honeymoon, I see a shadow at the far end of the room, sitting in that chair. It's him again, my friend Pollo, but this time he isn't smiling at me. He's chagrined because he sees that I'm uneasy. He can read my mind but he can't seem to understand my answer to the question he asks me over and over again, incessantly. "But, do you love Gin?"

Chapter 13

This is Alice."

"Pleasure to meet you." She's a lovely young woman with short hair, hazel brown eyes, a slender physique, and a determined smile that dazzles over a sky-blue blouse with turned-up white cuffs and a pair of dark jeans. Her shoes are serious and dark, possibly a pair of Tod's.

She seems perfect, almost to a fault, but I wouldn't want to trust my senses, which are somewhat befuddled as of this moment.

Giorgio smiles at me, pleased with himself. "I told her about what happened. You can go, Alice."

"Yes, thanks, but there was just one more thing I wanted to say. This job is very important to me. I like the way I see Futura growing, and I like what you've built so far. I'd never sell my soul for a handful of cash, and I'd never tell a corporate secret to others. If I received a more attractive offer, I'd come talk it over with you, and I'd try to find an accommodation." With that she turns to go and shuts my office door behind her.

Giorgio glances at me. "Well? What do you say? Do you like her?"

"In what context?"

"Professionally speaking."

"She scares me a little bit."

"You're afraid of someone who speaks the truth? That doesn't seem like you."

"You're right, I was just kidding. She seems reliable to me. She's direct, sincere, and transparent." I go and sit down behind my desk. "I'm just curious about one thing. How did you find Alice?"

"Research…" Giorgio knows what he's doing but I wonder what's involved in that research. Then he points to something on my desk. "If you don't believe me, take a look at her résumé. You place so much stock in the internet, but then when someone uses it the way it's supposed to be used, you become all suspicious and refuse to believe him because you think it's unreliable somehow. I applied the filters for what we needed and hit 'search.' I came up with roughly five hundred résumés. Then I narrowed it with my own filters, and Alice Abbati popped up."

"So what are these filters of yours?"

"Now you're asking too much."

"You're right. I was just wondering if there was something I missed."

"Well, how about this? She speaks perfect English, and she knows Chinese, and you know that it would be a great thing to grow Futura in China. Last minor detail, her father is a general in the Financial Police."

I look at him curiously.

"Someday that could come in handy."

"I sure hope not. I'd like to be able to just go on working without having problems."

"Sometimes the problems you have are because other people created them for you. That's why it could come in handy."

"Okay, fair enough. So, you know what I say?" I scan through her résumé, stunned at the sheer volume of her skills and achievements. "I say that Alice strikes me as truly the perfect assistant. Congratulations on your recruitment skills and hiring choices. We should give her a raise right away."

Giorgio starts laughing. "I can never figure out if you're actually paying me a compliment or if you're still just pulling my leg…"

"One thing or the other is correct. You be the judge."

He sits down across from me. "The strength of a company is the team that runs it. We're united, we're winners, and today is a very important day. By the way, how did it go yesterday? Can we talk about that?"

I look at him. I seem to glimpse Pollo sitting on the sofa to my right, nodding his head. All right then, there are two possibilities. Either I need to cut my drinking or go see a psychiatrist and admit that I'm having continuous visions. I open the grates and throw open the windows overlooking the garden. That way it's much nicer, and there's more light too. "Yes. It went well. I discovered in a single day that I'm a father…"

"You already told me that."

"But a father of two children, though!"

"Another one? I wasn't expecting that. I think you need to examine one aspect of your life. I know that you love women, but let me remind you that you're about to get married, and as if that's not enough, Futura is growing, and if you keep pumping out children like this, I'm not sure the company will be able to keep up with you so you've never, by any chance, heard of those strange objects made of latex that resemble balloons? We call them condoms, I believe."

"Don't worry. Gin is expecting the other baby."

"Then I'm happy for you. Should we be expecting more news of this sort today? Any other occurrences we might have forgotten to put into our calculations? No? I mean, I'm asking just in case there's anything I should know."

"As strange as you might find this fact, over the past few years, absolutely nothing has happened that might result in babies I wouldn't be well aware of, okay? I've devoted myself body and soul to Futura, and yet..."

"Two seems like a good number to start out with if you want to be a good parent, but there's time to see about things, right? Do you already have any ideas about the name?"

"Gin suggested Massimo if it's a boy...which would be so much easier, and that way I wouldn't get mixed up."

Giorgio looks at me in surprise for the second time. "Seriously? Babi and Gin don't know each other, do they?"

"Gin and Babi friends, sharing that sort of confidential detail? Nothing could be further from the truth. Why do you ask?"

"Thinking badly of others is a sin, but it's also often quite accurate."

"Nice."

"The late prime minister Giulio Andreotti said it, but

he's dead so it's in the public domain. You're free to use it if you like. Can I ask you something else?"

"Sure, why not?"

"Have you talked to Gin?"

"Not yet."

"Are you planning to do it?"

"I don't know. Yesterday, I was about to do it, but it was such a magnificent dinner, prepared with such loving care, that I didn't want to ruin it. Then I was planning to tell her everything after dinner, but she gave me the news."

"So you're never going to tell her?"

"I don't know. Right now I'm not sure what good it would do anyone."

"Right. Do you think that you'll see Babi again?"

"I don't know."

"But you do know that we have a meeting soon with the director of the network drama series and that you're going to have to make a pitch on everything that we presented?"

"Yes, I do know that."

"Good. At least there's one thing you're seeing clearly about."

Chapter 14

We walk in through the sizable front door of the head-
quarters of the Network and go to the counter where they
issue security passes. One of the three young ladies leans
toward us.

"Good morning. The director, Calvi, is expecting us,"
Giorgio says.

The receptionist quickly checks for the appointment
on her computer. I read her nameplate and discover that
her name is Susanna. So Susanna speaks to someone on
the telephone, replies "Thanks," and hangs up. Giorgio
pulls out his ID, but Susanna just smiles at him. "Giorgio
Renzi and Stefano Mancini, I already have you registered."
And a moment later, she's handing us two passes and
pointing us in the right direction. "Take the elevator to
the seventh floor."

"Thanks."

We head for the large glass doors, and we each slide our
pass through the electronic slot. We walk to the elevators.
When we reach the seventh floor, there's already a young
woman waiting for us.

"Hello there. Renzi and Mancini?"

"Yes."

"Please follow me."

We start walking down the long hallway. When we're about halfway down the hallway, the young woman turns to me.

"I'm Simona, and I wanted to thank you for the kind gifts you sent to me and my colleague. How did you guess? Do you know that, when I opened it, I was literally speechless? Thanks again." And she stops in front of the office, ushering us in and inviting us to take a seat. "Would you care for any coffee or water?"

"Just an espresso, thanks, and some still water," Giorgio replies.

"And for you?"

"Same for me, thanks." And I receive a smile of gratitude for a gift I had no idea I'd even sent her. As soon as she leaves the room, I turn around and look at Giorgio. "Excuse me, but would you mind explaining?"

"Good job, you came off handsomely."

"That I realize, but I have no idea what for or how."

"She's crazy about Alessandro Baricco, and her colleague is a huge Luca Bianchini fan. And you, an extraordinarily discerning human being, sent a copy of the exact right book to each young lady."

"Yes. Okay, but still, she seemed just a little too over-joyed, as if she were about to break into tears."

"Maybe that's because of the personal dedication that you managed to obtain from the authors themselves!"

"Are you serious? I managed to get personally auto-graphed copies of books by Baricco and Bianchini? Well, I have to admit, I'm quite impressed with myself…"

"It was only predictable that Simona would be just *thrilled* to meet you."

"In fact, I'd be thrilled myself. But how did you do it?"

Giorgio smiles at me. "You have to become impeccable, charming, loved, and desired. You are the boss of Futura, the company I work for. I only ask you one thing, seeing that Simona is very attractive and understandably swept away by your allure. For the moment, I'd avoid spawning any other children…"

We start laughing. I'm about to reply when at that very moment Simona comes back in, accompanied by another young woman.

"Here you are…" She sets the tray down on the table. "This is the espresso, and here's the water, and this is my colleague. She so much wanted to make your acquaintance."

"Pleasure to meet you, I'm Gabriella."

Not always is a good deed met with a good effect, and yet I am forced to admit, in the presence of Gabriella, that there is a certain perfection to life. She's tall, blond, and shapely with big blue eyes and a straight nose. She extends her lovely hand, which I cannot help but admire, and I reply, "The pleasure is all mine. I'm Stefano Mancini."

She blushes and looks down. "You made me so happy." Then she turns on her heel and leaves.

"My colleague is a little shy," Simona points out. "I'll have to ask you to be so kind as to wait for a few more minutes, and then you can go in." And she leaves us alone.

"You can just imagine, that Gabriella…you shook hands with her and now she's already pregnant!"

I punch Giorgio lightly on the shoulder. "Oh, just cut it out with this routine."

"Come on, let's be serious. We're about to go in." Giorgio opens the little sugar packet and pours it into his demitasse of espresso. "It's 11:05. We had an appointment at 11:00. Wait and see, it'll be at least twenty minutes before Gianna Calvi condescends to see us."

"Wait. How on earth do you know that?"

"She only reads Marco Travaglio, the articles in *Affari e Finanza*, and to be absolutely contradictory, Nicholas Sparks and his books about love and destiny. She's making us wait even though today's appointment was made possible, absurdly enough, by the very person who gave her her job. Do you understand how power works? She wants us to understand that, whatever happens, she's the one who counts, she's the one who decides . . . she's the one who dominates." And he gives me a cunning smile. That's just the way Giorgio does things. He goes straight to the heart of the problem, the enemy's heart, and laughs about it.

I drink my espresso, too, before it can get cold, and I sip some still water. I take a look at the three projects we're presenting, and I find a sheet of paper atop each of the three.

"Who wrote this?"

"Alice, this morning, without me having to say a word. She tells me that it's a little crib sheet on the plot, which ought to be useful for a quick review before the pitch meeting."

"It's a very well-done crib sheet."

"Next time you see her, I'd recommend you compliment her on it. We fire those who betray us, but we give the proper measure of appreciation to those who deserve it."

"Right you are."

I look at the clock. It's 11:28.

If Giorgio is right, then she ought to be calling us in any minute now. I realize that there's a text message on my phone. It's from Gin.

> Darling, how are you? Are you happy about yesterday's news? We haven't talked about it enough!

It's true. I didn't have the words to express my feelings. The words I could have said were silenced by the alcohol. But as usual, Gin hit the bull's-eye. We really haven't talked much about it.

It's fantastically wonderful! As soon as I send the text, Gabriella enters the room.

"Would you care for anything else? I brought you some chocolates. They're delicious." And she sets a gianduiotto down for each of us. We each pick ours up and thank her. "Come right this way, Director Calvi is waiting for you!"

I walk along beside her; Giorgio lingers behind. Before leaving us to our appointment, she turns her big blue eyes in my direction, puts something in my hand, and, blushing, tells me: "This is my phone number."

I slip the scrap of paper into my pocket, and Giorgio and I enter the office as the director stands up from her chair and waits for us at her desk.

"My apologies for having made you wait."

"Oh, don't mention it…"

"I'm Stefano Mancini, and this is Giorgio Renzi."

"Yes, I know Signor Renzi, but I've been very interested in making your acquaintance. I've heard very good things about you…"

How strange. There was a time when no one had anything to say about me but bad things. Either the world has changed or else I have. But this doesn't seem like the right time to focus on the issue, so I smile without any real conviction and say nothing more.

"Please, be seated. Have they already offered you something to drink?"

"Yes, thanks, an impeccable welcome. They gave us a piece of chocolate." I pull it out of my pocket. "In fact, I'm going to eat mine before it melts."

Giorgio looks at me and sits impassively. My behavior is in line with a specific and rational line of reasoning. Calvi made me wait half an hour to prove that she has power, so she can wait for me to eat my piece of chocolate just to show her that I have a tiny piece of power too, right? Giorgio hands me a tissue. I take advantage of the opportunity to wipe my mouth, and then I start to tell her about our three projects. I speak calmly and confidently, reinforced by the review of the work that I was able to do. The director listens to me and nods. Out of the corner of my eye, I see Giorgio, who listens until I'm finished.

"Very good," says the director.

I glance at my watch without letting her notice. Twenty-two minutes. I wanted to keep it under twenty-five minutes, according to Giorgio's instructions, and I nailed it.

"Your proposals strike me as very interesting," Director Calvi compliments me.

I try to explain the logic behind our projects. "We wanted to talk about women first and foremost. We're trying to write for them."

Giorgio had briefed me on the conceptual outlines that the new network management intended to apply to their programming, and our authors followed his indications to a tee. I don't know how he'd been able to get his hands on them, but seeing his success with the secretaries, I assumed he wouldn't be far off when it came to the rest of his information.

"Unfortunately, right now we have a great many projects just like these…" Calvi throws her arms wide, as if helplessly apologizing. "In any case, leave them with me, and I'll give them some thought."

Giorgio stands up, and I follow him.

"Thanks, madame director, let's talk soon."

"Certainly, gladly, and again, apologies for making you wait."

She walks us to the door and bids us farewell with a smile that drips with nothing other than formal courtesy. I see neither of the two secretaries, so we troop off alone toward the elevators. We walk past the waiting room, and I spot a group of people. Giorgio stiffens. A man turns toward us and recognizes Giorgio.

The guy stands up and smiles at him in a fashion that I find rather excessive. "Giorgio Renzi, what a surprise. How are you doing?"

"Fine, thanks. How about you?"

"Just great! What a pleasure to see you again. You have

no idea how many times I've thought about giving you a call." He clasps Giorgio's hand and shakes it vigorously. The man is short and stout with a trim little goatee and a pair of round eyeglasses. He's dressed strangely in a leather jacket, white shirt, black denim jeans, and a pair of dark Hogans on his feet. He seems pleased by this chance meeting. "Let me introduce you to my new assistant, Antonella."

Giorgio shakes hands with a petite blond woman with something about her that looks like the product of cosmetic surgery, maybe her nose and certainly the two in- flatable kayaks she has instead of lips. She flashes Giorgio a faint smile but hardly seems pleased to see him.

"And this is my editorial consultant, Michele Pirri." He points to a powerfully built, tall man with thinning hair, a puffy face, practically no neck. Let's just say that the trio leaves a lot to be desired, aesthetically speaking.

"Delighted to meet you." Giorgio shakes his hand too. "May I introduce my boss? Stefano Mancini."

"Ah, yes. Of course, what a pleasure. I'm Gennaro Ottavi. We've heard so much about you."

I smile but I really don't have much to say. I need to prepare some standard response, seeing that this seems to be a song on repeat play lately and I never know how to respond to it adequately.

Luckily, Giorgio comes to my rescue. "Well, great to see you. Now if you'll forgive us, we have an appointment."

"Yes, of course."

Giorgio precedes me, and we head for the elevators. At that very moment, the director's door swings open and out comes Gianna Calvi.

"Gennaro! Please, come right in."

We see them enter the director's office together, and as her door closes, Giorgio pushes the button marked G. Our doors close too.

"Who were they?"

"He's the CEO at the company where I used to work."

"Ah, right, you talked to me about him, but I've never met him in person. Did the director make them wait?"

"They're great friends."

"How do you mean?"

"Ottavi has given her a cornucopia of gifts."

"What do you know about it?"

"I handpicked them all."

"Ah."

We stand in silence as the elevator descends.

"Why didn't you stay on with him?"

"He used me as long as I was convenient to him. Then he decided not to use me anymore, and I had no shares in his company."

"But I offered you shares, and you refused the offer."

"You're right, but now I'm thinking about it." Giorgio rubs his forehead, and then with a determined attitude, he tells me, "I did the right thing by not having anything to do with him. For a while, I actually thought we were friends too."

We ride down in silence until we reach the ground floor.

"Are you coming back to the office with me?" Giorgio asks.

"No, I have a luncheon."

Then Giorgio extends his hand and stares at me with a cunning smile.

"Do you want my pass?" I ask.

"No, I want the note that Gabriella gave you," Giorgio says.

"Do you want to call her for a date?"

"No. But Futura needs to have a future. You have to start with the basics. An attractive young woman is working there, and, like I told you, I don't want any other surprises…"

"I wouldn't have called her," I say.

"You never know."

"'Temptation is a woman's weapon and a man's excuse.'"

"H. L. Mencken. Nice quote. But Oscar Wilde said, 'I can resist everything except temptation.' I really like Oscar Wilde and I follow his advice," Giorgio says.

So I reach into my pocket and pull out the scrap of paper and hand it to him. Giorgio tears it up and tosses it into a trash can nearby. "Trust me, boss. It's best not to have that number."

And so we bid each other farewell. Strange that he didn't ask me where I was going for lunch.

Chapter 15

Papà answers the door with a broad smile on his face. "Stefano! How nice! I was afraid you wouldn't make it! Come in, come in, Paolo's already here."

I walk into the living room and hand him a bottle wrapped in a trademarked wrapping paper that he instantly recognizes.

"Thanks, nothing better than Ferrari Perlé Nero spumante, but really, you shouldn't have," he says as he unwraps the bottle purchased from Bernabei, his favorite wine shop. "I'll open it right away, seeing that it's already chilled…"

I have to laugh. Oh, really, I shouldn't have, but he immediately wanted to check and see what kind of bottle I'd brought. "Of course, Papà, that's why I brought it."

In the living room, I see my brother, Paolo, and his wife, Fabiola, little Fabio drawing something and the stroller a little farther on with baby Vittoria fast asleep.

"Ciao," I say softly as I step closer to the stroller.

"Oh, you can shout at the top of your lungs when she's asleep. She never hears a thing. The only problem is when is she ever asleep?" And Paolo starts laughing.

Fabiola immediately upbraids him. "How would you

even know? He never hears her. Goes on sleeping as if nothing had happened, after all Mamma Dearest can go ahead and get up...But now everything's going to change, you understand that? This year things are going to go differently. Even if you have opened a brand-new office, I don't give a damn. I want to be with Fabio and keep an eye on him at swimming lessons, basketball practice, English lessons, and then for his homework. So I'm going to have to start being well rested, which means getting my fair share of sleep."

Paolo puts on a resigned expression, but he smiles. "I told her we could get a babysitter because I recognize that a mother's work is overwhelming and exhausting..."

"Go on, make fun of me," Fabiola scolds him.

"No, not at all, I'm deadly serious. But she wouldn't do it."

"Of course not. My children are going to grow up with me, not like some of the kids Fabio plays with who spend the whole blessed day with their nannies." I look at Paolo. He really did need a woman like her. She's making him grow up in so many different ways. What she wants is always plain and simple, and she never beats around the bush. You can butt heads with her, but you'll never misunderstand her.

"Ciao, Uncle. Look what I did." Fabio shows me a drawing.

"Very nice. But what is it?"

"How can you ask what it is? Are you kidding? It's the serpent Kaa from *The Jungle Book*!"

"Of course. I was just pretending not to recognize him. You did a great job."

"Ciao, Stefano. How are you?"

Kyra walks in. She's Papà's girlfriend, and it's been going on for at least a year now. She's Albanian and, more importantly, much younger than him. She must be about thirty. She's pretty, tall, and a little chilly. I don't like her much because she isn't friendly, but I've stopped worrying about that sort of thing.

"Just fine, thanks. How about you?" I ask Kyra.

"I'm doing great. I made a meal on the fly. I hope you all like it."

I'm tempted to ask her, *Wait a second. Why did you do it on the fly? You invited us here a week ago, so what else were you doing all morning?* But it doesn't matter. What's the difference? And I think about my mother. She'd have laughed at all these thoughts of mine and would have said, very simply, *Oh, come on, whatever. It will all be okay.*

So I go into the bathroom to wash my hands. There's a white basket with short, muddy-brown hand towels, and there's a bar of Ayurvedic soap. There are dried flowers in a smooth crystal vase and a small, framed painting by Paul Klee, or actually a lithograph. Everything seems impeccable. Kyra has completely renovated Papà's home. Who knows how much she got him to spend, and yet what I see I don't like. It smacks of the extraneous, fake, and gussied up. It seems like one of those display stores thrown together by some architect doing his first project and eager to prove that the minimalist style is ultrachic, but there's no heart in this home. But my father is happy, and that's enough for me, so we can both be happy, and after all, he's the one who's going to have to live here with Kyra.

I join them at the table, where Papà is pouring a glass of spumante, and Fabiola puts her hand in front of her glass.

"No, thanks. None for me. I don't drink."

"But I wanted to drink a toast."

"Just a tiny splash, then. Thanks."

"This is rice pilaf," Kyra points out. "These dolmas are filled with meat, in this case lamb, and here is a stew."

The last bowl is a strange and not particularly well-defined amalgam of foodstuffs. But further along, I recognize a bowl of fresh salad.

"Thanks. I think I'll just have a taste of everything."

I start with the rice, but only after Fabiola has served herself, of course. I'm not quick enough to get a fork to my mouth before Papà raises his glass in the air.

"Now then, I'd like to propose a toast."

We all raise our glasses and wait to hear what he has to say.

"First of all, I'd like to raise a toast to this day. It's been a while since we've seen each other, and we ought to do this more often because it's always nice to have you all in one place, even if your mother is no longer here…" He looks at Kyra for a moment as if to say, *You're all right with me saying that, right?* And she smiles without showing the slightest sign of annoyance. "We're still a lovely family, and in fact, we get along better now than we did before." He looks around at the rest of us, seeking our approval. I listen to him impassively, and of course Paolo is much more caught up in what he says.

"Certainly, Papà. How true."

And so, encouraged, he continues his little speech:

"Yes, so today I'm happy to have you all here, precisely because of how important my family is to me..." Stirred and emotional, he swallows. Yes, in other words, it's clear that he's about to say something important but doesn't know quite how to get it out. Anyway, in the end, he apparently decides to just go for it. "What I want to tell you all is that...Yes, that is, you're all going to have a little brother...Or maybe a little sister."

At that point, Paolo turns pale, but I smile. I can't quite put my finger on it but somehow that's exactly what I'd been anticipating. No, actually, I really expected my father to start talking about getting married.

Now my father is a bit more relaxed, and he lifts his glass in our direction. "Will you toast with me?"

"Of course, Papà." And I gently elbow Paolo. "Get a grip on yourself," I tell him softly. "It's good news."

"Yes, of course." Somehow, Paolo suddenly appears to abandon all his reservations. So we all raise our glasses.

"To your happiness, Papà."

"Yes..."

"And to yours!" Fabiola adds, with a smile at Kyra.

"Thanks."

Kyra looks at Papà, who immediately nods as if he'd forgotten. "Oh, right. We're getting married in July. In Tirana."

"Well, then, it's going to be a time of celebrating."

"That's right!" Papà is finally relaxed. "And now let's eat!" Then he turns to me. "I've heard that, in Tirana, they're doing a lot of work with Italians, a major TV network..."

"Yes, I know."

"You could take advantage of the fact."

"Certainly."

I don't tell him that they've already purchased several projects of ours. They wanted the writers, too, but after the first week, they stopped paying everyone. Almost everyone just came back home, though two writers did stay on.

"Try this." Kyra passes around a strange mishmash. "It's tavë kosi. It's very good. I make it with eggs, lamb, and yogurt. And you should also try some byrek..." And she hands around a savory cheese tart.

I take the tavë kosi with a spoon. Paolo waits to see me taste it first so he can tell whether it's a good idea to dare to try it, whereas Fabiola has an excellent excuse. "I'm on a diet." And she takes only a small bowl of salad. Little Fabio had already eaten at home before coming over.

I decide to taste everything on offer. After all, I'm curious to try. And so I eat while I watch Papà caressing Kyra's hand and telling her, "It's good, it's really good."

It's not true at all. He's lying shamelessly. He always insisted that my mother cook the same things every night; anything out of the ordinary would disgust him. Instead, with Kyra, he's turned into a human doormat. Is that the way we work, we men? Is twenty years' age difference with just any woman enough to turn us into such complete losers?

"How do you like it?" Kyra asks me.

"Excellent, that's really a distinctive flavor."

Actually, I'd happily eat a pasta alla carbonara or a pizza, but why not make them happy? Papà is happy, and so is she. But the spumante is excellent. I'm really pleased with my choice. And I'm happy that I didn't tell them that Gin is expecting a baby. Will it be a girl or a boy? Who knows, maybe Kyra's baby and our baby will grow up playing together. Even if their child will be my baby's uncle or aunt, whether my baby is a niece or nephew!

"Delicious, really good," I say, as I think to myself with a certain degree of confusion about just what our extended family is going to look like.

And I think about my mother and how badly I miss her. And at least, on this point, I'm being sincere.

Chapter 16

When I return to the office, I notice that the door to Giorgio's office is open. With one hand, he's pushing around the mouse of his computer, and with the other, he's talking to someone on the phone in a low voice.

"Yes..." And he starts to laugh. "Exactly. The last thing anybody needs... That's why you were paid." He nods his head in my direction and continues, "That's right, with my boss! And I'll bet it was easy! In fact, you should have paid *him*." Then he says something else I don't quite manage to hear, and then he ends the phone call. "Well, how was your lunch?"

"Fine. I was at my father's."

"Ah, and how is he?"

"Just fine. He's going to have a baby."

"Him, too? It's a family thing, then. You really have the gift."

Just then Alice walks by. "Would you like an espresso?"

"Yes, thanks."

"Yes, one for me too." And before she can turn to leave, I add, "Alice, thanks for the project synopses. They were very well done. And one more thing. Let's be on a first-name basis."

She smiles. "Thanks, but I'd just as soon remain somewhat formal."

"As you prefer."

She smiles. "So you found them useful, sir?"

"Yes, very."

"I'm really happy to hear it."

Alice walks toward our espresso machine, and Giorgio makes one of his perceptive comments. "Excellent, that means the work will just keep improving. See you later."

I go into my office, and on my desk I find a well-wrapped and sealed package. There's also a note in a sealed envelope. I open it.

You've always been with me, all this time. B.

Nothing but an initial *B*, but I have no doubt who it's from.

I step out into the hallway, and I call Silvia, the secretary who sits at the reception desk.

"Yes?"

"Who put this package on my desk?"

Silvia blushes. "I did..."

"But who brought it?"

"A messenger, around noon."

"Okay, thanks."

I see Giorgio lowering his eyeglasses, and in one hand he's holding several sheets of paper, possibly a project.

"How is it?" I ask.

"Excellent. It strikes me as first rate. I'll talk to you about it later."

"Okay. Later, then." And I shut my door again. I sit down at my desk and remain motionless for a short while, eyeing that package. Then I pick it up. I heft it. It seems like a book. Maybe it is one. But bigger than a book. So I finally make up my mind to open it. I unwrap it and sit there, surprised. This is really the last thing I was expecting. It's a photo album. On the first page, I find another letter.

Ciao, I'm so happy you opened the package. I was afraid you might throw it away without even unwrapping it. Luckily, I can see that's not the way it went. I always made two albums. I have one exactly the same as this one, maybe because I've always thought that someday this might happen. I'm happy in a way I haven't experienced in a long, long time. It's as if a circle is once again unbroken, as if what I'd lost so many years ago has now been found. When I saw you again, I felt beautiful, accepted, and welcomed in a way I've never felt before, or if I have, I no longer remember it. Yes, maybe that's a better way of putting it because, when we were together, I felt the same way. Now I don't want to bore you with more words. If for any reason, you decide to throw this photo album away, please let me know. I worked so hard on it, and I'd be sorry to think that something I worked on with such love should wind up in a trash can. B

Once again, the signature is nothing but that initial: *B.* I look at the letter, and I see that her handwriting has improved. It's nice and round, but it's lost that childish playfulness that she once had with certain vowels. No, Babi, your words haven't bored me. You've shed a different light on our life back then. The way I experienced you, what you meant to my life. How I was able to make you happy. How I was able to anticipate your bad moods and wait just the right amount of time to come back and find you. Difficult, demanding. With those sulky, pouty lips of yours.

"I warned you that this is the way I am," you'd said to me. You knew how to make me laugh. You knew how to prompt my patience, my tolerance, the qualities I never thought I had. You made me a better person. Or maybe you just made me think I was. During that time when everything seemed wrong and backward, upside-down and inside-out, when I was driven by a deep-seated simmering sense of uneasiness. When I constantly felt like a tiger in a cage. I was in continuous movement; I couldn't stand still, and all sorts of things were enough to push me over the edge into pure violence.

I look at my hands. Webs of tiny scars, knuckles knocked out of alignment, the indelible marks of faces that I ravaged, smiles gone forever, shattered teeth, broken noses, swollen eyebrows, split lips. Dirty punches, low blows. Fury, violence, savagery, anger, like a sky about to burst into a thunderstorm, a tempest.

Then, with Babi's peace and quiet, all she had to do was caress me, and it was as if it sedated me. Another type of caress, tender and sensual, kindled a different type of shiver in me. "We're a high-octane couple, erotically speaking, and that ought to be enough for you," she would say when I overdid it with high-proof beverages. There were times when she'd spew out the kind of things only an uninhibited, daring woman would say, but she was always amusing. Like the time she said to me, "You can work miracles with your tongue." She liked to make love and look me in the eyes while she was doing it. She kept them open until the wave of sheer pleasure made her shut them and let herself go without restraint.

"Only with you," she said. "But I want everything. I want to try everything."

I'm lost in ancient memories. I'm shipwrecked sweetly into a number of unexpected flashes of back then. Babi, so soft; laughing on top of me, sighing and her head tipping backward, moving faster. And then, stupidly, I get aroused as I envision her breasts, so lovely, two perfect miniatures that drove me nuts, perfectly sized for my mouth. She, all mine.

And as I linger over these last three words, it's as if I see the picture of her shattering into dust. I see her at the door with a sad smile, looking at me one last time and then turning to go. She isn't mine at all. She's never been mine.

And with that horrifying thought, I open the photo album. The first picture is a photo of the two of us. We're just kids. I had long hair, and her hair was blond, bleached pale by the sea. We were both tan and bronzed. And our smiles gleamed even brighter against that dark skin. We're sitting on the fence in front of her little house at the beach. I can still remember it. We'd gone there that last week in September when her folks had already gone back to Rome. We'd lived a day together as grown-ups, as if that house belonged to us.

We bought groceries from Vinicio, the only shop open there in Ansedonia, buying a few bottles of water, espresso for the next morning, bread, tomatoes, some cold cuts, and an excellent mozzarella that came from the Maremma. And then a couple of steaks, some charcoal, a bottle of red wine, a couple of beers— already ice cold—and a wrapper of big green olives. The cashier seemed astonished, so much so that she asked Babi, "So, how many of you are there?"

"No, these are just for the aperitif…" As if the fact that there were olives and beers for the aperitif justified all the rest. And then we sat out in the backyard of her house on Viale della Ginestra, just a few miles away from that house on the rocks where I'd taken her, blindfolded, for our first time together. "But I know this street. I've always come here to go to the beach, my grandparents have a house here on Viale della Ginestra, just a little farther on," she'd told me when she took off the bandanna.

"I always came here too. I have some friends who live in Porto Ercole, the Cristoforis. And I went to the beach in Feniglia."

"You too?"

"Yes, me too."

"Seriously, and we never ran into each other?"

"No, apparently not. I would have remembered."

And we'd laughed at destiny. So weird. We'd always gone to the same beach, but at the two opposite ends of it.

"Feniglia is long. It's a good four miles all in all. Every so often I'd walk the whole length."

"So did I!"

"And we never ran into each other?"

"We've run into each other now. Maybe this was just the right time for it."

I lit the fire in the little garden while she set the table, and then we settled in to bask in the last light of the setting sun. Babi had just taken a shower, and I can still remember that she was wearing the yellow sweatshirt that I'd bought in France, during a trip with my folks. Her hair was wet, which made it look darker, and smelled sweetly of having recently showered. And I remember that she was brushing her long, wet hair and had her eyes shut and that the sweatshirt was clinging to her legs, which poked out from underneath, while she was wearing a pair of Sayonara sandals and her toenails were perfectly adorned with red nail polish. In her other hand, she was holding a beer, and every once in a while, she took a sip. But I was the only one eating olives. Then, at a certain point, she set her beer down on the fence and took my hand and guided it up under the sweatshirt.

"But you're not wearing anything... You're not wearing panties..."

"No." At that very moment, a Vespa pulled up in the street below the house, and Lorenzo—whom everyone called Lillo, an asshole from the group of young people from Ansedonia who had always had the hots for her, though Babi had never given him so much as the ghost of an encouraging nod—dismounted.

"Ciao, Babi. Ciao, Step. What are you up to? Everyone's over at my house. Why don't you guys come too?"

And Babi was naked, and my hand was there with her, and despite his arrival, I hadn't stopped at all. Babi looked at me, and I just smiled at her, but still without stopping. Then she turned to look at Lorenzo.

"No, thanks. We're just going to stay here."

Lorenzo said nothing, and neither did we for a few seconds. I had the impression he was about to insist.

Then it finally dawned on him that he was the third arrival who made a crowd, and his presence wasn't needed or desired. "Okay... Have it your way." And without another word, he took off on his Vespa and vanished down the end of the street.

Babi kissed me and led me inside. After making love, we were famished, and we ate dinner at midnight. It was dark out and I rekindled the fire. We warmed up by drinking red wine and kissing each other hungrily, as if nothing could ever separate us. It was all so perfect that we'd happily have stayed there, together, forever.

Forever, what a terrifying word. So I turn to the next page, and I'm suddenly breathless.

Chapter 17

My son is in his crib with a baby-blue ribbon and a bracelet on his wrist to make sure there are no mix-ups, that we don't lose him. Number 3201B. A number and his face, the features barely sketched out in the flesh. It's the day of his birth, and he still has no idea of anything, much less the fact that his father, namely me, isn't there. As far as that goes, it's an ignorance we share, since I knew nothing about him either.

The photo carries Babi's words as a caption. *I wish you could have been there, at my side, today, July 18. You're both born under the same sign. Will he be like you? Every time I kiss him, hug him, and smell his hair, it will be like having you near me. You're here with me. You'reMineForever.* Without spaces.

One after another, I flip through his pictures, like a succession of different times, moments, and seasons in a flip book. I'd already seen some of these pictures on her Facebook page, but having them in my hands now, carefully curated and not just tossed out randomly, makes me feel like I'm part of something that I'd never have been able to imagine and to which I can't assign a name.

But he has one. Massimo in his high chair, Massimo

crawling on a light blue carpet, and Massimo wearing a funny T-shirt with the words I WILL SURF written on the chest. And for each picture, a note, a caption, a sweet thought that Babi added just for me. *Today he said his first word. He said Mamma, not Papà. It really touched me and I cried. Those tears are for you. Why aren't you here?* she writes, addressing a Step who isn't there, who doesn't know, and with whom she'd like to share all the most wonderful things she has.

Today he was such a good boy. He pushed himself up against the wall and started walking, one foot after another. Then he stopped, turned to look at me, and just stared, Step, I tell you... At that moment I felt like I was dying. He has your exact same eyes, your gaze, your tough determination. I stepped closer to help him and he pulled one hand away from the wall and, instead of taking my hand, pushed it away. You understand? It's you, no two ways about it!

I feel like laughing, and more, but I keep what's churning inside me hidden.

In the successive photographs, Massimo has a different look on his face. He's grown. *Today he ate every last bite, and without spitting anything up on me! It's a miraculous day. Just a minute ago, a motorcycle went by, and it reminded me of the noise yours made, when I could hear it coming from Piazza Giuochi Delfici and then down Via di Vigna Stelluti, and then Via Colajanni—which you'd roar down at full speed until you reached Piazza Jacini. The doorman Fiore would let you through, raising the barrier because he was afraid you'd break it. But that motorcycle that went by today wasn't you. Where are you, Step? Did you follow to the letter that song you loved so much:* "Try to avoid all the places I hang out in, places that you know so well…" *Well, you did it. We haven't run into each other even once. It's true.*

And in silence, I continue turning the pages of that photo album, his second, third, fourth birthday party, his hair growing longer, darker. He's skinnier and taller until I see the little boy I met in person just a few days ago. And to see him transformed like that, picture by picture, page after page, it feels like a moment I've already lived sometime, in a previous existence. I desperately try to remember, and my mind wanders through the past. I squint as if trying to focus on something that's escaping me. I feel like a man crouching down on all fours on a beach, both hands plunged into the sand, hunting for a beautiful woman's lost earring. Then, when I suddenly open my eyes again, the beautiful stranger disappears, while it's as if that memory reshapes itself right in my hands.

I'm right there. At Babi's house, on the sofa. *She leaned over, opened a drawer in a small white chest, and pulled out a photo album. We started leafing through it together, and in photograph after photograph, she grew too. As did my curiosity and my jealousy for everything I hadn't experienced…I made fun of her for how funny she looked when she was little, but I didn't tell her how much I loved every second of her life. The changes in hairstyle, those birthday parties and anniversaries now long since forgotten.*

There's one photo that she didn't want me to see. She wanted to skip it, and then we wrestled until I managed to win the battle. It was a picture where she was crossing her eyes. And I laughed as I looked at it. "Strange, that's the one that looks most like you." That same day, she got mad at me because I found a diary in her bedroom and started reading it. It wasn't long, though, before we'd made peace and we started making out. At a certain point, we stopped. She suddenly pulled away and raised her forefinger, holding it up to her lips. "Shh..."

"What's wrong?"

She walked over to the window and pulled open the blind. "My parents are here!" And quickly she walked me to the front door. And I was dying to spend more time with her.

"Hey. Can I come in?"

The door opens, and Gin pokes her head in. "Ciao! What are you up to? Am I intruding?" She asks the question with a broad smile.

"No, are you kidding? Come on in."

I barely get a chance to shut the photo album and put another file with a project in it on top of it.

"Darling, don't you remember? We have a very important appointment. I only came up because you weren't answering your phone..."

"It's true. I'm sorry. I'd silenced it."

"Come on, they're waiting for us."

"I'll be right with you." I shut the door behind me and call out to Giorgio. "We'll see you tomorrow. I'm probably going to be back very late."

"All right. Ciao, Gin."

"Ciao, Giorgio." And we leave the office and enter the elevator. Gin pushes the button for the ground floor. "Hey. Everything all right?"

"Yes, sure. I was just thinking about something."

"I'm sorry if it was something very important. We just can't reschedule today's appointment."

"No, don't worry. It was nothing important. An old project. I don't think it's any good."

"Well, if you want, we can talk about it so I can give you my opinion. You know, I understand a thing or two about television, okay?"

"I know that very well. You're a star. We should have picked you as a hostess. You were too pretty, though, and everyone would have been jealous."

"What do you mean I *was* too pretty?" And she punches me in the shoulder. "Listen, you little punk…" Just then the elevator door slides open, and the Parinis come in, an older couple from the third floor.

"Everything's all right, don't worry. We're about to get married, and this was just a dress rehearsal to make sure we're suited for it."

"Ah…" he says, as if he actually believes it.

Gin strides quickly toward the car, and I follow her, but I tell myself that I probably won't ever be talking to her about that other old project.

Chapter 18

Apologies!"

Gabriele, Gin's father, smiles at me in the rearview mirror.

"Not a problem."

Her mother greets me with a smile as well. We seem like a perfect family.

Gin gets in beside me. "He didn't hear the phone. He was all caught up in a new project."

Francesca turns to look at me for a moment. "So how's it going? Will we be able to see anything good on TV?" Her mother always talks to me as if I'm single-handedly responsible for all the television programming in Italy. "Especially when you consider that we're forced to pay the annual fee for state TV, you'd think they'd give us more options. They always put on the same old stuff."

And then Gabriele weighs in. "And that's not all. This time of year, they just show reruns. Don't you think it's time to be done with that? How much money has RAI taken from us Italians this year?"

"Well, two hundred and sixteen million euros."

Francesca whips around. "Seriously, that much? And you work for RAI?"

"Yes, but also for the Network, Medinews, Mediaset, Sky, and all the digital channels and the other networks."

"Ah…" And they lapse back into silence. Gin's parents exchange an uncertain smile, as if they wanted to get a better idea about something that strikes them both as somewhat nebulous.

"I think they must believe I'm rich. That I was quite the eligible bachelor!" I whisper into Gin's ear.

"You're such a dope." And she bites my ear.

"Ouch!"

As we turn down the Via Cassia Antica, the traffic has subsided, and Gabriele accelerates.

I can feel my cell phone vibrating in my jacket pocket. A text from an unknown number.

Did you like the gift? I hope so. I wrote something for you on the last page. Did you read it? Hey, don't throw it away. And let me know. Thanks. B.

I feel myself blushing, my heart racing, and I try to calm down.

"Who's it from? What's going on?" Gin has noticed.

"Nothing. Just work."

She smiles at me. "These days, stuff is really piling up. I get it and I'm sorry."

I try to reassure her. "Don't worry about it. I'll take care of it later, or at the very worst, tomorrow."

She gives me her hand. She squeezes mine tight and then she leans back against her seat and looks out the car window. Her father turns on the radio, and a song starts up, at random. It's "The Blower's Daughter," by Damien Rice. Gin recognizes it, and now I'm the one who takes her hand. It's the soundtrack to a film we've talked about a lot, *Closer*, about relationships, love, and betrayal.

After that film, I remember that she went into the bedroom and shut the door. I'd understood that she didn't want to be disturbed for a while. There are movies that inevitably open old wounds, scars that hurt exactly like physical ones do when the weather changes.

That evening, her mood had changed. So I'd gone into the kitchen to make dinner, set the table with the glasses and silverware, and all the rest. I'd made noise to ensure she'd hear me. I'd rinsed the lettuce, chopped the tomatoes, and opened a can of tuna. I managed not to cut myself. I'd put on a pot of water to boil and tossed in two handfuls of coarse salt. I'd picked up the wooden spoon and given it a stir. I managed not to burn myself. I'd pulled out a small, shallow pan to sauté the chopped onions and other fixings I might add. I'd turned over the Tetra Pak of diced tomatoes and patted it several times on the bottom. Then I'd opened it.

I'd opened a bottle of beer, and just as I was about to drink it, she came out of the bedroom. She was wearing nothing but one of my shirts. She was barefoot and had removed her makeup. Or perhaps tears had done the job for her. She definitely didn't want me to know that, if it was indeed the case. Or maybe it was just easier for me to make that assumption.

"Do you want some?"

She'd grabbed the beer without even saying thanks, and she'd taken a long swig before speaking. "Swear to me right here and now that you'll never see her again."

"She's married."

"That's not the right answer."

"I swear to you."

Then she took another swig of beer and hugged me tight. She just leaned on me, like that, in silence, with her face resting on my chest and her eyes wide open. I know that because I could see her reflection in the glass of the windowpane as darkness was falling.

"Take me out for a spin. Come on..." she'd suddenly said to me. "I'm drunk."

So I took her in my arms. "Here, I'll dress you." And I enjoyed myself picking something out for her, rummaging through her armoire. I'd taken off her blouse, and she was just wearing panties and a bra. And even though I felt a surge of desire, I knew that would be a mistake. So I'd slipped a T-shirt over her head, then a pair of short socks, and finally a pair of jeans. I'd put on a pair of running shoes, tying the laces carefully and lovingly, and then when she was about to go into the bathroom to put on her makeup, I'd stopped her, taking her by the hand.

"Just stay the way you are. You're beautiful."

"All you do is lie, Step. You're a disaster. You're no longer able to distinguish reality from make-believe."

"I really like you like this. I'm no liar. I've always told you the truth about everything, for better or worse."

"That's true."

We'd climbed onto the motorcycle and fled from the city, avoiding traffic and racing quickly out to the seashore. We'd stopped at Maccarese, at the first restaurant we found that was open, which turned out to belong to a chef who had a TV show. Strangely, the place was empty, and the proprietor had recognized me. We'd met and talked about the idea of doing a *pilot, but nothing had come of it after all. I'd been smart enough to call him, explain what had happened, and tell him how sorry I was, and that I hoped there'd be some future opportunity to work together. He'd been happy to get the call, even if the news wasn't the best.*

"I've been to lots of meetings. And more than once, it hasn't turned out well, like this one. But no one ever called me to tell me so, the way you've just done. Thanks."

"Well, it seemed like the very least I could do."

"No, you've got true grit, kid. You've got what it takes. Come see me any time you want, Filippone in Maccarese. Everyone knows me here."

"Certainly, gladly."

But I never thought about him again. Instead, that evening, we just happened upon him. He remembered me right away, and he greeted me with genuine warmth.

"Sorry, folks…I just opened the restaurant but there's no one here this evening because I'd told everyone I wasn't opening until next week…" Then he stepped closer to me and whispered, "I really wanted to come work. I was sick and tired of being at home. You understand what I'm saying, right?"

I'd nodded, and so he'd given us the table closest to the water and left us alone. That time it was all my doing, I thought to myself when Filippone came over to tell me that dinner was on the house.

The sound of the waves, the starry evening sky, the wine and the grilled fish had all calmed Gin down. She looked at me with that sweetness in her eyes that didn't take long to look back over everything that had happened, to turn it into sadness, so I'd laughed and joked and distracted her, talking to her about this and that and more or less everything, and, in the end, I'd kissed her. Once we were back home, we made love, remaining wrapped in each other's arms in that bed all night.

I pick up my phone, and I delete the text message. I don't ever want to see Babi again. But as the last notes of Damien Rice vanish, I'm no longer all that certain.

Chapter 19

It isn't long until we arrive at San Liberato. We drive up the steep road, and then we're looking out at all of Lake Bracciano. The reflections of the sunset make the atmosphere warm and inviting. It's as if everything all around, the vineyards, the trees, even the church, had been dipped in orange dye. The atmosphere is calm and untroubled, a place of great and idyllic tranquility.

When we come to the little piazza, Gabriele parks the car. We get out. Laura—the secretary and administrator of the place and, reporting directly to Pettorini, the chief organizer—comes right out to meet us. First of all, she shows us around the church. It's small and unadorned, but the light of the setting sun creates a perfect atmosphere, making the place look especially warm. There is seating for roughly a hundred people inside, while the altar, where the ceremony will take place, is on a small dais. Our friends and family will see everything from below.

Laura explains how she's thinking of bedecking the setting. "Here I'd put some calla lilies, at the front door too, while here, on the floor, white daisies in large bunches, and along the edges of the altar, white roses..."

Francesca and Gin nod. Laura specifies "Long stem."

They both smile together. "Yes, of course, naturally."

Gabriele and I listen as calmly as can be, and he trots out one of his truisms. "There's no two ways about it, weddings fascinate women greatly and moderately worry men."

I nod, quite amused, even though deep inside a strange thought suddenly strikes me. What does it mean when he says weddings "moderately worry men"? I mean, yes, but just how moderately? But I decide not to pursue the matter any further.

Then Manlio Pettorini arrives, arms thrown wide and a glowing smile on his face, with thinning hair but a slender, powerful physique. "Gabriele! How nice to see you!"

And they hug with what looks like sincere affection, a real bear hug that makes anyone watching imagine how many significant experiences they must have shared over the years. Gabriele points at Gin.

"Here we go, my Ginevra. You remember her, don't you?"

Manlio Pettorini slaps his hands together. "Of course I remember her. How could I forget? But how she's grown! Mamma mia!"

"My wife Francesca..."

"Yes, of course. How are you?"

"Fine, Manlio, thanks. And how are you?"

"We can't complain."

"And this is Stefano Mancini, the husband-to-be."

Hearing myself introduced like that has an absurd effect on me, but I smile and extend my hand in his direction. He immediately seizes it, clasping with enormous strength.

"Wow, you don't know how lucky you are. Do you know how much people envy you? When this young woman came up to see us in Rosciolo, in the village, you should have seen the line of young men in front of her house. She couldn't get through the door to leave!"

"Yes, I know. It's true, I'm a lucky man."

And Manlio Pettorini looks at me with great satisfaction. "That's right! And now, by all means, let's all sit down at the table because I'm curious to know what you think of it."

Gin locks arms with me. "Oh, lucky man, be a good gentleman and walk me to the table."

"Certainly, lovely peasant girl with a long line in front of your house…"

"Dummy." And she elbows me in the ribs.

"Ouch…" I say in a subdued voice.

"Look out now. I'm a peasant girl with a mean right hook…"

"Yes, I know. I can feel it!"

And we all sit down together at a large table under a gigantic fig tree with broad leaves. The sun reflects off the lake, and the view is marvelous from this corner of the town.

Pettorini explains exactly what he has in mind. "All right, then, I'll put the kitchen back here…" And he points to the far end of the lawn, which is opposite the location of the church. "But the tables will be arranged right here, under the trees, which will make it less muggy and more comfortable. Overhead we'll have awnings, for the same reason, and hanging lights. They'll all be connected on a single string so that each table will be illuminated but not excessively so."

Gabriele looks at him with great satisfaction. "Manlio really knows how to do his job."

"You're making fun of me, aren't you? I love the work I do. And now, at last, I can do it the way I like. Not like when I organized dinners for the Italian Senate at Palazzo Madama. Can you believe it, there it was the ushers who decided what we'd eat on all the most important occasions? And you can't imagine how passionate they were about the choice of wines!"

"And so are we!" Gabriele slams his fist on the table, pretending to be quite demanding himself.

"Ah, of course you are!" And they laugh together.

Then Pettorini summons the waiters. "Come on, men, bring the primi piatti. All right, then, I've prepared three first pasta courses, so that whichever one you don't like, we'll scratch it off the menu, okay?"

"Manlio, anything you make we're sure to like…"

"All right, then whatever you love a little less! I already had an idea of what I'd make, but I can't decide everything all on my own. For that matter, you're the ones who are paying."

"Oh, true, but if you decide and there's a discount, then we'll trust you!"

And they laugh again as the primi piatti start to arrive.

"Now, this is spaghetti alla chitarra with truffles and mushrooms. And this is ravioli filled with minced vegetables and ricotta with sage and butter, while these are buckwheat paccheri with cherry tomatoes, olives, and spicy olive oil."

"It all looks delicious," says Francesca.

"Yes." Gin smiles with a nod. "It smells fantastic."

And from then on, it is a succession of truly delicious dishes, served with great care and intense attention by a small crew of very young waiters.

"They've all gone to hospitality school," Pettorini points out.

Then there are samples of the wines, sherbets served as palate cleansers, then the entrées and a whole flotilla of potential side dishes.

"Careful not to overeat," Gin whispers. "There's still plenty of things to sample…"

"But this vitel tonné is incredible."

And at the very same moment that I say it, I realize why I like it so much. My mother always used to make it for me. Her vitel tonné was exceptional, just like this one, the meat was lean without so much as a speck of sinew, always beautifully sliced, usually very, very thin indeed, making it even more tender. The sauce was made with super-fresh eggs, vinegar, and just a dash of sugar, at least that's what I think I gathered from the conversations I overheard in the kitchen among women about the secrets behind certain dishes. And so we go on eating while the sun sets once and for all over the lake and all around us lights blink on.

"Yes, it'll be more or less like this. With white lamps at the base of each and every tree and then yellowish-orange lamps down there at the end to create more of an atmosphere."

It all strikes me as very beautiful, and this last sauvignon they had us taste is chilly and impeccable with a very delicate fruity aftertaste. Then come new strawberries and raspberries with homemade whipped cream, light and delicious with spoonfuls of melted chocolate dripped over them. Followed by a semifreddo allo zabaione, a frozen dessert that's basically a chilled mousse flavored with egg yolks, sugar, and Marsala wine, and another hazel-flavored semifreddo. To conclude, excellent espressos.

"All right, then I'd set up a table down there with drinks, light ones like beer and wine, and hard alcohol, cocktails and such, which are certainly an attraction at any wedding...Oh, who knows why it is, but you young people, the happier you are, the more you feel you need to drink!" Gabriele nods in some amusement. "At least we were drowning our sorrows in alcohol, not our happiness!"

"Yes!" Gin laughs. "It's true."

"And instead, at table, I'd serve these amari." And he has an Amaro del Capo, a Filu'e Ferru, an Averna, and Jägermeister brought to us.

"Some of them are well-known, others less familiar. Almost no one knows about gentian, but it's really fantastic. Just give it a try."

And he pours us a sip in little amaro glasses.

"You're right. That's delicious."

"It's a digestive. And I suspect that's going to come in handy!"

And Pettorini laughs because, if you consider everything they decided to serve us, it was a lot. Various antipastos scattered around the grounds. There are tables with prosciutto and other deli meats, then mozzarellas, burratas, chunks of parmesan and other selections of French and Italian cheeses. A number of fried foods on offer at various points, where there will be full-fledged fry stations for fresh shrimp and baby octopus, panella, or bread dough fried in olive oil, cherry mozzarellas, tiny red and white arancini, breaded fried olives all'ascolana, stuffed with sausage meat, and little meat croquettes. All that for the appetizer.

Then two primi, first courses of spaghetti alla chitarra tartufo e funghi (square-section spaghetti with truffles and mushrooms) and paccheri pomodoro e olive (oversized penne with tomatoes and olives). Then come two main entrées, filetto di chianina (the Italian equivalent of a kobe-beef filet) and seabass. All sorts of side dishes, potatoes, vegetables from chicory to broccoletti, and three different salads, one with walnuts, pine nuts, and chunks of pineapple, and then desserts and fruit.

Francesca and Gin chat with Pettorini about the selection of different types of bread, with a few other details about the wines, and by this point, it strikes me that everything has been decided in the best of all possible fashions.

"Ah, look, Don Andrea is arriving."

We turn around and see a priest walking toward us from the far end of the garden, illuminated by the dying sunlight coming over the lake. He's striding briskly. I see him smile and shake his head from a distance.

"Here I am, here I am…" He looks at the carts next to our table. "I see that I missed quite the meal."

Then Gin stands up and greets him affectionately.

"Don Andrea, what a lovely surprise! I didn't know you were coming, or we'd certainly have waited for you."

He pulls back a little after the hug and gazes at her curiously. "So you couldn't find a little church any farther away? I practically melted my Simca's engine to get up here!"

As Gin sits down, Pettorini laughs. "I can just imagine all the wrong turns!" The two men shake hands. Then Pettorini points at him. "You can't imagine how many weddings he and I have done together!"

"And they're all still rock solid!"

"Seriously?"

"Yes, absolutely. I always have a nice little talk with my bride and groom before I marry them. In fact, have you two had too much to drink?" He looks at us with a smile.

"I'd definitely say not."

"Just the right amount," I toss in.

"Have you had a nice hot espresso?"

"Yes."

"Then let's have a nice little chat. I'll start with you." And he points at Gin. "Do you have anything you need to tell me?"

Gin blushes, perhaps thinking about her belly. I smile, but I act nonchalant. Don Andrea must see all sorts of things.

"Well, now, let's not waste time here. Let's head over there, where we can talk more comfortably."

"Don't you want anything to drink?" asks Gabriele.

"No, no, I never drink while I'm on the job."

"At least an espresso..."

"No, otherwise I just won't sleep tonight."

Gabriele shrugs, defeated.

Gin gets up from the table, and before walking away, she looks back at me and gives me a smile that I'm guessing means *I think I'm going to tell him*. She follows Don Andrea to a table at the far end of the garden. There they sit down together.

Now I see their silhouettes as if sketched against the lake behind them. The waters of the lake seem to have turned into a violet blackboard. Gin is waving her hands, laughing, and moving her head. She's cheerful, buoyant, and above all happy. What about me?

How am I? And it almost comes natural to me to reach into my pocket and pull out my cell phone and look at it, as if I were looking for my answer there. Nothing, no messages. Silence.

This, too, is an answer, after all. So I get a small glass, I pour myself a little Amaro del Capo, and I sit back down. I sip it slowly. Not far away on my right, Gabriele and Francesca are talking to Pettorini. He's showing them tablecloths. Then everyone looks at a cloth sample, they nod, and they seem to have come to a final decision on that choice. Manlio Pettorini nods too. *That's the best one. You're right*, he seems to be saying without words.

"Hey, everything all right?"

I turn around. Gin is right in front of me.

"Yes, just perfect. Really a wonderful evening."

"Yes." Then Gin sits down beside me. "I told him."

"You did the right thing, if you wanted to tell him."

"Yes, I think it's the right thing to do."

I don't know what she means. I don't know how it can be the right thing to do, but I say nothing. I take another sip of Amaro del Capo and sit in silence.

Then Gin picks up my glass and drinks a tiny sip of her own. "That's strong."

"You shouldn't drink that."

"I know, but come on, rules are made for breaking, every once in a while. Anyway, look, Don Andrea is waiting for you."

"Okay." So I stand up and head over to him.

Gin shouts at me from a distance. "Hey, cheer up. You look like you're going to the gallows!"

I turn around and laugh. Then I sit down across from Don Andrea.

"You did look pretty resigned."

"Yes, but not too resigned."

He smiles at me. "That's true. I'm happy to hear what Ginevra just told me."

"So am I."

"Seriously?"

I'm caught off guard for a moment. "Certainly. I'm about to marry her, and I'd made up my mind long before the unfortunate accident."

He starts laughing. "Yes, I know, I know . . . Well, listen, Stefano, there's something I want to tell you. There's a special confession that's considered necessary with a priest before being married. If you say a certain thing, then one day this marriage could be nullified. And no matter what, the priest is obliged to maintain the sacramental seal of confession."

Then there's a moment of silence, as if he means to

let me have a little time to think it over, to make my decision.

"Lots of people say something intentionally in order to be sure that, whatever happens, they can always have the marriage nullified at some later date." Again, he sits there in silence. He turns to look toward the lake and, without turning to me, he asks, "All right then, do you want to tell me anything? Do you want to confess anything?"

And I'm surprised by what I say next.

Chapter 20

When I get back to the table, I feel relieved.

"Beautiful evening, no? What do you say, my love?"

Gin squeezes my hand tight. "Yes, really nice."

"Did you like what we ate?"

"I did, a lot. In fact, I loved it. It was really perfect. Everything was delicious."

She gives me a sidelong glance as we get in the car. Then she laughs. "Are you sure? You haven't changed your mind, have you? Don't leave me standing at the altar! We're not going to have one of those strange weddings where the bride is just left waiting for the bridegroom... right?"

"No..."

Gin throws both arms wide as if frightened. "Help! You just uttered the vaguest 'no' I've ever heard. Not a hundred percent convinced. A very dangerous 'no'!"

I can see her mother laughing. They're sitting in front of us. Gabriele's driving, and he must certainly have overheard.

"Hey, no..."

"Oh God, this one was worse than the last one! No, no, no. You're going to leave me standing at the altar!"

And she jumps on me, laughing and punching me in the shoulder.

"Ouch!"

"Well, that's nothing! Maybe you've forgotten that I've done plenty of boxing, and I'm deadly serious about it, you know. I'm not kidding around! Well? Spit it out!" She ducks under and punches me in the hips, hitting but basically just tickling me. "Talk!"

"What am I supposed to say?"

"That you'll get to the church even before me and you won't play any weird tricks on me!"

"I swear to you, cross my heart and hope to die." And I kiss my fingertips, twisting them together in front of my mouth.

"That's no fair! You see, you crossed your fingers. You're the usual old liar!"

"Come on, I'm just kidding. Can you imagine me showing up late? You're the one who's always made me wait for you."

"Well, you're right about that..." Then she turns serious again. "You really talked for a long time with Don Andrea."

"Yes."

"You had a lot of things to tell him."

"He wanted to listen. We talked about film."

"Come on, can you really never be serious with me for even a minute?"

"What do you want me to say? It's all covered by the secret of the confessional."

"It is for him. You're allowed to tell whatever you want!"

"Now you're the one who won't be serious."

Gin sits in silence. She turns and stares out the car window.

But only for a short while. Then she changes her mind and turns back to me.

"That's true, you have a point." She has a bright smile on her face now. "I hope it was useful to you in some way."

"Yes, I like him. He's a super nice guy."

"Of course he is! Do you think I'd choose a horrible old ogre for my wedding? Here, look at this. He gave me some readings to do in church, so we can choose the ones we want."

"Ah. So are we going to be praying this evening?"

Gin smiles at me, and then says in a low voice, "Of course. What else do you think, you know, my folks are right there!"

"I wasn't talking about here in the car. I meant later, at home."

"You're such a dope. They're taking us to your office. You have your motorcycle there, don't you? Grab it, and we can go home, okay?"

"No, let me go up to the office for a bit. I need to read some things for tomorrow. Then I'll join you."

"Okay."

"Okay, you can just drop me off here, Gabriele. Thanks."

The car slows to a halt. I open the door and get out.

"Thanks for everything. See you soon."

They say goodbye to me. I plant a kiss on Gin's lips, and I shut the door. The car takes off, and I head for the office. All the lights are off in the building. I take the elevator, ride up to my floor, and open the door. There's no one around, silence reigns. I turn on the light, and then I shut the door. I walk over to the espresso machine and switch it on.

I won't stay too late, but I'm looking forward to this. I pick up the remote and switch on the stereo, tuning the radio to FM 102.7. "One song you remember, one song you live." It seems like pure chance, but a song by Ligabue, "Certe notti," is playing. I don't think that it's an omen.

I head for my office, and I see that the door is shut, the way I'd left it. I go in and turn on the light. On the desk is the project that I'd used as a decoy. When I pick it up, I find the photo album underneath it. It seems as if no one's touched anything.

I go back out into the hallway, and I make myself an espresso. When it's ready, I go back to my office, shut the door, and sit down at my desk. I pull my cell phone out of my pocket and set it down next to the photo album. There's nothing. No texts, no messages. No phone calls. So much the better.

I blow on the hot espresso and look at the photo album lying closed in front of me. Maybe I ought to listen to the advice Don Andrea gave me. But there's nothing I can do about it, my curiosity is too extreme, so I take a sip of espresso, and then I set the demitasse down at one side of the desk. Then I look at it and, somewhat obsessively, push it farther to the right to occupy a bit more of that empty space, and then I turn the handle toward me.

Then I open the photo album.

Chapter 21

And I find myself back where I'd started. The photographs of a little boy growing up, becoming taller and taller, smiling, making funny faces, whining, laughing like a fool. Trying to ride a bike, succeeding, tearing down a hill with the wind in his hair and hands clutching the handlebars tight. A boy who looks like me.

And I never experienced any of that. Another man experienced it. But in these photographs, that man never appears. You'd almost think that he doesn't exist. Not so much as a hand, not a shoulder, not a snippet of any part of him, not even an object that might represent him. Maybe it's no accident. Maybe Babi edited the pictures expressly for my benefit.

But when I get to the last page, I see it. There's just one picture with him in it. Him, the guy who thinks he's that little boy's father. And when I see him, I'm stunned, speechless, gasping in disbelief. I hadn't recognized him on Facebook. It's Lorenzo.

It just can't be. I was determined to know nothing about it, not the day, not the church, not even the reception, and above all, I was determined not to know who he was.

And now I discover that it's Lorenzo—Lillo. An asshole. A guy who'd been pestering her ever since they were kids, the classic suitor who's been carrying a torch all his life. Who, usually, in the personal history of all women, just stays the friend, a guy you're happy to run into again, just by chance, a pleasant happenstance, who married someone else, not the young woman he was head over heels in love with. But that's not how it went with Babi.

I do my best to remember anything else about him. He was a solid soccer player. I'd seen him occasionally on the beach at Feniglia, but he didn't have much of a physique. His legs were short, his shoulders were broad, and his hair was a little curly. His eyes dark, and one tooth chipped. I look at the picture. Yes, he hasn't changed much. His hair is just a little shorter, and he's dressed a little fancier. One time, we were alone at the beach house, and he dropped by, to see Babi more than to see the two of us. He'd invited us to a party, but Babi had told him she didn't want to go. I just remembered it.

I can hardly believe it. So he tried and tried, and in the end, it worked out for him. And I can imagine them together, the way their relationship began, where it took them, where he gave her the first kiss, where...*No, Step. Enough is enough. You can't keep doing this. Stop your mind, force it to move far away from all this, for fuck's sake. Just set fire to your memories, all the pictures, and the excruciating pain that it all causes you.* And slowly that all happens.

It's as if I were sedating myself. A strange feeling of calm suddenly settles over me. It's like a sudden sprinkle of rain, and then all the clouds vanish. The sun shines brightly again, but there's no rainbow. Or else like a stormy sea, dark and raging with towering waves that break over everything in their path, and then a few seconds later, you see those same waters flat and serene, like oil or, even better, like a tabletop. Just like that, my breathing settles and slows. It's done now.

Once, when Pollo saw how angry I got on account of Babi, as if she and she alone could really pluck the strings capable of making me foam at the mouth, he told me something. *"You want to know something? Something you might not like, but which might be the real reason that you've gone completely overboard for that damned young woman?"* And then he just stopped and stared at me.

In the end, I just broke out laughing.

"Why are you laughing?"

"Because of the way you said 'that damned young woman.'"

"But it's true. Just look at the shape you're in." And he'd reached both arms out to me, pointing at me with both hands. *"You're out of your mind! All right then, do you or don't you want to hear the brilliant conclusion that I've finally come up with?"*

I threw my leg over the saddle of my motorcycle and sat down. "Okay, let's hear it."

He'd smiled at me and taken a seat on his bike, in turn. He sat there, without a word, for a little while, and then, before I could ask him again, he'd finally piped up: "Just four words: resign yourself to it."

I'd stepped off the motorcycle, and with one hand, I'd waved him away. "A fine conclusion! You and your brilliant ideas."

"You underestimate me. Remember those words: resign yourself to it."

And now I'm here, looking at the last photo in this

album, and as if that wasn't enough, the picture with that asshole, of all people. And yet, I remember that one and only time we'd even talked about him. That day.

"But you can't be jealous of a guy like that, Step. You just can't. He's nothing but a friend."

"He annoys me, plus he's always coming around to see you. He doesn't even take into consideration the fact that you're with me."

"That's not true. He takes it to heart. In fact, he's inviting us, not just me!" Babi looked at me with a smile and caressed my cheek. *"Have I convinced you?"*

"No."

"So now what?"

"So now I'm thinking I'm going to have to give him a beating. That way everything will finally be clear."

"Cut it out now. You drive me crazy when you're like that."

There. I really would have done the right thing by beating him to a pulp back then. Who can say, maybe things would even have gone differently as a result.

No. It wouldn't have changed a thing. In fact, I find myself thinking about something that I'd forgotten. And yet we'd talked about this too. He's rich, very rich, goddamned rich, so rich that, as soon as he was done with college, he'd opened a chain of intimate apparel just to diversify, he liked to say.

And Babi had told me how things had worked out in that family. The guy's grandfather had started a long-distance bus business in the Marche region. He'd built up a network of coach lines where there was no other public transportation connecting far-flung, godforsaken towns that had no other alternatives. And so he'd started earning big money, and he'd plowed his earnings back into his company, extending out into neighboring regions like Molise and Abruzzo, continuing to pile up cash. By the turn of the 1980s, it had become an official, government-sanctioned transportation network, extending all the way north to the region of Emilia-Romagna.

From there, the family had been especially good at investing their money, opening a number of companies, and what had definitively crowned their efforts at empire building was the company that managed advertising spaces for all of Italy. Anything that anyone advertised on a billboard or posterboard in even the most tucked-away, overlooked spots would inevitably and by obligation make reference to their company.

This man's son, who was therefore Lorenzo's father, had done nothing more than to consolidate all of that without changing an iota of what he'd inherited. And so Lorenzo was bound to inherit the company, no matter what ability or hard work he might bring to the table. Then he might earn a little more or lose some of his wealth, but he was really going to have to work extraordinarily hard to destroy an empire like that.

Yes, I remember perfectly when she told me about it. So, tell me, Babi, is this what your life has actually become? That night in the car when you told me the news that you were getting married, I'd been left speechless. You looked at me, and you told me, "It's never going to be the way it was with you, but the way it was with you had become impossible."

And I'd continued to sit there in silence for a moment. I even thought you'd said that to me as a way of making me feel better, after we'd finished making love—or maybe it was really just a random fuck. Who can say. They seemed like the right words to put a definitive end to that chapter together in our lives.

But I do remember that, before I left, you told me, "But after all, life is work, children, and friends, and in the end, love is just ten percent of the whole thing."

And when I heard that, I died a little bit, and I wondered to myself, *What the hell am I even doing here? She's getting married.*

And I felt ashamed. I felt dirty, and I thought about Gin, her clean, bright self, and what I'd already done...

And when you turned on the radio, it almost seemed as if you were just killing time to keep from kicking me out, but you couldn't wait for me to go. Maybe because you knew that you were lying, that you were being the actress that you are, that those words didn't come from you, they came from your mother. She's the one who forced you to marry Lorenzo, or maybe I should say, Lorenzo's bus lines, his advertising company, and his underwear shops. That remains my pleasurable delight, a justification that maybe it's easier to accept as the truth.

I'm about to shut the photo album when I realize that, on the facing page, directly opposite the photo of that asshole, there's an envelope. *For you.*

Chapter 22

Well, I don't know what to call you anymore. I'd like to call you sweetheart, darling, or even my love. But I know that you're no longer mine. And yet, there was a time when you were, when you'd have done anything for me, anything and then some, even more than what any other reasonable person could have imagined, a normie, as you used to call them. And you weren't normal, or really, I should say, you weren't ordinary. You were and you remain special. But there are times when that can be uncomfortable, an inevitable, insurmountable challenge. At least, that's partly what you were for me.

Maybe it was out of fear, maybe because I wasn't courageous or because I didn't know how to say enough is enough, no more beating around the bush, he's mine and I want him. Maybe I should have said that. But now what has been is what is. There's no point crying over spilled milk. I've tried desperately to have you here with me, every single day, and in a certain sense, I've even succeeded. You were with

me at every moment of every day, even when I was
talking to my girlfriends, or listening to music, or
laughing or else miserable—whatever my state of
mind, you were still there with me.

Then, when Massimo was born, everything became
so much easier because, every time I looked at his
mouth, his smile, those eyes that every now and then
would stare at me even before he knew how to talk, I
could glimpse your gaze, your love, your curiosity—
they were the same eyes that searched inside me for
who knows what. Yes, I'm certain that when you
laid eyes on that photograph of Lorenzo, when you
discovered just who had become my husband—that
is, if you hadn't tried to find out before that—you
must have said, "You see? I did the right thing when
I beat him up!"

I smile when I read that part. At least in that detail she
knows me and understands me.

Lorenzo has always loved me, he's always wanted
to be with me, and when we started dating, I
realized that he has certain qualities that are ideal
in a man you'd want to marry. He's generous, kind,
and reasonably attentive. Do you remember what I
told you about that? As far as I'm concerned, your
marriage only takes up a small portion of your actual
life. The rest of it is work, friends, and children.

Actually, you'd talked about love, and you'd only
assigned it about ten percent.

But then, just the other day, I watched an old movie again. *Meet Joe Black*. And when I got to that scene, when she's in the helicopter with her father and he asks her if she loves Drew, and his daughter says little or nothing, then the father tells her that he wants her to be swept away. He wants her to be deliriously happy. Because if you don't start with someone you can't live without, what are you going to end up with?

I've watched that scene so many times that I know it by heart, but the first time I saw it, I burst into tears. I sobbed and sobbed, and when Lorenzo came in, he was worried. He asked me what had happened, but I couldn't even bring myself to speak. So then he got mad. He insisted I tell him because he thought something might have happened to Massimo. But really, something had happened to me. No one ever explained things to me like that, no one ever stopped me. In fact, my mother basically forced me into marrying Lorenzo with a very subtle form of brainwashing, making it clear to me every single day what my life could be like, what a woman's life could be like, every day filled with loving attention, beautiful possessions, and then, to have a child...

Of course, when I told her that I was pregnant, there was never the shadow of a doubt about who might be the father, even though, a few months ago, we were having dinner at my folks' place, and at a certain point, Massimo just broke out laughing and he sounded exactly like you. When that happened, my mother stopped and looked at him. At first, she laughed, too, but then her face changed. Really, it transformed, and it was as if a thought had suddenly gone through her head. She turned to look at me, and there was a spark of understanding in her eyes. Then she said to me, "Your son is very handsome."

And I said, "Yes."

And she said, "I wonder how he'll turn out."

And after that, we never said another word about it. After watching that movie, I realized that I needed to see you again, and that I had actually always known that this moment would arrive eventually. For that matter, I started collecting duplicate pictures of Massimo from the very first day, from when he came into the world, and I kept them so I'd have them the day I finally met you again.

The scene from that film was as if someone had held up a big mirror in front of me and I'd suddenly been able to get a glimpse of my own life. And then, the fact that I broke down and sobbed like a baby until I just couldn't speak, well maybe that can give you some idea of what I saw in that mirror. Nothing, an absolute void, except for my son. I'm not saying that there's nothing in my life, nothing to make me feel that I'm living the life that I want to live. Sure, I have a beautiful home, a shiny new car, lots of parties, plenty of friends, but every single day it's as if all that only served to sharpen my pain, making me feel all the more keenly how empty and pointless my life has turned out to be. We even thought about trying to have a baby sister or brother to keep Massimo company, but we couldn't make it happen.

The thought of this attempt they made suddenly ties a knot in my stomach. It blocks my respiration, and it makes me suddenly feel like throwing up. But I manage to get past that point, and I feel like tearing that letter up into shreds, so great is the annoyance I feel because of the story she tells me without a thought for the consequences. *We couldn't make it happen.* And then I conjure up the image of an awkward, demented attempt, conceived only for that purpose. And I see a dreary act of sex, a miserable orgasm, a passive woman on the verge of boredom, pretending to take part, like the finest actress in a soft porn film, or maybe not so soft, after all. And then I see that dope of a young man, that useless husband getting busy on top of her, or underneath her, or from behind... Why didn't I give him a good sound beating at the time? I knew it then, and I know now that you always have to listen to your gut, to your instincts, that's the best advice you'll ever get.

So what now? What does my instinct tell me? Here I am, with this letter in hand. I still have half a page to read, and I can just glimpse on the other side of this sheet of paper. What surprises may lie in wait for me in all those words? They lurk there, like menacing soldiers concealed in trenches, ready to attack, to strike, to end me, to destroy. I already know that I won't be able to resist, whatever may emerge in the coming lines, I'm still determined to go ahead and read them. So I turn the page and go on reading.

Anyway, enough of that, I don't want to bore you with
my private and personal issue. But there is one thing
I want to tell you, namely this: ever since the night
I rewatched *Joe Black* and I thought back to you, I've
done nothing but imagine us meeting again, what it
would be like, where it could take place, what you
would be like. Would you be surprised, would you
be happy to see me or would you be angry, or worse
still, would you be indifferent? And then, when it
finally did really happen, I couldn't do anything but
look into your eyes. Yes, I was trying to read your
emotions, what you were feeling when you saw me
again after all these years, or to put it in the terms
you like so well, "Is the flame dead or is it still
smoldering?"

I persuaded your secretary to help me out. I told
her a few things about us, and she embraced our
story passionately. She told me that we were missing
an important opportunity but that it would never be
too late. She struck me as a good person, conscien-
tious, quick on the uptake, and capable. You hired
an excellent assistant.

Sure I did. Too bad she doesn't work for me anymore.
And she has you to thank for that fact.

She refused to tell me anything about you. I have
to say I tried everything I could think of to get
her to talk, but I couldn't get a word out of her.
As far as that goes, she was a model of discretion.
Maybe you're in a relationship, maybe you're dating

someone, maybe you've broken up with someone.
I don't know. I know that you're not married. I
saw that you don't wear a ring, and anyway there's
nothing about you being married on the internet or
anywhere else. But the most important questions I
want to ask are these: Are you happy? Can we talk?
Can we see each other? Could you please think about
that? I'd really like it.

No two ways about it, this evening, everyone seems to
be worried about my happiness. Just then, my cell phone
beeps. It's a text message.
I open it. It's from Gin.

My love, what are you doing? Don't work too hard!
Soon everything's going to be even crazier. Come
home...I want you.

I smile. I fold up the letter. I put it away in the photo
album, which I hide in my bottom drawer.
Do you all want to know? Well, maybe I'll tell you
another day. This whole story just strikes me as a giant
dramatic Hollywood potboiler, of which I'm unfortunately the unknowing protagonist. I wonder what's going
to happen. And to paraphrase Joe Black again, *I'll only
find out by living*.

Chapter 23

 ood morning, everyone."

I walk into the office with a positive attitude, a bundle of good cheer, neither of which is justified to tell the truth, but I've decided that the best way to confront this day is not to think about it. Then, we'll see. Something will happen. The time will come when I'll make a decision, or else, just maybe, everything has already been decided.

"Good morning. It's a pleasure to see you like this." Alice walks over and hands me some papers. "I've put down all your appointments for the day, and these are some letters that just came in."

"That's great. Thanks." I head toward my office.

"Would you care for an espresso?"

I turn to look at her with a smile. "Yes, thanks, why not?"

And off she strolls. I have to say that she's really quite attractive with barely any makeup, very interesting in her simplicity.

"Everything okay, boss?" Giorgio calls out a hello from his office.

"Everything's okay."

"No news? No new arrivals...?" As he asks the second question, he moves his left hand in midair, as if caressing a ball or perhaps miming a round belly.

"I shouldn't have told you a thing. And I'm never going to tell you anything again, for fuck's sake. I had to go and hire a comedian to work in my office?" And I shut my door.

There's no present of any kind on my desk today. Well, that's good. I don't think I could have handled any other revelations. And there's nothing strange in the morning's mail either.

No. What's this? A letter for Stefano Mancini. It's not written on a typewriter or by computer, and it must have been hand-delivered because there's no stamp on it or any other postmark. I study the handwriting more carefully, and I don't think I recognize it. I pick up the switchblade knife I keep on my desk and use it as a paper knife. I open the envelope.

Dear Signore Stefano Mancini,

My name is Simone Civinini. I'm a young man, just 23, and I'd really like to do the work that you do. Since you haven't been working in this field for long but you started from the bottom, I'm sure that you'll recognize in my words two fundamental things: ambition and enthusiasm.

I'd very much like to meet with you. I'm enclosing a project of mine and leaving you my phone number and email address. If it can be of any interest to you, I'm available to do any small jobs you might have for me, any routine

tasks. But if you think it might be appropriate someday,
I'd very much like to work as a TV writer for you.

When I said that you started from the bottom, I wasn't
trying to curry favor. I've been following your career ever
since you had all those problems at TdV, I know your
whole history. So I'd be happy to meet you in person. In
any case, let me thank you for reading this far.

At the bottom of the letter, I see his phone number
and email address. I look at his street address. He's from
Civitavecchia, but he must spend time in Rome too or
else he might just be here on a business trip. Or I guess
he could be staying with someone, given that he delivered
this letter by hand.

The enclosed project is titled *Who Loves Who*. It's an
amusing title, if nothing else, definitely not run-of-the-
mill. I start reading. The program is a fifty-minute format.
The game proceeds in a succession of separate blocks that
are very easy to follow. It's well written, simple, and
direct, without a lot of flourishes and complications. So
I go on reading. The idea involves six men and seven
women, or else seven men and six women, who each tell
the story of a moment from their lives, something that
happened with their boyfriend or girlfriend or else their
partner or spouse. The way they met, their first date, their
first kiss, the first time they made love, where it was or
the strangest story about it.

Each contestant has to sort all the other eleven con-
testants into the correct couples on the basis of the stories
told by all the others. If they guess all the couples, then
that means they've also identified the extra contestant.

At this point, they only have a minute's time. There's no storytelling left. They just have to be incredibly lucky because they have to choose among a few people singled out in the audience which of them is the love interest or partner of that extra thirteenth contestant. If they're able to guess that person as well, then it's a full sweep and they win it all.

When I'm done reading the letter, I'm really satisfied. It's incredible that this twenty-three-year-old writer has invented a format that could be a real game-changer, and not just for the Italian market, but for the whole foreign market as well. So I leave my office and go to see Giorgio.

"Look at this." I set it down on his desk. Just then, Alice arrives in silence but with her usual lovely smile, bringing us a couple of espressos.

"Thanks."

She leaves us alone. Giorgio takes the letter in his hand.

"What's going on? Some sort of special request?" He cocks an eyebrow, hinting at who knows what.

"Yes, a ransom note."

For a moment, he looks at me, baffled.

"Come on, I'm just kidding. It's an idea from a young writer, and it's not bad at all, if you ask me. It would be a great get, just what both the Network and Medinews are looking for to spice up their programming."

"Seriously, something that big? And written by a young writer?"

"Yes."

"Italian?"

"Yes."

"How young?"

"Twenty-three. He's never worked in television before, and he's chosen us as the company to pitch it to."

Giorgio is reading the project's cover letter. He starts laughing. "He chose *us*? He chose *you*! He's a big fan of yours. These days, you just can't turn around without landing on silk, you know…"

I shake my head. Then Giorgio stands up, walks around me, and shuts the door. We're alone. Then he sits down on the sofa. "I have two things to tell you. No, make that three."

I sit down in the armchair facing him. "I'm all ears."

"Well, first of all, I've found out that Ottavi made two wire transfers to the director Gianna Calvi."

"Ah. And he makes it that easy to catch him red-handed?"

"He sent them to the account of her boyfriend's mother." Giorgio is really something. I can't begin to imagine how he got his hands on this kind of information, but I have to tip my hat. It must not have been easy.

"What's more, he gave her a Rolex, the latest model with diamonds, and a week's all-inclusive stay for two at the One and Only."

"What's that?"

"One of the most exclusive resort villages in the Maldives. There are only sixteen bungalows on the island, and each one comes with a butler and all-inclusive in-room service as well as a first-rate spa. I think it runs around three thousand euros a day."

"Oh, great! I was thinking of going when you told me about the sixteen bungalows. But now that I know about the three thousand euros a day, I don't think I'll go after all."

"Okay. Now let's do this. If we manage to win the foreign market with at least ten countries for two new formats and we're also able to place a drama series, then we absolutely have to go there, okay? It's an incentive to achieve that result. Do you know that many American companies set out the various objectives they want to achieve at the beginning of the year? It turns into a sort of race to grab the highest prize."

"All right, I'm in." The objective is so ambitious that I'm perfectly sure that we're not running any such risk.

"Put it there."

I shake hands with him anyway, very willingly.

"Fine. Now, let's move on to point two. The producer played very dirty, and we, if you're in agreement, won't play any cleaner with him."

"But what he's doing is straightforward corruption. I'm sorry, I'm not interested in veering in that direction."

He smiles. "Good, that's what I wanted to hear. But I needed to hear it. We won't give anything away, but we'll do our best, one way or another, to place that drama series."

"I don't want anything illegal. I don't want to depend on anyone else. I don't want to be open to blackmail."

"And you won't. I assure you, you're not risking a thing, not you and not Futura."

That was an important point to make. Giorgio is a responsible man.

Then he looks at me as if he'd just had yet another bright idea. "Then let's do it this way. The responsibility is all on me. I'll act on my own, not as Futura. I still have something to settle with Ottavi, and it's something I would have done eventually. It was just a matter of time. The only thing is, I don't want to tell you anything. I don't want to involve you in any way."

I smile at him. "I have no idea what you're talking about..."

"Excellent, perfect, that's exactly right. And now for the third thing, the most important thing to me..."

I stand, pick up my bottle of still mineral water, and take a long sip. He waits while I drink. Then I sit back down in the same chair. Concerning this last item, he seems uneasy. I wonder what he's about to say.

"Well, then...I really like this company. I like what we've done together and what we're doing now, and what I hope we'll do in the future. But there's one thing I'd like to make clear." He pauses briefly, and I'm careful not to hurry him. "If by any chance you think that sometimes I joke around too much, if there's anything you're not happy with, just let me know. There are many people who make a fatal mistake, if you ask me. They keep in too many things. Precisely because they didn't know how to deal with things as they came up, one thing at a time, in the end they have to deal with an explosive, uncontrolled situation, and at that point, the relationship is no longer fixable. Now, that's something I don't want to see happening between the two of us." He looks at me. He seems to have finished, and he heaves a sigh of relief as if, one way or another, he had finally gotten a weight off his chest, and he shifts comfortably in his seat.

I smile at him. "Everything's okay. There's nothing so

far that's bothered me. I think I would have told you if there had been."

"Even when I joke about this sort of thing?" He refers to the belly again.

"Of course not. Even in those cases, you make me laugh, and you cut through the tension."

"Good, I'm glad."

I start to get up.

"One last thing." He changes his tone of voice now.

"Yes, tell me."

"If you ever needed any advice, or you wanted my opinion, or you felt like letting off steam...or anyway, if you wanted to share something, I'm here."

"But I already have!" I open the door.

"Then don't worry about a thing here. Go and get ready to get married," Giorgio says.

"Thanks and so long. I'll see you later."

Chapter 24

When I wake up, the house is silent, except for music playing quietly on the clock radio. It's ten a.m.

"Gin, are you here?"

No answer. She must have woken to the alarm. I head for the kitchen. Breakfast is laid out, cereal, a block of Brie, a honeydew melon, already sliced, bread ready to pop into the toaster, and a note.

Good morning, darling. Eat hearty. It's your last day as a single man! By tradition, we aren't supposed to see each other today. So tonight you'll have to sleep at your father's or brother's place, but don't come back here. It's bad luck! I know your father has a suit for you. I'm dying to see it! Now, the bachelor party. I know Guido is planning it but take it easy. I need you in decent condition to legally say, "I do"! I love you, and if everything works out, I'm planning to marry you. Gin.

I fold up the letter and start eating breakfast. Then I shower, shave, and get dressed, and soon I'm ringing my father's doorbell.

"Here you are, at last! I'm not going into the office

today. Paolo is on his way. He told me to let him know when you arrived. He wanted to say goodbye."

"Yes, okay, but I'm not leaving for America or shipping out for war. I'm just getting married..."

"Well, that's a form of warfare." And he starts laughing like an idiot. I give him a frosty glare.

"Oh, look, Paolo is here." He leaves the room and comes back beaming, arm in arm with my brother.

"Hey, Stefano!"

"Ciao." I stand up, and we hug. We chat idly for a while, but when I stand up and announce that I'm leaving for the office, my father holds up his hand.

"Hold on, hold on!" And he hurries out of the room, coming back with a garment bag. "Here's the suit."

"Aren't you going to model it for us?" asks Paolo.

"No, tomorrow, with the music and lights," I reply, dismissively. "Tonight's my bachelor party, and then I'll be staying at the Hilton. Can't see the bride before the ceremony, you know!"

I head for the office, work a full day, and then check into my room at the Hilton. I lie down, ready for a quick nap before the evening's entertainment, when the phone rings.

"Good afternoon. Signor Guido Balestri is downstairs, waiting for you."

"Yes, please tell him I'm on my way down."

I put my shoes back on, grab the key, shut the door, and call the elevator. Then, as I wait, I wonder what the hell kind of bachelor party lies ahead. Then a wave of panic washes over me. Oh my God! This is my last night as a single man. I'm getting married tomorrow.

Chapter 25

Hey, what's all this?"

Guido is leaning casually on the hood of a black Mercedes E-Class sedan. "This car is taking us to a delightful surprise."

"I like that."

"Then get in."

I climb into the front seat, beside him.

"No, no, you get in back. I'm your chauffeur today."

"Even better."

I get in back, and Guido takes off, driving calmly, like a pro. "All right then, put this on." He hands me a black sleep mask. "You can't see where we're going. Orders from Mr. Big."

"Who's that?"

"The guy who helped me to organize all this, a friend you know who's given us the keys to a world you can't even begin to imagine…"

I pretend to be afraid. "Take me home!"

Guido laughs. "Too late! You're my prisoner. Put on the mask and pipe down!"

I put on the mask, and, after a while, I crack the

window to get some fresh air. I open my mouth and take a deep breath, filling my lungs. I taste the life outside the car. And I recognize the smell.

"Hey, we're heading for the seaside." I imagine Guido looking at me in the rearview mirror.

"No fair. You took off your mask!"

"I don't need my eyes. I can smell the sea."

The car keeps rolling, the air buffets my face, and the road rises and falls, rocking me gently into sleep.

Later, though I have no idea how much later.

"We're here. You can take off your mask."

Jesus, I don't know how long I've slept, but the sun is setting. "We're at the port."

"Yes, and there's a boat waiting for us."

I get out and see that I'm at the Porto Santo Stefano Yacht Club. A hundred miles away from Rome.

We board a Tornado 38 that peels away fast from the dock, heading straight out into open water, quickly accelerating to 30 knots. On we roar, until, just as the sun sets off Feniglia, we see a large, brightly lit yacht.

"Here we are."

Incredible. I didn't expect this. As we tie up to the side of the yacht, heads appear looking down on us. It's everyone.

"Here he is! About time!"

There's Lucone, Bunny, Schello, and all the rest. Even Marcantonio and still other friends. I look at Guido, stunned.

"Excuse me, but just how big is this yacht?"

"One hundred thirty-eight feet."

"And how did you get it?"

"Who cares? Just enjoy it!"

"They aren't going to arrest us, are they?"

Guido laughs. "No, no, stop worrying. It's a favor from an honest person. And we're not going to fight. Because there's thirteen of us, and I invited fifteen girls!" And sure enough, the party unfolds with girls and champagne and seafood and music and dancing.

Guido takes me up to the top deck of this three-decker behemoth: "Just look at that view…"

We're in the bay off Argentario. I see the long beach of Feniglia, where I kissed Babi for the first time, and then the hill above, dotted with houses. Some of those villas have their own private steps down to the sea. I look at the villas, one after another, down to the farthest inlet. There it is, the perfect villa, the highest, perched atop the rocks with its own dizzying staircase. That's where Babi had her first time. I cast my mind back.

"Are you happy?"

"So very happy."

"So happy you could reach up and touch heaven with your finger?"

"Much, much happier than that. At least ten feet higher than heaven."

"What are you thinking about?" Guido drops right into the middle of that memory.

"About how beautiful those villas are."

"The way things are going, one day you'll buy one of them. Maybe that one all the way down on the end!"

"Yes, maybe so."

I turn to Guido and ask, "Okay, I won't ask again. But just tell me one thing, Guido... What's the catch?"

He laughs. "You think there has to be one?"

"Yes."

"Well, that depends. Maybe it'll be tomorrow!"

"Ha! Good one." But I'm not laughing.

Chapter 26

There's been an endless procession of fresh, delicious grilled seafood, and my friends and I have been digging in heroically. After dessert, washed down with what seems like gallons of champagne, we all stand up and head for the prow. A fantastic combo strikes up the music, and the girls start dancing. A few newly formed couples head for various cabins.

Marcantonio, Guido, Lucone, and Bunny have found a roulette wheel, or maybe they brought it with them. In any case, they've set up a mini-gambling den at the center of the dinette. Shouts of excitement greet each bet.

Out of nowhere, the ship's siren sounds. We climb up onto the deck and crowd the railings, looking out over the water.

The night sky is clear, glittering with stars arrayed around the big full moon. And in the endless bowl of perfect dark blue, fireworks start to explode. Red, yellow, green, purple, one inside the other, incessantly. They sail straight up from the sea, up, up, up, and up, high overhead, one hundred, two hundred, even three hundred feet over our heads, spreading out like huge umbrellas, and before they have time to fade away, others explode beneath them, shattering and then crumbling down into the water below. The colors change constantly: red and orange are soon transformed into cascades of white and green. One after another in an explosion without end.

"Bravo!" "Beautiful!" "Stupendous!" Some whistle, others clap their hands, and I hear the popping corks on more bottles of champagne, as if this were New Year's Eve.

The ship's horn sounds again, twice. The girls all start filing off the yacht as if on command, and apparently that is exactly what the twin toots of the horn signaled.

Guido comes over. "Well? Did you like your party?"

"Loved it."

"Good, I'm glad to hear it."

He hugs me and then turns to head off toward the tender along with everyone else. The party is clearly over, and the tender is filling up. I start to follow him, but he holds up his hand.

"No, no." He smiles. "You, the commander, and the crew are staying the night. Enjoy this one-hundred-thirty-eight-foot yacht. There's a suite just for you. It's been locked all evening, they just opened it up. No one else has been in it."

"Wait, I don't understand. Why this yacht, who...and tomorrow?"

Guido smiles and climbs aboard the tender.

"Enjoy your last bottle in your suite. And tomorrow, when you wake up, there's a speedboat waiting to take you to shore. If you're up for it, that is..."

Without another word, he heads away from the yacht,

following after all the others. The pilot revs the engine, follows a wide curve, and disappears into the night.

I see the captain waving to me from a distance. "Good night." And he too vanishes into his cabin.

Silence, solitude. The boat seems empty; all my friends have left. The crew must include at least eight seamen, but there's no one around. It's spic and span, clean and gleaming. They did their work discreetly while the others were still celebrating. Never intrusive, busy and efficient.

I walk back through the dining room and head slowly toward the last cabin near the bow. On the teak door is the single word: SUITE. I open the door. The cabin is enormous with a king-sized bed. On a small coffee table stands an ice bucket with a bottle of Cristal champagne. Next to it is a rose, and next to it, a note. *For you.*

And then I see her, reflected in the mirror.

"I suspected for a moment that you might be behind all this...But just for a moment."

"Were you hoping?" Babi smiles. She's dressed in a silver-sequined dress that shimmers and gleams with even the slightest movement. Her hair is black and short with long bangs over her blue eyes, made up perfectly to stand out even more distinctly.

"No, I never hoped it. I dismissed the idea because it seemed nonsensical."

She's wearing high heels, and her skirt is short.

"Last time we were in that house. You remember?" She points to Ansedonia, outside the big porthole, across that dark sea, a hill dotted with twinkling lights here and there.

"Yes, we were. And yes, I do."

"That was the first time we made love, and it was beautiful."

"Yes, Babi, and it was a long time ago."

Now she moves slowly. "Do you like this yacht?"

"Yes, very much."

"I'm glad to hear it. It belongs to my husband. I never come aboard. But tonight I was happy to be able to put it to good use."

"What did you tell him?"

She steps close, brushing against me, but then grabs the bottle behind me.

"Sit down, Step, and I'll pour you a drink."

So I go over to the sofa as she opens the bottle.

"I just told him I wanted to throw a party. He didn't ask why or with who—he's an ideal husband. He's far away right now, and most of the time." Then she pops the cork and pours two glasses full of Cristal, offering me one. She looks at me, smiles, and raises her glass. "To our happiness, whatever it might be."

I say nothing, clink glasses delicately, and then look her in the eye as we each take a sip.

"Do you like me with my hair dark like this? You didn't recognize me at first, did you?" She says nothing more and just smiles at me. "It's a wig. I wore it for you. I wanted to be your last girlfriend, your last kiss as a single man…" She continues looking at me as I drain my glass of champagne and set it down. She stands up, picks up the bottle, and fills both our glasses again, handing me mine.

"May I?" And she points at the sofa. She wants to sit down beside me. She wants to seduce me.

"It's your boat."

"But unless you give me permission, I won't do a thing."

I look at her without speaking for a moment. She seems calm and collected, and maybe she really would do whatever I told her. I pat the sofa cushion. "Be my guest."

She steps closer, sits down, and takes another sip of champagne. Then she picks up a remote, dims the lights, and turns up the music. Then she leans forward, slowly starts to unbuckle the straps on her shoes, and then takes them both off. Now she's barefoot.

"Oh, there, that's more comfortable. I put on this wig because tonight I don't want to be Babi anymore. I'd like to be anyone else, but a girl you like so much that you can't resist me and so you decide to spend a special night with me. Will you give me that gift?"

And she looks at me, her eyes intense and languid, her lips slightly parted, and I stare at her mouth, her teeth, her smile glimmering in the dim light. How many times have I dreamed of that mouth, how many times have I shattered armoire doors with my fist because you were no longer mine, Babi?

"I'm getting married tomorrow."

"I know, but tonight you're here, with me."

She places a hand on my chest and lets it slide down onto my belly. Then she pulls me to her and leans toward my face. She opens her mouth next to mine and inhales my breath as if she wants to live on me.

At that moment, Gin appears to me, her big, kind eyes, her laughter, the letter with this morning's breakfast, her parents, Don Andrea, the choice of both church and menu, the words spoken, the promises made. And I feel guilty, wrong, and I wish I had the strength to stand up and walk away, but I do nothing. I just close my eyes.

I've had so much to drink. And it's as if I could hear someone laugh and say, no, you're right, it's not enough of an explanation. But Babi is wearing the wig, she's a different person now, it's a stag party like any other, it's just one last roll in the hay, nothing more than that...Sure, that's right.

But I know that that isn't true either. Babi takes my right hand and guides it up her legs, up up under her skirt. She lets me feel how much she wants me. Then she climbs up on top of me and straddles me, closer than ever.

"Love me, come on and love me still, just for tonight. The way it once was, or even more than that..."

And we kiss, losing ourselves.

Chapter 27

I won't bore you with my awakening aboard the yacht, the trip back in reverse in daylight, and then my shower and shave and dressing in my suite at the Hilton. It all seemed like a dream until I found myself in the all-too-real church, at the altar, facing Don Andrea.

The music seems to swell as the people all take their places and the church fills up. Then from the light-drenched forecourt, I see Gin enter through the portal, arm in arm with her father. She's beautiful, beaming, in a white gown, her shoulders bare, the veil long. And her happiness overwhelms me, sweeps me away, removes my every doubt, even the slightest uncertainty.

Babi was nothing but one last bout of sex, a bachelor party saturnalia with lots of free-flowing champagne and a lust for fun. Whereas this is my life.

Gin walks through the crowd, past the pews, beaming with contentment, and the music seems almost deafening, and everything is perfect. Yes, now I'm capable of answering that question that everyone kept hammering away at. I'm happy. I'm very happy.

Chapter 28

The next morning, Gin and I wake up at the hotel. We have a lovely breakfast in the garden, and I have to say that, luckily, my hangover seems to be a thing of the past. I have no headache, and, not having had a lot to eat, I feel light and unburdened. Paolo and Fabiola helped to organize the details of the honeymoon trip, and everything is taken care of and perfect. We leave this evening at nine o'clock. They left all the paperwork for me in the room.

"Fiji, Cook Islands, and Polynesia, a magnificent trip. We'll be traveling around the world, and we'll be gone, all told, for three weeks."

"Look at that. There are even brochures and guidebooks. Your brother certainly takes care of things down to the slightest detail."

"It's Fabiola, and she must surely be giving him a hard time because this is the honeymoon trip she would have wanted to go on when they got married."

"Well, where did they go instead?"

"A week in France, in Épernay."

"Well, still, that must have been nice. There's plenty of

excellent champagne. Maybe that's not the absolute ideal after the stress of getting married though."

"It's just that my brother was working as an import-export consultant for French champagne, so he wanted to be there to keep an eye on all the technical aspects."

"Really? I'm surprised to hear that she didn't divorce him on the spot when she found out that detail."

"You're not allowed to say a critical word about our honeymoon, though. It was a gift from my mother."

"Yes, and it's wonderful." Gin throws her arms around me. "I'm happy, Signor Mancini, very happy indeed. And I'm especially happy to be your wife." She lifts up on tip-toes and kisses me on the lips and then smiles. "And I even brought you a new swimsuit, seeing that the hotel has a pool. I'm going swimming right away because the last few days have been seriously stressful, and I'm ready to relax."

"And I'll come with you."

So we spend the rest of the morning doing nothing but relaxing. I alternate between an inflatable sky-blue air mattress and a navy-blue canvas lounger, but I especially get lost in watching clouds passing slowly overhead. Gin reads magazines while I leaf through newspapers, skipping the crime pages or anything else that features human evil. I'm looking for relaxation today, as far as the darker side of existence is concerned. I don't want to think. My mind neither falters nor wallows anywhere.

A bird sails through the sky overhead. Then I hear a car horn. An automobile is climbing the hill. Then it stops in the large garden where I hear the engine die, a car door slam, and then I see him arrive at poolside: none other than Giorgio Renzi.

"Well, how are my little lovebirds? Are you ready to set off on your honeymoon? I'll take you to the airport if you don't mind; that way you can get ready without haste but also without excessive dawdling. I wouldn't want you to miss your flight and all the various connections that follow. Your brother told me all about it last night. It's going to be a fantastic trip, and, what's more, he's a genuinely nice guy."

"You're trying to get me out of the way, aren't you? I wonder why you two are trying to sideline me. You're definitely not telling me everything..."

Giorgio sits down at a poolside table. "If you want the full picture, we're in negotiations with Spain, Holland, and Germany. But let's not get ahead of ourselves. Maybe there will be good news awaiting you when you return home.

"Even better, tomorrow afternoon I have an audition for Dania Valenti. I'll let you know as soon as I'm done. You see? I want to spare you this kind of nonsense."

"So you're saying I can leave without a worry in my mind?"

Chapter 29

Let's go pack our bags. Otherwise, Giorgio will show up here and catch us unprepared."

I get down two Samsonite suitcases and start packing. Gin and I roam through the apartment, bumping into each other occasionally and far more often calling out questions from room to room.

"Where are the swimsuits, anyway?" I ask.

"Where they've always been, the last armoire at the end of the hall, in the top drawer, where you'll also find bathrobes and towels."

"They've always been there?"

Gin starts laughing. "Always. Every now and then, they've jumped into the washing machine, but they've spent most of their time right there."

"Okay, good to know."

And we go on picking out T-shirts, shirts, shorts, shoes, and at least one jacket each.

"Will it be cold there?" she asks.

"In Polynesia?"

"I mean, I don't know, at night?"

"Only if you have the AC turned up too high. Let's head downstairs," I say.

No sooner does Giorgio ring the doorbell than we're already out the front door. He helps us to load our luggage into his VW Golf, and minutes later, we're speeding through Prati on our way to the Via Aurelia, heading for the airport in Fiumicino.

"Excited?"

"Delighted!" Gin is sitting in back, in the center seat. "It's all I've been waiting for this past whole month, to leave on our honeymoon."

Before long, we see signs for parking at Fiumicino airport.

"Here we are."

Giorgio slows down and pulls over to the side of the road, near the signs for departures. "Do you have everything? Passports, identification, tickets?"

"Yes, everything we need."

Giorgio helps us get our suitcases out of the car, gives me a hug and Gin a kiss, and then waves goodbye. "Have fun, newlyweds. I'm not going to bother you. If you need anything, just reach out."

Chapter 30

We land in New Plymouth and catch a quick connecting flight to Fiji. After roughly nineteen hours, Gin and I finally arrive at Nadi International Airport.

Then we board what looks like a London taxicab in terms of size, though certainly not color since it's fire-engine red. The cabbie drives fast through the streets and roads. Along our route, there's plenty of vegetation and animals, ranging from cows in their classical color combinations to parrots in the most spectacularly fanciful hues. There are lots of people riding bicycles. Along the road, kids play next to fountains and faucets, spraying water in all directions and filling colorful balloons. They're dressed in khaki or dark blue shorts that are unfailingly very, very loose, paired with sleeveless shirts that are almost always white. The taxi drives onto a wharf, and as it rolls along over those wooden planks, the sound that arises is a deafening melody.

"Here we are. We've arrived," I say.

Out we go. Waiting for us is a large white motorboat. A very tall, hatless gentleman helps us aboard after loading our suitcases.

"So long, Mr. Noodle." We say goodbye to the driver, who had told us that this was his nickname. Then the motorboat pulls away from the wharf, and once we're outside the little marina, it takes off at full speed with a growling roar. I look at Gin sitting on the upholstered bench. She looks tired. And in fact, we've been traveling for quite some time.

"How are you doing?"

"Fine." She does her best to smile at me.

"Sit farther inboard. That way you won't get wet, and the wind won't hit you as hard." To help shelter her, I sit down beside her and wrap my jacket around her shoulders.

"There." She really smiles at me. "Now I finally feel well and truly married."

About two hours later, we arrive at Monuriki, where at last we receive our reward for the long and exhausting trip. We find that we are the proud possessors of a beautiful bungalow just a scant stone's throw from the sea. The house is partly carved out of the living rock and partly built on the sand. There's nothing but greenery all around, a small hedge dotted with sky-blue flowers—the inside of each bud is bright yellow—and it's surrounded by a low white fence. The sand blows all the way up to the large picture window.

Inside, the house is cool and super modern. There's a great big plasma-screen television set, high-tech speakers, and a king-sized bed. There's a bottle of champagne to greet us, along with a bowl of strawberries, kiwis, and grapes. An elegantly attired valet shows us how to use all the equipment, including the Jacuzzi in the bathroom.

The tub is set in the rock and has a view of the water through a large, round window.

In the days that follow, we walk around the island over and over, a stroll of just a few miles. We often eat in our room, with a waiter available at all hours and impeccable service. At night, we go to the island's one restaurant where the tables are set far apart and there's never any noise or bustle. There aren't many people eating because there are only about ten bungalows on the island, and there are other couples on their honeymoons just like we are. Practically speaking, during the day, it's as if each couple has their own beach, all to themselves. We have the time of our lives.

Chapter 31

Every time I come back from a trip, Rome looks so different to me." I set the suitcase down outside the front door and rummage for my keys.

"Sure, but you're talking about when you were just a little boy and you were gone for three months at the beach." Gin is carrying nothing but a light backpack slung over her shoulder and a fanny pack with her most vital possessions strung around her waist.

"Yes, that's true."

As I find the keys and open the door, I'm reminded of Anzio, the teenage summers I spent on that long beach and the first octopus that I netted at night with my grandfather Vincenzo and cooked just minutes later in the house we rented mere yards off the water's edge. And Mamma and Papà, who'd spend the evening sitting on lounge chairs to watch the sunset and the swallows darting and diving through the air and then just listen to the voices of the customers buying shaved ice and choosing their flavors, tamarind or sour cherry.

Those were carefree days, and my parents were cheerful and happy and never quarreled, and sometimes we'd all sing songs together. When you're little, you're happily and selectively blind—all you see are the good things, and if something's off-key, you don't even notice it because all you can hear is the music of your heart. What kind of life will I be able to give to this son of mine? Will I have another?

I carry the suitcases inside and set them down on the bench in the bedroom. "Gin, I'm going down to check the mail," I say to escape for a few moments.

"Okay, and I'll start unpacking the suitcases." Then she stands in front of the mirror and turns to look at her profile. "I can start to see a bit of belly." And she says it with a smile, happily, her face betraying some slight signs of weariness. I assume she's just tired from the trip.

"Yes, but you're still beautiful."

Gin whips around and glares at me angrily.

"What's wrong?"

"If you're this good at telling me lies, that must mean you practice saying them, and you're probably lying to me on a regular basis."

"You're so suspicious. I'll be back up in just a minute. I'm not like those guys who say they're going downstairs to buy a pack of cigarettes and then they vanish forever…"

"Only because you don't even smoke."

I riffle through the mail, but it's just promotional brochures, bills, and a few letters for Gin, but nothing strange with my name on it. So much the better. I wonder what Babi knows and how she's dealing with everything that's happened, if she's still thinking about me or if it was really just a one-nighter, a fling. I wonder if she meant what she said. Such lovely words.

I stop on the landing and shut my eyes. I see her again, her hair tangled, from time to time covering her face, her smile, her tears, on top of me, talking, telling me her thoughts, her dreams, her fears. But it's too late now, Babi. There are things that have a special magic because they happened then and there and are confined to that moment.

I open the front door. "It's me. I'm back."

I shut the door, trying my best to leave all those thoughts out on the landing behind me.

Chapter 32

I set the mail down on the coffee table in the living room. "There's a few letters for you!"

Gin picks up the mail and leafs through it. She rips open an envelope. "Look at this, twenty percent discounts at La Rinascente department store. They have my number. Why do they use up all this paper instead of sending me an email or a text? Poor old trees! I swear to you, every time I open an envelope that could have been avoided, my heart bleeds for them." Gin and her love for the natural world. Then she opens another envelope.

"I can't believe it! It's an answer from the Merlini law office. They've invited me for an interview!"

"Nice."

"Yes, but of all times, just when I'm pregnant. Usually women get hired and then they get pregnant. Whereas I do the exact opposite. How smart does that make me?"

Gin and her work ethic, her sense of duty.

"But you look great. If you don't know, no one would say that you're pregnant."

"Would you cut it out, you con artist? What are you going to teach this baby on the way?" She touches her belly. "To lie? To be dishonest? And then they'll turn it around on you, you know that? Don't you think it's much better to be clear, straightforward, and sincere? I can't imagine people who just tell lies all day, especially because then they have to remember to keep their stories straight, which is the hardest thing about it. You can remember the truth perfectly because it happened, but lies are much harder because you just made them up."

"Oh, good Lord, you remind me of Giorgio. I just hope I don't start getting you two mixed up."

"How do you mean?"

"I wouldn't want to start turning over the projects I think are promising to you and then, when I'm feeling it, I start kissing him."

"You're such a dope."

"We're seeing him tonight. Try not to fall asleep, that way we can get right back onto our time zone without too much jet lag."

"I'll try."

We exchange a light kiss.

"If you need anything, give me a call. I'll be in the office or maybe somewhere nearby, at the most."

"Okay, sweetheart, have a good day."

Chapter 33

Gin walks into the medical building and heads over to the elevator in the lobby. She summons it, and while she waits, she muses that, in the old days, anything could happen, anyone could pick an argument, but no matter what, Step would have come. Then she enters the elevator, pushes the button, and the doors shut. Okay, she thinks, but now he has more responsibilities.

She rides up to the floor, steps out, and walks over to the receptionist, who checks for her name. When she finds it, she points Gin to the waiting room. A short while later, the doctor arrives. "Ginevra Biro?"

"Yes, that's me."

"Come this way, please."

Ginevra follows him into a small room where a nurse is waiting.

"Lie down here, thanks. Now I told you that I wanted to draw some blood. You're still fasting, right?"

"Yes."

"My assistant will do the draw. Are you afraid of needles?"

"No."

"Good."

"As long as they're not too long."

"This one's not too long."

A young woman bares Gin's arm, fastens a rubber strap around it, taps her forearm, finds the vein, and inserts a small needle. The first test tube with her name on it fills with blood. Ginevra watches without the slightest fear as the nurse replaces test tubes one after the other until they're all filled with her blood.

"All done, doctor."

"Fine, thanks. Now please leave us alone."

The doctor takes out a tube of gel, opens it, and spreads some on the tip of the probe. Then he gives Gin a series of instructions:

"Uncover your belly, please."

Gin raises her blouse and pulls down her pants with a loose, elastic waist, chosen especially for this visit among the assortment of maternity clothing that she's purchased. She turns to her left and sees the visuals of the sonogram on the screen.

The doctor reassures her. "I warmed up the gel so you wouldn't jump in the air, neither you nor your baby. There now, do you hear the heartbeat?"

Gin, thrilled, nods her head while the doctor measures the fetus's limbs and shapes and transcribes that information onto a document in an open folder. "All one hundred percent normal, and it's growing. I can see the sex too. Do you want to know or would you rather keep that a surprise?"

Chapter 34

As I enter the apartment, I hear Gin's voice from the living room. "Well? How did it go?"

She is sitting with her feet on the coffee table, a cushion behind her head, very relaxed as she watches the TV, which is playing with the sound turned down.

I tell her how my day went. Then I ask, "Tell me, how did it go at the doctor's?"

"Excellent. Perfect measurements, growing normally... and I even found out the gender."

"Wow, I can't believe it. At last!"

Gin picks up a folder lying next to her on the sofa and hands it to me, but when I try to take it, she yanks it back just in time.

"No, I'm not giving it to you. You should have come to the appointment!"

"It's not like I forgot. I really couldn't. Giorgio was in Milan, and there was no one else who could solve this problem. Believe me, I absolutely had to stay."

"Of course, big producer..."

"Silly."

Gin extends the folder in my direction once again. I try

to grab it, but she's faster than me, and by twisting her wrist down ever so slightly, she makes me miss it again.

"Hey, stop it. You're being awful!"

"Tremendously awful and tremendously vindictive. All right, then, let's play a game. Let's see if you can guess the gender. After all, it's right here in black and white. If you guess right, then you can choose the name. If not, I decide. You up for it?"

"All right."

Gin smiles at me. She sets down the file on the backrest of the sofa, right in front of me. I look her in the eyes and try to suss it out.

She raises one eyebrow. "I'm not giving you even the slightest hint."

Suddenly, inevitably, dramatically, I'm reminded of Babi. How did she convey the news to her husband? Did she know the baby's sex the first time she went to the doctor? And when she found out, did she tell him right away? Did she wait for him at home or did she text him the minute she left the gynecologist's office? Did she send a picture of a boy baby, a blue bow, a pair of light blue baby shoes, or the symbol of masculinity with the circle and the little arrow pointing up and to the right?

"Well? What are you thinking about? It's a boy or a girl, you can't go wrong! It's not like I'm asking you to guess the exact weight!"

I smile, but I'm annoyed. I try not to let it show, but a sense of uneasiness rises up out of the depths. That little boy who lives with Babi and her husband is my son. And so, out of a sense of contrariness, without even really thinking about it, just to give an answer and ward off all that unpleasantness, I tell her in a rush. "It's a girl."

And Gin sits there with a piece of raw fennel snapped off in her mouth and then goes back to chewing. Eventually, she says, "Good job. Damn, though, you're always lucky!"

"Oh, well, I had a fifty-fifty chance. It worked out for me. Okay, then, let's see...Here, how about this? Gertrude! I love Gertrude as a name. It's so uncommon, yet it's a significant name. Gertrude was a queen, Hamlet's mother."

"Where do you get these things? Riccardo doesn't know them. Maybe from Giorgio? I liked you better when you were ignorant! Are you seriously thinking of naming my daughter Gertrude? Just listen to the sound of it..."

"It's beautiful, it's unique, and it's special. I won, and so I get to choose the name."

"I was just kidding! And after all, Gertrude was also the name of the Nun of Monza."

"Seriously?"

"Certainly! You wouldn't want to have such a sinful daughter..."

And we go on sampling potential girls' names. Giorgia, Elena, Eva, Giada, Francesca, Ginevra like her mother, or even Gin, Anastasia, Anselma, Isadora, Apple, like the daughter of Chris Martin and Gwyneth Paltrow, or even the name of Madonna's daughter, Lourdes Maria.

We go on joking, but all this reminds me of the time that Babi and I snuck into that house on the sea and found the robes with two initials and, after taking a swim, put them on and started inventing the most ridiculous names, the more ridiculous the better. In the end, there we were, Amaryllis and Siegfried, embracing as we looked up at the stars, happy, so happy that we felt like we were at least three meters higher than heaven.

I feel a knot in my stomach. Will I ever be able to get free of her, of every thought, memory, joy, or sorrow, of all that universe of emotion that, over the years, has meant that it's been carved so damned deep into my flesh?

Chapter 35

Babi walks out of little Massimo's room.

"I sent you a dozen red roses, and you didn't even text me to say thank you." Lorenzo is standing in the middle of the living room.

"I was out all day, and I knew you'd be home later. I needed to check Massimo's homework."

"We have a nanny to do that."

"I want my son to grow up in contact with me. I want him to hear the sound of my voice. I thought you knew me. I don't like having nannies around the house. When we were little, my sister and I never had one."

"We can afford them though."

Babi glares at him angrily. "My folks could afford them, too, but they preferred not to." She walks over to the roses, arranges them to give them a little more room in the vase, and then picks up the card on the table next to them. *I love you more than ever.* She folds it back up. "Thanks. They're beautiful."

"Do you know what they're for?"

Babi says nothing. She picks up a few action figures from the floor where Massimo had been playing with them.

Lorenzo looks at her, with her back to him. "Because today is our monthiversary. It's from the first time we kissed. It was at night, and we were up on the Gianicolo Hill. We got out of the car, it was cold, and you said to me, 'Hold me tight.' So I did. I embraced you, and we stood there like that for a while. Then I kissed you, and you laughed, and you asked me, 'So what does this mean? Are we going steady now?' And I told you, 'No, it means I want to marry you.'" Lorenzo smiles, pulls out a pack of cigarettes, and lights one. "So? Do you remember?"

"Perfectly. Just like you never remember not to smoke indoors." Babi walks out on the terrace. Lorenzo picks up an ashtray and follows her. He sets it down on the parapet and stands near her. They remain in silence, looking down on the passing cars on the Via Nomentana. There's a bit of traffic. Over a distant roof, the flag of an embassy waves and beyond that lie the magnificent vaults of the church of Santa Costanza.

Lorenzo looks around. "The terrace has turned out perfectly. I like the lighting too. Shall we sit down?" He points to a sofa near several potted strawberry trees and a maritime pine, illuminated with faint blue lights.

Babi goes over to him while Lorenzo walks to the light switch to dim the terrace lights ever so slightly. When Babi turns around, she can't see him, but then she hears the melody of "Meraviglioso" by the Negramaro coming out of the speakers, filling the terrace with atmosphere and sound. A second later, Lorenzo appears with a remote in one hand, smiling at her.

"Turn the music down. I'm afraid that if Massimo wants something, we won't hear him."

He shows her, in his other hand, a baby monitor with the green light indicating that it's turned on. "We can hear him for sure with this." He sets it down on the low table in front of her. "Do you want something to drink?"

"A coffee, thanks."

Lorenzo goes inside, but he's back in a few minutes with a tray. On it is the espresso for Babi and a bottle of Talisker scotch with a short glass and a bowl of ice cubes. He sits down, fills the glass with ice cubes, and pours himself a generous amount of whiskey, practically to the brim. Then he takes a long sip, leans back in his chair, spreads his arms, and looks up at the sky. "I'm constantly traveling, but I can't settle down. There's just too much to do and see, but actually, I wish I could just stay here, by your side."

"But even when you're here in Rome, we still never see you. You never come home to eat, you don't go to pick Massimo up at school, and at night, you always have something you're doing for work or with your friends. All that makes me think you must have a girlfriend on the side."

"If only."

Babi turns and looks at him in surprise, baffled.

Lorenzo drinks a long slug and finishes the glass of whiskey. He fills his glass again and takes another long sip. Then he pulls out the pack and lights another cigarette. "I've had you stuck in my head since I was just a boy. I've chased after you all my life. I pursued you, I called you, I courted you, and I invited you to parties. You've always been my obsession."

"I never thought I'd meant so much to you. So

aren't you happy your dream has finally come true? You married me."

Lorenzo finishes his glass yet again, fills it back up, and takes another slug. Then he takes a drag on his cigarette. "I didn't marry you. You're the one who married me. In fact, you only married a part of me, the part you needed to fill up the space that I could occupy in your life. I still don't quite understand why you needed me, of all people. Why you chose me. Maybe you wanted to punish me for something."

Babi starts laughing. Lorenzo pulls her to him and kisses her. For a moment, she lets him do it, even though she never parts her lips. Then he lifts her skirt, touches her legs, tries to spread them, and slides his hand into her panties, but she resists, clamps her legs shut, and refuses to let herself be touched. Lorenzo exerts more effort, crams his leg on top of hers to try to part them, and at that point, a sort of wrestling match breaks loose.

Then, all of a sudden, Lorenzo pulls away because she's bitten his lip. "Ouch."

"You were overdoing it."

"I want you."

"Not like that."

"Do you realize how long it's been since we've made love? More than eight months. Don't you understand that I still love you? What do I have to do to make you understand it? You're the only woman I desire, that I long for, the only one who gives me a thrill."

"I'm going in to check up on Massimo." Babi walks away, steering clear of him.

Lorenzo watches her leave. "I wish you loved me even a tenth as much as you love him." Then he picks up his glass and drains it at a single gulp.

Babi goes in. Even a tenth, she thinks to herself, would still be too much.

Chapter 36

Gin wakes up early and goes to the kitchen. She knows that Step had an appointment early that morning. She finds a note propped up against her morning breakfast mug.

Break a leg today, with a kiss from me.

So she pulls out her cell phone and texts him.

Thanks. And a kiss right back at you.

But she notices that the double WhatsApp check mark, indicating the message has been read, fails to appear.

Gin makes breakfast, putting a kettle on to boil and taking tiny bites of a piece of melba toast. Then she leafs through the paper, lingering over an item or two, and studies the entertainment page.

She hears the water come to a boil and then pours herself a pot of green tea, bobbing the tea bag in the hot water before carrying the teapot to the table with a hot pad to keep from burning her fingers. She pours out a mug, adds a teaspoon of honey, and stirs it while chewing on another slice of melba toast. She glances at the clock. She's contented and thinks, *What a wonderful time of my life this is. Aurora will be born soon, and we'll fix up her room, Step's work is going great, and he's so much more even-tempered, and today, to cap things off, I've been called in for an interview after sending around my résumé.*

Gin showers, dresses nicely, and climbs into her Fiat Cinquecento L. She feels utterly calm. Soon afterward, she's on Viale Bruno Buozzi, heading for the interview. She immediately finds a parking spot, which strikes her as a sign that her luck is good today. She locks her car and walks into the gorgeous office building. The entrance is all marble. On either side of the majestic staircase stand two large and lovely potted plants. To the right sits the concierge at a desk, checking the morning's delivery of mail.

"Good morning. I'm expected at the Merlini law office."

"Of course, take the second elevator, fourth floor."

"Thanks."

When Gin reaches the office, she speaks to a young secretary with a pageboy hairdo, seated at the reception desk.

"Good morning. I'm Ginevra Biro. I have an appointment with Carlo Sacconi."

"Yes, come this way." The young woman stands up and leads Gin down the hallway.

Gin follows her, looking around. It's a big office, crowded with young lawyers, male and female, hard at work.

The young woman stops in front of an open door. "Counselor Sacconi, here is the person you were expecting."

Gin walks in. A man who looks about forty stands up and walks around his desk to greet her.

"A pleasure to meet you! Come in, come in, take a seat."

Gin sits down, and the man shuts the door and then walks back to his desk.

"I'm pleased you could come in. It seems like good news. I'm guessing you haven't taken another position, is that right?"

Gin smiles. "That's right. I've accepted only one offer, my newlywed husband's offer of marriage!"

"Ah! Well, congratulations."

"I'm still recovering from the wedding. It took a lot of planning, fun but exhausting. Luckily, we had a relaxing honeymoon afterwards."

"Where did you go?"

"Fiji, Cook Islands, and Polynesia."

"That must have been magnificent. My wife and I vacationed in Mauritius, but we didn't really like it. But we're interested in going to the Seychelles."

"I've heard that's beautiful."

"Yes, there's the island of Praslin, of course, but we hear that the really gorgeous place is La Digue."

"My husband told me the same thing." Soon Gin finds herself chatting amiably, surprised at how comfortably the interview seems to be going.

"Maybe we'll run into you there on our next vacation."

"Yes, coincidences do happen."

"Well, you have a follower here in the office," Counselor Sacconi says. "None other than Counselor Merlini himself. He read your thesis on digital intellectual rights, and he thought it was phenomenal. What do you say to that?"

"I'm delighted. I wrote that thesis with excitement and enthusiasm, and I'm glad to hear that Counselor Merlini liked it. But to tell the truth..."

Counselor Sacconi holds up one hand to keep Gin from saying another word.

"Say no more. I don't want to find it's a law office we're on good terms with. I don't want to make a misstep. We would offer you an internship, an expense account, and a weekly stipend. I'm not saying you're hired, but close to it. I've been expressly told as much by the counselor. I don't have to talk to anyone else to offer you this position." Then Counselor Sacconi looks at Gin with a smile. "I certainly hope that you're interested in accepting our offer, signorina."

"And I hope you can accept my conditions. I have a daughter."

"Would you like us to take her on at the firm as well?"

"In twenty years or so, maybe, but for the moment she's studying right here, inside of me." And she pats her belly to make matters perfectly clear.

"Good for you, best wishes. I'll mention it to Counselor Merlini, but I'm sure it won't be a problem. We'll work with you, and I'm sure we can come up with a solution, or at least a series of solutions."

Gin is surprised by that response. "Absolutely, I'm pleased to hear it. So you'll let me know?"

"Definitely, and quite soon." Counselor Sacconi stands up and walks to the door. "Come, let me see you out."

They leave his office and follow the hallway back to the reception desk.

"Well, let's stay in touch."

"Thanks for coming by. I appreciate your honesty." The lawyer turns and leaves.

The secretary clicks the door open, and just as Gin walks through it, she barely misses slamming into a young man. "Excuse me."

"No, pardon me...Ginevra! What a surprise! What are you doing here?"

It takes her a few seconds to recognize him. "Nicola! Ciao!"

They exchange cheek-kisses.

"I'm here for an interview. You?"

"I work here." Then he points to the plaque on the door. "You see? Or maybe you don't remember my surname."

It's true. His name is Nicola Merlini. *How could I have missed that? But I haven't seen him in forever. I have an excuse.* "You're right, I just didn't think of it."

"Not a problem. Shall we have an espresso? There's a café downstairs."

They ride down in the elevator, and Gin looks at him curiously. Nicola had a crush on her, and they were about to see if they could work things out enough to become a couple, but then Step burst dizzyingly back into her life.

"It's been forever since we last talked. We haven't even run into each other by accident."

"Well, I'm glad it finally happened today. How did the interview go?" Nicola asks.

"Well, I think..."

"Sacconi knows what he's doing." They walk into the café. "What'll you have?"

"A decaffeinated espresso."

"Decaf and a regular espresso, black, for me, thanks."

Suddenly, a lightbulb goes on for Gin. Couldn't Nicola have spotted her résumé and insisted she be hired? "Nicola, you're not involved with me getting this interview, are you?"

"Absolutely not."

"You know that, if I find out that you pulled any strings, for that reason alone, I wouldn't accept."

Nicola smiles. "I know that about you, and it's one of the things I like best. But I had nothing to do with it. I'd heard my father talking very favorably about a new thesis, but I had no idea it was yours."

Gin savors her espresso with special enjoyment now.

Nicola looks at her and smiles. He really still likes her. He's glad he talked his father into taking her on.

Chapter 37

Come right in, please."

The secretary ushers Gin into a small waiting room where other expectant mothers are sitting, their bellies all more or less swollen. Some are so big with child that they're certainly about to give birth. They're looking at their cell phones, reading newspapers and magazines, and one is playing with her four-year-old daughter.

"But why are we giving him the same name as Grandpa? When I say Hugo, am I talking to him or Grandpa?"

"To both," her mother replies with a smile.

"Oh."

"Signora Biro?"

Gin stands up and walks toward her.

"This way, please. Dr. Flamini is waiting for you."

"Thanks."

She walks in, and the doctor looks at her and nods. "Good morning, Ginevra. Please, have a seat."

"Thanks."

He sits down in his turn. "Now, then…" He opens a folder. "Have you been uncomfortable? Pain? Nausea? Do you feel particularly tired?"

"Well, yes, tired and exhausted, actually.."

The doctor takes off his eyeglasses, sets them down on the desk, clasps his hands together, leans back in his chair, and shuts his eyes for a brief moment. Then he opens them again and looks at her. Gin suddenly stiffens, realizing that something's not right.

The doctor tries to smile, but even his mouth looks uncertain. "There's a problem."

Gin feels her heart start to pound fast. She can't catch her breath.

"With the baby girl?"

"No. With you."

And then, absurdly, she's suddenly calm again. Her heartbeat slows, as if deep inside she had said to herself, *Oh, all right. In that case, everything is fine.*

The doctor puts his glasses back on and takes a sheet of paper out of the file folder.

"At first everything seemed fine, but then I spotted a tiny swelling caused by a swollen lymph node. So I ordered further tests. I was hoping I was just being a stickler, that it was just a minor inflammation, but that's not the case. You have Hodgkin's lymphoma."

Suddenly, Gin has a pang, and she immediately feels herself trying to sense what she's feeling inside. She searches for the least discomfort, but there's nothing. Nothing at all. She looks up at him, stunned, and is tempted to ask, "Are you sure there hasn't been some sort of mistake?" But she says nothing and instead starts turning her questions to a higher force, to fate and to destiny. *Why me? Why now? Why now that I'm expecting Aurora?*

The doctor looks at her, and she sees in his gaze not the slightest chance of a mistake.

"I ran your tests twice. I was hoping against hope that I'd made a mistake, that the data were wrong. But I hadn't, and they weren't."

They sit in silence for a few seconds, and Gin sees everything she's done in the past few months flash before her eyes, her wedding, pictures with her guests, the honeymoon, the sonograms—as if everything were suddenly drained of color. Then she shakes herself, trying to snap out of that state of torpor, trying to regain equilibrium and lucidity.

"Well, what are we going to do now?"

The doctor smiles at her. "We're in luck. These pregnancy exams have allowed us to catch it in time. We're in an early stage. So we can start immediately with a series of chemotherapy and radiation therapy. It should clear it up completely."

"What about the baby girl?"

"If we are to begin this course of treatment and beat the tumor, we're going to have to interrupt your pregnancy."

Gin is stunned. To lose Aurora, to lose her like this, after just seeing her for the first time, after hearing her little heart race, after hearing those first few tiny kicks. Never to see her, ever again, at all, in the first place. Never to have met her at all.

"No."

The doctor looks at her in astonishment. "What do you mean, no?"

"No, I don't want to lose my daughter."

After a moment, he nods. "It's your decision. Do you want to think it over for a moment? Talk it over with your husband, with your family?"

"No, my mind is made up. What could the consequences be if I wait out the next few months?"

"Well, that's hard to say. The lymphoma might follow a very slow course. In that case, it wouldn't be hard to start treatment after your daughter's birth. But it might turn out to be quite aggressive, and then it would be much more challenging. Still, you need to think carefully. This cancer is no laughing matter. I would prefer to insist and have you start treatment immediately."

Gin shakes her head. "No."

"If we start now, we'd have an eighty percent chance of remission. In five months, that percentage will drop to sixty."

Gin ventures a faint smile. "That's not a bad percentage. I would have thought worse."

Dr. Flamini forces a smile. "You're a positive, sunny, bright young woman. Keep thinking like that. Your soul can have a tremendous influence on the state of your body, especially when it's sick…" Then he smiles and pats her hand in a fatherly manner. "Don't be too hard on yourself. Think it over. And if you change your mind, just forget about what you said today. You can always have the baby later, when you're better."

Gin smiles. "We can tell ourselves all the lies we want. Then she'd be my second daughter. You said it yourself. I'm an optimist. I hope to have both things go my way."

Chapter 38

I'm on the train to Milan. Giorgio booked me a seat in business class. It's so exclusive that I have the compartment to myself. I have an appointment with the famous director Signor Calemi to sign a few profitable contracts, if everything works out. That would give Futura quite a growth spurt.

I look at my watch. Gin had an appointment with the doctor to see how Aurora is doing. She should be out by now. I call her, and she picks up on the first ring. "Wow, that was fast! I thought you'd be in the car or half-naked in front of your doctor."

Gin laughs. "Don't exaggerate. At the very most, I let him look at my belly. I just had to do a quick sonogram. It took no time at all, and I'm already home."

"Great. How did the exam go?"

"Just fine. Aurora is healthy and growing. I got a look at her sucking her thumb. He took a picture. I'll send it to you in a minute."

"That's so great. What about you? All good? Are you worried? How do you feel?"

"I'm in great shape. This afternoon, I'll take my

first swimming lesson for expectant mothers. Trying to stay trim."

"You're incredibly trim."

"The doctor said to keep your hands to yourself for now," she says.

"I'd like to know if he really said that. I'd like to have been a fly on the wall."

"I'm sorry, my mother is ringing the buzzer. Let me call you back later."

"Certainly, my love, don't worry."

Chapter 39

I pull a bottle of beer out of the fridge and open it. I turn on the TV and watch the newest show that Futura has produced, *Lo Squizzone*. It came out perfectly. It's the second episode, and I imagine our numbers will drop a little. They always drop a little on the second episode. Still, we'll see. With a different host, it's like a different show. As I'm watching, I hear the door open. "Gin, is that you?"

"No, sweetheart, it's a burglar."

I get up to greet her with a smile on my face. "It's true. You're a thief who stole my heart." And I wrap my arms around her.

"Listen, you've been a screenwriter, and now you're a producer, but I think you've always been and always will be a con artist, a sly dog who's used the same scripts over and over again. Come on, let me see our script. Where do you keep it?"

I tap my forehead. "It's all hidden in here..." And then I place my hand on my heart. "And here."

She pulls away from me, shoving me hard in the chest. "I'd seriously like to get in there, rip all the doors off their hinges, and see what's tucked away in those safe-deposit boxes!"

I start laughing. "Just think if they were completely empty, and there's nothing at all there. What a tragic, disappointing discovery that would be."

"I'm so afraid."

"Well, you'll never know." I head for the kitchen. "Do you want some beer too?"

"If only. No, just a fruit juice, thanks."

"Okay, coming right up."

I fill a glass with fruit juice, my own glass with beer, and I head back into the other room. "Hey, you didn't tell me much about your doctor's appointment today. How did it go? I was on the train, and the reception was terrible. After that, I had to hurry over to the studios. Sorry I didn't reach out to you before this."

"Fine, everything looks normal."

I spot a dark cloud on her face. "Are you sure?"

"Yes, I'm positive." She opens her bag and hands me a file folder. "These are the results from today's examinations. Growth up by ten percent, she's in magnificent shape."

"Great, I'm happy to hear it."

I take a look at those sheets of paper. I read the measurements taken, I look at the photo of that tiny body, and while I'm distracted by the beauty of everything we're creating, I fail to notice the sadness that's suddenly pervading Gin.

⌒

Eleonora answers the phone without even bothering to look at who's calling.

"Ele, what are you doing?"

"Gin! What a surprise! Nothing, I've only just returned home."

"Do you want to come down?"

"Wait, are you downstairs?"

"Yes."

"I'm on my way."

A second later, Ele is stepping out of the front gate. She looks at Gin and studies her in silence, uncertain what to say, what to think. Then she starts to fumble out somewhat pointless words, just to start the conversation. "Well?"

"Nothing."

"Don't try telling me 'I was just in the neighborhood' or I'll kill you!"

Gin tries to put on a brave smile. "I'm scared."

"Of what?"

Gin stands there for a second in complete silence and then realizes that she can't do this. She can't talk about it.

"Maybe I'll be a bad mother."

Ele shakes her head. "Listen, if you aren't going to be a good mother, the most I could hope to do is take care of a goldfish, and even then, I couldn't be sure I wouldn't wind up drowning it."

They embrace, and Gin whispers, "Stay close to me, all right?"

"Always. Even if, sometimes at night, I will still be going out with some guy named Marcantonio."

Gin pulls away. "Excellent! I'm so happy for you! See if the two of you can make it last this time, though!"

And they go on chatting like that, joking and kidding around. As Gin laughs, she realizes that she's filled with a bottomless sadness. *I can't even talk to my best friend. I can't tell her about my problem. I'm not telling her anything, I'm laughing and laughing, but I feel like crying.*

Later, Gin drops by to say hello to her mother.

"Hey, what are you doing here? I heard your keys in the lock and thought it might your father coming home early."

"No, no, it's me. I'm still allowed to have a set of keys, right? I was fourteen when I got them, but I don't want to give up my set."

"Of course, they're yours, and we're keeping you for-ever, baby doll."

When she hears those words, Gin has to make an effort to keep from bursting into tears, and at that instant, she realizes how fragile she is. So she turns away and invents an excuse. "I need to get something from my room..." She hurries down the hall, vanishing from her mother's line of sight.

A short while later, having regained her equilibrium, Gin reappears with a smile on her face.

"Hey, everything all right?"

"Yes, I wanted to get this book. I remembered I had a copy, and I felt like reading it." She shows her mother *Three Bedrooms in Manhattan* by Georges Simenon.

"Nice. I liked it when I read it."

Gin turns to leave, and as she walks away, she thinks to herself, if I don't tell my mother about this, then who can I tell? As she thinks it though, she answers her own question. You know what she'd say. She'd tell you to start treatment right away. She doesn't want to lose her daughter any more than you want to lose yours.

Gin suddenly feels a surge of strength, and she turns around with firm conviction. "Ciao, Mamma. Let's have dinner together sometime soon, okay?"

"Sure."

Beaming, she leaves the apartment. Gin steps into the elevator, pushes the button, and as the doors slide shut, looks at herself in the mirror. Well, one thing is certain. *I've improved as an actress.* Then she decides to go for a drive around the city, heading nowhere in particular, turning on the radio and singing, doing her best to avoid red lights. When she does have to stop, every now and then, she can feel people looking at her. She looks straight ahead and just sings along to the radio. In the middle of a verse about the meaning of life, she suddenly bursts into tears. *Why me, why now of all times?* And she feels terribly alone.

Gin lacks the courage to share her pain with anyone else. What she wants right now is to be held, loved, and helped, to have no options, no choices available to her. But maybe that's what horrifies her more than anything else, the thought that she could change things, make a different decision. *But I want Aurora; I want Aurora more than anything else. And then I'm sure that everything will be all right anyway because God can't... He couldn't... He wouldn't...*

~

"Gin?"

"Huh?"

And suddenly she's just woken up. She finds herself staring at Step. He's standing in front of her, smiling.

"What were you thinking about? You had such a strange look on your face. At first, you were so tense, as if you were in the middle of some terrible argument, and then at last you smiled as if you'd found a solution for everything." He lovingly strokes her face.

"Yes, that's right."

"Are you sure that everything's okay?"

"Yes, everything's fine."

"You want to go out tonight?" he asks. "I have an invitation to a party for a new Fox channel."

"No, thanks, I'm a little tired. I had an exhausting day today. It's just the new job. I'm not used to it."

"All right, whatever you say. I'm going to take a shower."

Gin finishes her fruit juice. *I really do need this job at the law firm. Working will keep my mind busy, and most important of all, Dr. Flamini is right: my mind needs to remain calm and sunny for the baby.*

Chapter 40

Babi hears Lorenzo enter the apartment. "Hi, I'm home!"

She meets him in the dining room where only one place is set with two covered dishes. She's wearing a long black dress and carrying a small handbag, with her hair pulled up into an intricate hairdo. Babi notices her husband's appreciative gaze and smiles at him. "Leonor told me you'd be coming back, so I had her make you some cold pasta, mozzarella and tomato, and vitel tonné. There's salad, too, or else you can have some spinach warmed up. I chilled a blanche for you, if you like that, or else there's a Jermann or a Donnafugata. Anyway, there's plenty to choose from in the wine cellar. I didn't open it because I didn't know which you'd prefer."

Lorenzo steps closer to her and smiles. "A blanche is perfect. You chose just right." Then he caresses her arm. "You're so beautiful. Do you want to keep me company while I eat?"

"No, I'm sorry, I'm going out. Massimo is asleep in his room, so try not to make noise. But if you want to go out, don't think twice. Leonor is here keeping an eye on him, and if there's any problem, she can reach us both on our cell phones."

Then Babi turns to go, but Lorenzo grabs her arm and restrains her firmly. He squeezes her arm tight, intentionally. "You're my wife. You can't just do as you please. You never even told me you were going out."

"I didn't know you were coming home. I thought you'd stay out again tonight...with Annalisa Piacenzi."

Lorenzo turns pale and lets go of her arm. "So you're seeing Stefano Mancini again, your beloved Step. He saw me at Da Vanni, and I was with Annalisa, but he just jumped to unwarranted conclusions. What a pig. He's just doing it so he can get you into bed. The man just can't get you out of his mind."

"I'm not seeing him, and I'm not in touch with him, and even if I'd run into him, he wouldn't have said a thing. Too much of a gentleman, but that's something you wouldn't understand. My computer wasn't working today, so I used yours. You left your chat open with all your lovely fantasies and everything that's really happened between you two. Congratulations. You even told her that I want to make love on our terrace, that I insisted, and that you basically told me no. If it helps you, use me for your purposes. But be careful. Our son has learned to read, asshole."

Babi turns on her heel.

"You're not going anywhere." Lorenzo grabs her arm again to keep her from leaving.

Babi whips around at blinding speed and slashes his hand with a diagonal cut from her handbag, drawing blood. "Don't you so much as dare to touch me ever again, don't dream of it. I took a screenshot and copied the chat, and I've already sent it all to my lawyer. I hope that we can conduct this divorce in a civil and polite fashion. Let's maintain decent relations for our son's sake. But don't you ever dare to interfere in my life again or try to boss me around, or I'll ruin you. I assure you that I know all I need to do it." Then she smiles at him. "If you're angry, don't bolt your food and don't drink too much. Massimo would be sad if anything happened to you. Have a nice evening."

Lorenzo stands there staring at her, while she grabs her jacket and leaves without looking back. Babi waits for the elevator, hoping and praying not to hear that door open behind her, with Lorenzo thinking of something else to say. The seconds pass, and she starts to feel better, lighter, happy with what she's said and especially what she's decided. How could she ever have dreamed of marrying a man like him? She shakes her head, and as she steps into the elevator, she starts laughing, giddy with relief.

Chapter 41

When I arrive at the film studios on Via Tiburtina, there are plenty of cars already lined up. I roar past them all and pull up to the passageway reserved for motorcycles. I'm the only one using this entrance.

An attendant approaches me, carrying a guest list. "Good evening."

"Good evening, Stefano Mancini."

He scans the first page but sees nothing because it clearly ends before the letter *M*. He turns the page and finds me there. He jots down a quick check mark next to my name and flips the first page back over. "Yes, of course, here's your name, sir. So just head all the way down and then take your first right. You'll find Sound Stage 7, and that's where the party is being held."

"Thanks."

I shift into first and putter along slowly past the sound stages. A number of beautifully dressed guests must have parked outside the studio, and they're walking in the same direction. Others are waiting in their cars, in a line of traffic. Every so often a young woman impatiently gets out of a car and, without so much as a goodbye, heads off toward the sound stage.

I pull up at Sound Stage 7, park, and lock my motorcycle. I put my helmet into the luggage box, next to the spare helmet, and I start walking too. There are a number of elegantly attired bouncers at the door to the theater. Ten of them are holding guest lists. They clearly don't want the guests being held up at the door.

"I'm Stefano Mancini." They find my name immediately.

"Excuse me, you need to put this on." A young woman fastens a bracelet around my wrist and then smiles. "With that on, you can get in everywhere."

I thank her and turn down a hallway. I hear the music pumping loudly. When I stride through the big hangar door, I see there's an ocean of people with sweeping spotlights blazing over the guests, coloring them green, blue, and yellow.

There are young men dressed up as ancient Romans and wearing masks, dancing in high cube platforms scattered throughout the space. They're bare-chested and their muscles, completely smeared with oil, stand out sharply in the glare of the lights, creating quite a scene. Behind ranks and ranks of counters along the side of the room, there are scantily clad pseudo–vestal virgins serving an endless succession of drinks and cocktails. There are even more of them clustered in a central bar in the center point of the party.

The guests, thirsty and eager, clamor for libations. There are waiters strolling the room, collecting empty glasses. I don't see anything to eat. The caterers have clearly invested heavily in the drinks menu with the general philosophy that many of the guests will be dieting but everyone is happy to drink.

The party snakes through the entirety of Sound Stage 7 and then continues in the adjoining sound stage. Backdrops and props have been used to establish a unique location for the event. I recognize a house from the sixties, the interior of a submarine, the façade of a palazzo, and a room that must have been home to a maniac in the tradition of Hannibal Lecter or perhaps the movie *Hostel*, given that the set is crowded with all sorts of instruments of torture but also plenty of leather masks.

"Ciao, Stefano!"

"Ciao." I smile at a young woman hurrying past with two others. I cross paths with a few noted journalists, a few other faces familiar only to business insiders, and I greet them all, but stop to chat with none of them. I continue my wandering, carried along in this little convoy of guests, more or less unknown to me. Here and there in the tossing waves of ordinary civilians, the face surfaces of some formerly famous VIP in bursts of "where-are-they-now?" nostalgia.

Then Sound Stage 7 narrows into a short tunnel, and we are spewed out into Sound Stage 8. The lights are different here, and so is the music. There's a DJ with headphones that she holds up to her left ear. With her right hand, she works the console. She's half-dressed in military attire, and beneath the fatigues, she wears a white blouse and black lingerie, perhaps trying to be the female version of a strange mix of Bob Sinclar and David Guetta. She's surely being paid a small percentage of what either of them would get, but the music isn't bad at all. Everyone's dancing and moving to the beat.

At the center of this sound stage, there's an elevated

space, like an oversized boxing ring, standing about five feet above the floor. A small stairway leads up to it, and at the top, a bouncer checks IDs and ushers guests in or turns them away. Behind him is an array of black sofas, coffee tables, and ottomans, all teeming with an array of people designated VIPs for the evening for unimaginable reasons.

As I walk past, I see, seated on a sofa—between a handsome young man with long hair and the young managing director of the Network, Aldo Locchi—none other than up-and-coming actress Dania Valenti.

She sees me, excuses herself, and hurries to the edge of the elevated ring. "Hey, ciao! How nice to see you here! Is Renzi here too?"

"No, I don't think so."

"My cell phone battery is dead. If you talk to him, could you tell him I'm here? I don't even know how I'm getting home tonight. Did you know that Calemi might drop by later? He had a dinner, but he said he'd catch up with me. Do you want to stay up here with us for a while in the private seating?"

"No, thanks, I'm just looking around..."

"Okay, whatever you say. I'm staying here."

And she turns to go, wearing black leather short shorts, a denim jacket, a shimmering silver blouse, and a pair of low evening pumps. "Maybe I'll head down for a few dances..." Who even knows whatever else she would do, it seems gratuitously obvious, and then, before I have a chance to turn around, I run into *her*.

"Ah, it really is you. I saw you from a distance, but I couldn't be certain. Ciao."

Babi smiles at me, more beautiful than ever, with her blue eyes, her elegant black dress, and her hair pulled back. Her beauty seems almost out of place compared to what I've seen so far in here. Her delicacy, her shoulders, her shapely arms, the tiny dots of white gold that she wears.

She steps up and kisses me on the cheek. I shut my eyes. Even her perfume, so delicate and fresh, has nothing to do with everything else that surrounds me. Or am I alone in seeing things this way? All I manage to ask is "What are you doing here?"

Babi laughs and shakes her head. "This time I had nothing to do with it! I swear! It's not my fault that you're here, I didn't send an invitation to you. It's just pure chance that we've run into each other."

"Yes, I believe you..."

She heaves a sigh of relief. "Well..." And she points at the oversized *F* logo of the channel, projected on the walls, engraved on all the glasses, even adorning the sides of the VIP boxing ring. "Do you like how it turned out? I did it. I was invited as graphic designer."

"Yes, it's very original. Nice work."

"Thanks."

Then we fall silent in that deafening wall of music. But at last, Babi gives in and asks the question she's probably been saving since the beginning. "Are you alone?"

"Yes." And I'm tempted to say more, but for some reason unclear to me that's all that comes out. And as if that wasn't bad enough, I find myself adding, "What about you?"

"Yes, so am I."

"Okay."

She looks at me with a smile. "Well, maybe I'll see you again."

"Yes…" We stand there for a few more seconds. Then I smile at her and walk away. But then I can't help it. I turn around and watch her climb up into the VIP area. Then I slip intentionally away into the crowd. I must have nothing left to do with her. There was nothing between us that night. Still, I know that's not how it was for me.

I continue walking through the crowd. Now the music seems louder. I want to lose myself, vanish, annihilate my own existence. Why am I here? I pull a note out of my pocket. *Come, I'm eager to see you. Pietro Forti. Marketing Director. P.S. I'm at the Temple.* I look around and spot a broad staircase that follows a curve and then vanishes upward into the shadows, in a large ancient edifice. It looks like a strange blend between the Parthenon and a Roman temple, with a hint of Buddhist architecture here and there. I start to climb the steps when I see him walking toward me.

"Ah, here you are at last. How are you, Stefano?" Pietro leans closer. "Can I introduce you to our CEO Arturo Franchini, the sales director Sonia Rodati, and our head creative, Flavia Baldi?"

I shake hands all around, and I smile, but in the buzz of conversation and the relentless pounding music, I manage to hear only a few snatches of names and the importance of their titles, despite the way Pietro Forti emphasized them. They offer me a drink, they tell me how much they liked the "game" of the families on vacation, which they absolutely want to buy. They want to do lots of other projects with us and say that Futura is a company that works well, which is exactly what they need. I nod.

When I finish drinking the champagne, the young woman at our table smiles at me and refills my glass. I thank her, and then I lean closer to them to make myself heard. "I'm so glad to hear all this, and I'm sure that we'll work successfully together. I'll come see you all soon." That seems to reassure them so I stand up, walk to the edge of this strange, elevated temple, lean against the railing, and nod my head in time to the music, but actually I hear nothing.

I look down. The people are dancing, moving, flailing. Some of them seem to be dancing in slow motion, others are moving too fast. Still others seem to be completely out of step.

Then I see Babi. She's sitting on a leather sofa, talking to a young woman. They're not laughing. If anything, they seem to be chatting about work. Babi nods in agreement about something as the young woman moves her hands. She must be explaining something.

Then a young man arrives, stops in front of them, and stands there, talking for a while with Babi. I see her smile, and he hands her a slip of paper. She takes it and reads it. He gestures to ask if he can sit down next to her, and Babi nods and makes room. The young man sits down and smiles at her. He's courteous, his hair long, his shoulders broad. He must be an attractive guy.

The other young woman appears to excuse herself, stands up, and leaves them alone. They say goodbye. Then the young man summons a waiter. After the waiter leaves with their drink order, the young man leans close and whispers something into her ear.

Babi seems surprised. First she was smiling, and now she's turned serious.

At this point, I don't wait for her response. I hurry down the stairs. I push people aside and slalom through the crowd, trying not to slam into any of the dancers. I can't even say whether or not I'm successful. I no longer hear anything, feel anything, neither pain nor anything else. All I know is that I have to hurry to her side.

And in a flash, I'm at the foot of the staircase leading up to the ring. The bouncer, seeing me arrive at a dead run, braces for impact. When I reach the top of the stairs, he steps forward and blocks my path, trying to stop me. I say nothing. He looks me in the eye, shakes his head, and says, "Excuse me?"

I smile and throw my arms wide. Luckily, just then he spots the light blue bracelet they gave me at the front door. "Ah, forgive me." And he lets me through. I look around among all the sofas until I spot her. The guy is still talking into her ear, close, far too close, and every so often he smiles at her and almost seems to lean in toward her mouth, and she lets him do it. She listens and nods. I can't help it. I see red. I stride over to Babi, and I take her by the hand. "We have a problem. I need you to come with me. Please excuse us."

I don't even get a chance to hear the guy's answer. I take her away with me. I drag her down the staircase, into the dancing mob, surrounded by new arrivals, through flows of people pushing in the opposite direction, bumping into us but then letting us past. And we seem to be the only ones moving against the stream, avoiding people, stepping to the left and the right, and so on, without stopping, toward the exit.

When we're outside of the sound stage, I see a dark corner. I head straight for it, and only once I've reached it, do I stop. There. Standing facing each other, we recover from our hasty escape. She's panting, and her eyes are intense. I'm looking at her in silence, and I realize that it's as if not a second had passed since the last time we saw each other.

Then Babi smiles at me. "I was hoping you were looking at me. And I dreamed of you carrying me off, away from here."

And so I kiss her, unashamedly, thoughtlessly, rebellious master of my own life. We go on kissing like that, just like a couple of youngsters who've just slammed the door shut right in the world's face, two young people who just want to be left alone on their own, who've been waiting for this moment all their lives, because people in love don't know fear.

And her kiss is unlike any other. It's love, it's a never-ending story, it's all my tears and all my sorrow, it's my happiness and my life, it's damnation and desire, it's a death sentence and it's unconditional freedom. It's everything I want, it's everything I can't go on living without.

Chapter 42

A short while later, Babi and I arrive at my motorcycle, and I barely have time to see Valenti leaving, holding hands with a man who looks to be about twenty years her senior, but that's certainly none of my business. We put on our helmets, and in the blink of an eye, we're out of there and roaring through the night wind. She has her arms wrapped around me, holding tight just like back then. She's not afraid because she's used to the way I drive, and so she abandons herself entirely, placing her trust in me. Every so often though, she squeezes me a little tighter. I can't believe the wonderful sensation I'm experiencing: the two of us, together again.

Babi slips her hand inside my shirt, running her fingertips over my skin, gently caressing my abdominals. Like me, she must feel the need to touch, to feel that it's all real, it's all true, we're not dreaming this.

I turn my head to look at her, and I give her a smile. "Where are we going?"

"Head for the Via Aurelia. I have an idea," Babi says.

Then I see her take out her cell phone and send a text message to someone. I continue driving, following her directions. Half an hour later, a barrier gate swings open, letting us through. We drive a little farther, and then I see her before me. The *Lina III*. I help Babi off before putting down the kickstand and getting off in my turn.

The captain of the yacht is awaiting us by the gangway. "What a pleasure to see you both again."

We take off our shoes and board the yacht. The captain steps closer to Babi and tells her in a low voice, "I sent everyone to bed, as you requested, and I arranged to have everything ready, exactly as you wanted it."

"Perfect, Giuseppe. You have no idea how nice it is to have someone you can always rely on."

"Well, unless you need something else, I'm going to turn in. Anyway, ring the bell; there's always someone available to help you."

Babi smiles at him. "I've already asked you enough, and at the very last minute. Sleep well, and thanks."

"Good night." Giuseppe vanishes down a hallway that leads to the crew cabins on the lower deck.

"Come on. Let's go up."

This time it's Babi who takes me by the hand and leads me up a broad spiral staircase, carpeted in a soft ice-white wool pile. We reach an area surrounded by picture windows with soft, pale blue lighting. The sofas are upholstered in light-colored leather, and on the deck, there's a gorgeous powder-blue-and-beige carpet. There's also a large cabinet, and in it is a plasma-screen television set, a gleaming steel fridge, and a Bose sound system with an iPod.

Babi hits a few buttons, searching for something, and

then turns around and grins at me, like a mischievous little girl. "It's my playlist."

She sets the iPod down in its base just as I hear the first notes and then those words, *Will you think back to the angels...*

"You remember this?"

"Of course I do. We used to listen to it all the time. We were crazy about Tiziano Ferro. And this song."

"That was our song, from when we first met."

And Babi sings with him, *"While the news about the two of us goes distractedly by..."* And she continues singing and moves giddily to that melody until I stand up and I sing with her. *"Of dark nights... when there's no time, when there's no space, and no one will ever understand..."*

And we look each other in the eyes, and we sing to each other, to ourselves, to the sleeping world that pays us no mind. *"Because it hurts, hurts, hurts like crazy to die without you."* And we embrace, and we continue listening in silence to this splendid song that talks about the time we've wasted and how badly that "without you" has hurt us. And in our eyes, I see sorrow and pain and joy and happiness. I see everything I don't know, I see her jealousy, her desire for me to be hers forever. Then she squeezes me tight, very tight indeed, as hard as she can, and she whispers into my ear as the song is coming to an end, "Please, I'm begging you, never again without you."

"Yes, never again."

And as if that had been the greatest, most earth-shaking oath ever sworn and she felt something like shame at having dragged it out of me, she pulls away from me and, without looking me in the eyes, asks me, "Would you like something to drink?"

"Yes, whatever you've got."

Then she opens the fridge and rummages around in there before turning to me and smiling as if shy at this new intimacy of ours. "Here..." And she puts a craft beer down in front of me—a L'Una—and a small glass of rum. "It's Zacapa XO." Then she hands me a large glass. "You can drink the beer from this, the way you like it."

I follow her instructions. I fill the glass with beer, and then I let the small shot glass full of rum drop into it, and it slides down the side, wobbling as it sinks, and then clinks to the bottom and is lost in the bubbles. I drink it with gusto, savoring every detail of this moment. Then Babi walks over to me, I put my arms around her, and we start to kiss. I'm immediately aroused.

"What are we going to do?" she asks.

"I don't know...But could we just not think about that right now?"

She laughs. "You're right, I always have the worst timing." And she straddles me, climbing onto me and hiking up her skirt.

Chapter 43

I took Babi home, and now I'm driving slowly through the night. I'm starting to see the faint light of dawn when suddenly I remember those words.

"Are you happy?" The question still echoes in my head. Don Andrea was sitting in front of me, eyes shut in silence. He waited for my answer. The more time that went by, the more that silence became burdensome, uncomfortable, agonizing. It was as if it were an embarrassing echo of everything we'd carefully side-stepped, avoided saying entirely. Far away, I heard the sound of some night bird, farther off the cheerful chattering voices of Gin and her parents, Francesca and Gabriele.

Then all at once, Don Andrea's voice, low and serious but, in its way, lighthearted, had cut through that silence. "Do you understand the question I asked you? It's not really that hard to answer. I just asked you if you're happy." And he opened his eyes and turned to look at me, eyeing me calmly, as if the answer he waited for was the simplest thing in the world. But we sat there in silence, and then, at last, he smiled at me. "Well, if it takes you this long to answer, one way or another, you've already answered me. I'm very sorry to hear it."

"It's not so simple."

"*I know. It seems like an easy question, but it's actually very complicated because it entails so many things.*"

"*I really wish I was.*"

He looked at me and started laughing. "*Who wouldn't want to be? There's a beautiful film on this topic, Gabriele Muccino's* The Pursuit of Happyness.*"

"*Yes, I've seen it…*"

"*So have I.*"

"*The star of the picture, what's his name, the rapper and actor…*"

"*Will Smith.*"

"*Exactly, he manages to find happiness, and you know why? Because, having nothing as he does, he only needs very little. But people who have a lot have a harder time finding happiness. Pirandello said that true happiness is having limited needs. Camus said that you'll never be happy if you keep trying to find what happiness consists of. I think that every one of us knows what would make him truly happy. It all lies in having the courage to be happy. In other words, to quote Borges, 'I have committed only one sin in my life. I have been unhappy.'*"

And we returned to our previous silence. This parish priest is a very unusual guy. He loves film and great quotes, and I like him. *And then, as if he were a longtime friend of mine, and I had to laugh at the mere thought, as if Pollo had been reincarnated in him, I started to talk.*

"*Gin is a wonderful young woman. She's beautiful, she's sunny, she's fun, she's sensible, she's intelligent but she's not sly, which, if you ask me, is a gigantic plus…*"

He nodded as he listened to me. "*Yes, you're right. I know her well.*"

"Ah, of course you do. Right. I was forgetting, she chose you to celebrate our wedding."

"Exactly…"

He smiled at me, so I went on. *"And I'm sure she'll make an excellent mother."*

"I couldn't agree more. She seemed very happy."

"And so am I."

"Oh, good, I'm glad to hear it."

And then I uttered the words I'd never imagined myself speaking. *"But I'm afraid."*

Whereupon Don Andrea laid his hand on my arm and gazed at me fondly. *"Fear in a case like this is a noble sentiment. In reality, you're afraid because you care about her."*

"And her parents and the child we're going to have. I'm afraid that I'm not going to be up to it."

"Lots of people who don't have half the fine qualities you two share have done it."

Then I told him the truth. *"The other day I ran into a woman, by pure chance. I hadn't seen her in years and years, and I was hoping never to see her again, as long as I lived. Especially because of what I felt for her."*

"And what you still *feel for her."*

"Yes."

Don Andrea raised an eyebrow, shut his eyes, and nodded his head. *"That puts a different light on things. It's hard to be happy in that sort of situation."* Then he looked over at Gin, who was laughing with her parents. Her father pulled her close and hugged her, and her mother cried out in concern. We could hear her voice from where we were. *"Gabriele! Take care. Don't overdo things. You're going to hurt her!"*

"Come on, we're just playing!"

Don Andrea resumed talking without looking at me. "So what do you want to do? Do you want to postpone the wedding until you have matters clear in your mind, or do you want to cancel it entirely?"

"No, we're expecting a baby."

Then he turned to look at me. "That's good news, isn't it?"

"Yes, very good news."

"But if you let that baby grow up with parents who are unhappy, who fight and all the rest of that, you'll make the baby unhappy just like the two of you, and it might be something the baby carries with them for the rest of their life. If you really love this baby, that's not something you can do."

I remained silent, and Don Andrea went on. "Strange that you haven't asked me the one question I often hear in cases like this."

My curiosity got the better of me. "What's that?"

"Is it possible to love two women?"

I couldn't help but smile. "Actually, it had occurred to me, but it seemed absurd to ask a man like you that sort of a question."

"Good, because it's a despicable question. It's nothing but an excuse for someone who doesn't know how to face up to their own responsibilities. Anyone who has that kind of indecision needs to learn to make their own choice, leave the woman they think they love, with all the attendant pain and possible unpleasantness, and have the courage to be happy with the woman they know they love. Because, deep down, we always know everything."

"We're expecting a baby. Gin is wonderful, and the life I want to build would have to be with her."

"Good, I'm glad to hear it. So you've thought it over, you've used your brain, and you've made your choice. But then, after

*the years go by, don't start having regrets, don't start dreaming
about how your life could have been. It would only be a useless
thought because there's no way to know, it might have gone much,
much worse." Then he shook his head. "But first and foremost,
you must never again see that woman."*

Then I smiled.

"What is it?"

"That's exactly what I'm afraid of."

*"I haven't known you long but I think I understand the way
you're put together. If you decide that's how it's going to be, then
that's how it's going to be. It's your life. Now let's go back and be
with the others." He stood up, took a few steps, and then turned
to look at me. He waited for me to catch up with him. Then he
locked arms with me and smiled. "Have I convinced you?"*

*"No, what I'm afraid of is that the young woman in question
might prove to be stronger than my own willpower. For that
matter, if it really was that easy to make choices of the sort
and just straight-out succeed, then all those confessions, all those
Hail Marys, and most important of all, you yourself would be
completely unnecessary. My sin, if I ever do sin, is your reason
for existence."*

Don Andrea looked at me, but this time he didn't smile.

Chapter 44

Hey, hi there!" Gin enters the kitchen all sleepy. She's wearing a light nightgown and has her hair pulled back with a hairclip that she's just putting up. "I didn't hear you come in."

"I was quiet as a mouse. I didn't want to wake you up."

"Well, you didn't."

"Do you want some coffee?"

"No, I'd prefer tea. It's gentler."

"I'll make you some right away."

I can sense Gin looking at me even though I have my back to her as I fill up the teakettle. I rinse it, fill it again, and put it on the flame.

"How did it go last night? Were there a lot of people?"

"So many people. It was nice, but you wouldn't have enjoyed it. Too much smoke, everyone jammed together. They definitely invited too many people."

"Did you meet many people?"

"Practically everyone." That seems like the only way to answer without telling a lie, but at the very same moment I say it, I feel a flood of shame. The problem isn't who

I met or what I did, it's what I feel. I try not to think about it.

"I had a long chat with the director of the channel, Pietro Forti. He wants to take some of our shows. I'm really happy with how it went."

"And I'm happy for you, my love." She steps close and caresses my hand before leaning forward and kissing me. It's a light kiss that barely brushes my lips, and yet I feel much guiltier at that moment than I did last night, with everything that happened then.

I smile at her as she sits back down. I wonder what she can be thinking. I hope she hasn't become suspicious for some reason. I don't think she heard me come home. Practically speaking, I barely had time to take a shower and have breakfast.

"Hey, everything all right? What are you thinking? You seem distracted." I say.

"Nothing... Actually, yes, I am thinking something, namely that this tea is taking forever!"

"Oh, no, no, don't worry. It's boiling now!" So I turn off the stove, open the tea bag, dip it in, and bob it up and down.

"Not too much. I don't like it very strong."

So I take out the tea bag, just as she's requested, and I set it in the sink. Then, with the hot pad, I pick up the teapot, and I fill a cup of tea for her. "There, it's ready."

She gets out the honey and then dips that spiral implement that keeps the honey from dripping into the honey pot. She turns it and then puts it into the cup.

"Well, I'd better get going. I have an appointment at the office."

"Okay, have a good day. I'll be at the law office. See you tonight. Goodbye, my love."

And this time, as I kiss her, I feel less guilty. No two ways about it, human beings are just that way: they get accustomed to everything and the opposite of everything.

Chapter 45

I see Babi arrive from a distance, striding briskly, and then she stops and looks around. But she doesn't see me. I'm sitting at a table by the bar, savoring both the cold beer and the bracing sight of her. She looks well rested with just a hint of makeup and very little lipstick. She seems more grown-up, and only now do I really see that. Or perhaps it's because I've finally accepted the way I feel about her. I love her. And there's nothing that could be better than to find yourself shipwrecked in love, helplessly caught in the riptide of a specific, ineluctable destiny, adrift in your desire for one person, abandoned in dreams of her without any other thought.

I pick up my cell phone, and I text her.

Even God is surprised at how well He's painted you. It's strange that a city this size lets you go around...You're a threat to public order, you're a disturbance of the peace.

Babi reads it and starts laughing. Shaking her head, she types something on her phone. A second later, I receive her answer.

Quit pulling my leg. Where the hell are you, anyway?

At a table by the bar, right in front of you.

When she reads this last text, Babi turns to look at the bar, searching for me among all the people. At last she sees me. Then she smiles in that way she has, a devastating glare of beauty so dazzling that any restraint or inhibition I might still have is instantly set aside. If someone smiles like that, it's as if they'd said "I love you" right out loud on prime-time TV, emblazoned it on the side of the Colosseum, carved it right into the face of the sun.

I stand up when she reaches my table. "You're so beautiful."

"Yes, sure. Ciao, you wannabe poet."

We plant kisses on each other's cheeks, like a pair of casual friends, but the spark of desire that I feel zap between us would be enough, I believe, to short-circuit Rome's entire urban power grid and set it on fire, worse than a modern-day Nero.

Then we both sit down, and she starts laughing. "What game are you playing at? You asked me to meet you here...Leaving aside the fact that you were just lucky Massimo's at school and I wasn't busy..."

"I *am* lucky."

"And I know that." She smiles. "We both are, but you

didn't ask me to drop everything and rush over here just
to have an espresso together, did you?"

So I lay some money down on the table, stand up,
take her by the hand, and lead her away with me.
"Come on."

We walk in silence along Borgo Pio. In the distance we
hear church bells chiming.

"If those are wedding bells, then it sounds like trouble
for both bride and groom."

"Yes, I couldn't agree more."

"So what now? Shall we pretend to be tourists and just
go home with a smile and a handshake?"

"We've done that before."

Then she leans toward me and steals a kiss. "But I'd do
it again. With you, I do everything all over again every
single day and never get tired of it." She touches my arm.
"Do you know that I desire you madly? I've never felt
anything like it. I've never desired anyone as much as I
want you right now."

I shut my eyes. The idea of someone else in her life
tears me apart. I can't think about it. It's behind us, over
now, as nothing compared to our happiness. I must be
able to do this. I've done much harder things. Am I not
capable of crushing tiny, useless, minuscule shadows of
her past with my sheer will? I have to be. So I pull it out
of my pocket.

Babi looks surprised. "No... Where did you find it?"

"It's been with me all these years." I smile at her. "It's
been waiting for you."

She touches the threadbare, ragged-edged blue bandanna, a relic of history, an epic souvenir of her very first

time. She presses it to her face and inhales the beauty of that memory. Then she gazes at me, her eyes glistening. "What fools we've been."

"Let's not think about it." I take the bandanna and unfold it. "May I?"

And Babi turns back into the young girl of those days. She turns around, lets me blindfold her, and gives me her hand. We start walking again.

"Don't let me trip and fall, okay?"

"No, of course not."

I smile, but she can't see that. Then a dog barks at Babi, and she recoils, throwing her arms around me.

The owner yanks the dog back on its leash. "Down, Rocky, down boy."

Babi asks, "Was this Rocky big and mean?"

"Naw, just a dachshund!"

Babi laughs. "Sorry I missed that!"

I continue leading her by the hand, ignoring all the curious glances.

"Okay, stop. We're here."

"Step, we're not married. What if someone sees you and tells your wife?"

"It was a rehearsal for a commercial, that's all."

Babi seems almost wounded by the facility of my lie. "You didn't use to be like this."

"That's your fault." Then I realize that I've offended her. "I'm sorry, I'm an oaf. I'll never say anything like that again, but we've done this now. Watch out for the step."

"All right."

I help her into the elevator. I shut the doors and open them again when we've reached the penthouse.

"Hey, this isn't a surprise party with my whole family, is it? I don't know that they'd like it."

"No!" I laugh. "After all, this isn't your birthday...Or is it?"

She tries to hit me, but I dodge the blow in time. Then I grab her arms. "Come on, I was just kidding...Stop here." I shut the elevator doors and open the front door to the penthouse. "That's it, a little farther. Okay, stop right here."

Then I shut the door behind her, reaching up to undo the bandanna. Babi slowly opens her eyes, squinting in the dazzling daylight until she grows accustomed, and then gasps in surprise. Stretching out before her is the dome of St. Peter's, the red terra-cotta rooftiles of the buildings along Via Gregorio VII, and the vista of Via della Conciliazione.

"I know you like penthouses, and this one's the highest one there is. And these..." I hand her a keychain emblazoned with the letter *B*. "...are your keys. I don't know how this will go, what will happen, and I'm not trying to hurt anyone. But I don't want to live without you."

Babi says nothing but just gazes at the magnificent panorama stretching out before her. We're on a grand terrace, high above the other buildings.

She smiles and points at the Vatican. "Let's hope we have his benediction."

But we both know we're sinners. We have no interest in repentance. When you love like we do, you know you've already been absolved of your sins. Isn't this the love God spoke of? I'd give up everything to be able to go on experiencing it.

We walk silently through this immaculate, renovated apartment. "It was only just redone, no one else has lived in it. It's where we're going to live, and we'll color it with our love."

Then Babi steps forward and throws her arms around me. "I love it. It's just the way I'd have done it. It's a dream come true. I know this is wrong. I know I'm making a horrible mistake. But this is what's going to make me happy."

And we kiss, at the center of that bare-walled living room, in that empty apartment without curtains or paintings but full of light, fun, and reckless passion. Like the sea at sunset, calm and peaceful, with who knows what tempests impending. But not now. Now we're happy, at peace, the way we always should have been.

"Come with me." And I take her to a closed door, and I open it. There's a bed with new, dark silk sheets and, on the nightstand on the left, a vase of red roses and a bottle of champagne with two glasses, still wrapped in paper.

"So, shall we start over?"

"No need. I've never stopped. I love you."

"Tell me again."

"I love you, I love you, I love you."

"But this time, don't change your mind."

Chapter 46

And suddenly my life changes in a way I could never have believed. Or perhaps it just goes back to what it always ought to have been.

And so we furnish the apartment. We arrange to meet in shops to buy curtains, carpets, and sheets, but no television set. Every day, at lunchtime, we eat together, and we consider some new piece of furniture for our little penthouse.

"Do you like these drinking glasses?"

"I do, a lot." So she puts them away in an antique cabinet that we found in a Trastevere junkshop.

Then I shrug. "Maybe we can use them someday, if we have guests."

"Yes, definitely."

But we both know that that can never be.

⸜

The days go by peacefully in our Borgo Pio penthouse.

"Tonight, Gin is having an all-girls dinner at our place,

so I can stay out if you like. Shall we do something at our penthouse?"

"At last I can cook you something delicious. Yes, I'll see you there, then?" Babi sounds happy.

"All right. If you like, I can do the grocery shopping while you put Massimo to bed. That way you can hurry straight over."

"Yes, sounds like a great idea."

"Okay, then text me everything you need, and I'll go to the supermarket and then we can meet there."

"Okay."

I continue working away at a few different projects when I hear the ping of an incoming text.

Parmesan cheese, arugula, avocado, lettuce, a green tomato and a red one, red onion, an apple, a pear, a bunch of grapes, a bottle of maraschino cherries, and a bottle of Pinot Grigio…Does that remind you of anything?

I read what she's planning to make me and notice that she's tossed in lots of things. I answer immediately.

Hey, are you planning to fatten me up like the classic husband?

Yes, the way to your heart is through your stomach…And that's not all!

I send back a laugh. Hahaha.

Anyway, you don't remember a thing. This was the
first dinner you made for me . . . No two ways about
it: pearls before swine!

Do you expect me to remember something from
who knows how many years ago?

And we go on joking back and forth by text as if not a
day had passed since then.

⌒

A short while later, I'm at the supermarket near Corso
Francia. There's not much of a crowd so I find a parking
space right away. I shop and pick up a bottle of blanche as
well as a fine red, a Tancredi. Then I check out. I pay and
leave with two bags of groceries.

Before I even get a chance to put the groceries in the
car, I hear a woman screaming.

"Help! Stop! No! Help! No!"

Not far away, two young men are trying to snatch
her purse. She's screaming her lungs out, kicking and
wrestling, clutching her purse to her chest, and when
they try to pry her arms loose, she winds up on the
pavement.

I set down my groceries, and in the blink of an eye,
I'm on them. They don't even see me coming. I punch the
first one straight in the right cheekbone. I can hear the
bone crack beneath my knuckles and watch his head snap
back. I tackle the other guy with a straight-legged kick,
smashing into his hip so hard that he drops to the ground.

He tries to get back up, but he slides on the gravel as he tries to scurry out of my reach.

I pick up a big rock from the ground, hurl it, and hit him square in the back. Then I pick up a bottle, ready to face off with them, but they take off as fast as their legs will carry them, heading for the darkness of the streets running under the Corso Francia bridge. So I go over and help the woman to her feet. "Are you all right? Not hurt? They're gone, don't worry, put your weight on me."

But when I get a good look at her face, I recognize her, I'm left speechless When destiny makes an effort, it's just unbeatable.

⌒

I open the front door to the penthouse. "Babi, are you here?"

"Yes, in the kitchen, making food for my lovely husband." I join her and set the bags of groceries down on the table beside her.

"Smells delicious…"

We exchange a kiss, and I notice that she's dressed very fancy. She's wearing a navy-blue skirt, high heels, a silk blouse, and a long necklace of dark stones. She's wearing an apron over it all.

"Is this what you wear to cook?"

"Usually I just cook in a negligee. But for you, I've made an exception!"

I get a Corona out of the fridge and open it. I sit down at the table and take a long drink.

"Well, I hope I got everything you wanted. I'm guessing this was a test to see how I did…"

"Exactly. Let me take a look." She opens the bags and peers in. "Perfect, looks like I really am going to marry you."

"Look out, miracles do happen! Do you know who I rescued a few minutes ago?"

"Who?"

"Your mother."

"My mother?"

"Yes, she was shopping at the same supermarket. At the exit, two thugs attacked her and tried to snatch her purse."

Babi's expression changes. "Was she hurt? Is she okay?"

"No, no, she's fine. She calmed down, and I helped her back to her car."

"I can't even call her because I would have no way of knowing about it."

"True."

"Absurd. What did you say to each other?"

"I asked if she was all right. She said that she was delighted to see me, that she found me more irresistible than usual, and that she absolutely wanted to reward me. But I told her that I couldn't because I had plans, to eat dinner with and make love to her daughter."

"What a dope. Be serious."

"I treated her like a woman who'd been attacked. I was courteous, I asked her if she wanted me to see her home, I gave her a bottle of water, and when I could tell that she was better, I walked her to her car. She said, 'You rescued me. I thought you were in cahoots with those two hooligans.'"

"I can't believe it! My mother is the worst. She just never gives up."

So I finish my beer. Then I stand up, and as she cooks, I hug her from behind. I take the spoon out of her hand, and I turn off the flame. She turns around and falls into my arms.

"What are you doing?" She looks at me with a curious smile.

"I rescued the mother. My reward, at least, is the daughter!" And I take her by the hand, leading her away with me.

⌒

Eleonora looks curiously at Gin.

"What's wrong? You seem perfect. You have a nice round belly, a stupendous face, more beautiful than plenty of times in the past, and I can finally tell you that!"

Gin starts laughing.

Ele shakes her head. "Listen, I'm not kidding. There were days when you were really a wreck."

"Oh, don't tell me that because, if you do, I'll have Aurora right now, here at home, and you'll have to take care of it all."

"No, no, forgive me. I was just kidding. I'm sorry. Stop laughing, be serious."

Gin regains her composure, sits down properly on the sofa, puts both hands on the pillows, and tries to pull herself back so her butt is comfortable and she can sit up straight.

"Do you want some help?"

"No, no, I'm fine now." Then, after sitting in silence for a moment, she says, "I think that Step has a lover..."

"Oh God, I thought it was something really bad…"

Gin stares at her in astonishment.

"No, I mean, I was worried about your health, or the baby girl, you know…" Then she must realize how much pain Gin is feeling for what she just said. "I'm sorry. Tell me everything. I can really be a fool sometimes. What makes you think it? Have you found something?"

"No, it's just a feeling. He's never there for lunch. He always used to come home. Sometimes he stays out late at night, he's always busy, he never calls me, he never texts me, and we haven't had sex in the longest time."

"Gin, that's just normal. You're pregnant, maybe he's worried about Aurora. He's just being thoughtful, and you ought to appreciate the fact that he's not like other men who don't care, and even if you have a big belly and it's uncomfortable…I mean, they'll jump on you if you can just fog a mirror!"

Gin shakes her head. "No, there's nothing that you can do about it. Even when things are at their worst, you can still joke about it. You're just a disaster."

"What are you saying? I'm keeping up your morale! How am I a disaster?"

"Well, you are a disaster though. The situation is complicated, and you always turn it into a comedy."

"All right, then, let me share the right side of things, the positive side. Well, for starters, Step is working hard, thanks be to God. He's earning nicely, he's no longer getting in fistfights, and he's got his head screwed on straight. He cuts a fine figure, he's well dressed, he's an enviable companion, hot and attractive, I can safely say it. And now Aurora is on her way.

"So everything that's happening or isn't happening, like the sex, is all absolutely normal. You're the one who's getting paranoid without a single reason. Do you have proof? No, because if you have no proof, then the court cannot take into consideration your motion!"

Ele picks up an ashtray and slams it down twice on the glass top of the coffee table sitting in front of the sofa. "The session is adjourned!"

Gin leans forward and tries to stop her. "Look out! The session may be adjourned, but you're still going to shatter my coffee table!"

⌒

"Ciao, Mamma."

"Ciao."

Babi and Raffaella exchange kisses at the door before moving into the living room to join Daniela and her father.

"Ciao, big sister, how punctual! Didn't you run into traffic? Corso Francia was jammed solid," Daniela says.

"I went the other way. I took Ponte Milvio," Babi says.

"No two ways about it, you're clever…"

"Care for a tea?" Raffaella smiles at her daughters.

"Gladly!"

Soon they're all sitting on sofas in the living room. Babi is greedily munching on one of the cookies that she brought to share.

"Fabulous, really delicious." Claudio takes all the credit.

"I found them. They're English," Babi says.

Raffaella issues her verdict. "Too much butter. They're bad for you. And after all..."

Claudio looks disconsolately at his two daughters. "I've been getting things wrong all my life."

Daniela picks up her teacup. "Not so, you got one thing right. You married her."

Babi is tempted to add, "And if you hadn't, who else would have taken her with that personality?" Instead, she limits herself to smiling and adding a simple "Right!"

Raffaella smiles wanly. Then she finishes her tea, sets down her cup, wipes her lips, and looks at her two daughters. "Well, we've called you here today because we have a serious problem."

Babi and Daniela stop smiling. If their mother is coming out with phrases of that sort, it must mean that things have truly hit rock bottom. It could be a problem with someone's health, maybe Papà is really sick, Babi theorizes. In fact, he does seem particularly tired. Or maybe someone's threatened them, but for what possible reason?

Babi can do nothing at this point but listen. But Raffaella doesn't seem to know how to begin. She hems and haws, trying to find the right words. She appears embarrassed and perhaps even ashamed.

Claudio tries to reduce the tension in the room. "Don't you worry now. It's not as bad as it sounds. It's just that we've lost all our money..." Then, as if trying to make the news easier to digest, he tries to joke about it. "We've become paupers."

Babi and Daniela are speechless. On the one hand, Babi is relieved because she'd imagined much worse, but on the other hand, this news seems unthinkable.

Babi is the first to speak up. "How did it happen?"

Claudio tries to clarify. "We made some risky investments."

"*You* did." Raffaella displays anger and contempt.

Claudio nods. "It's true, it was my fault, but only because a friend of mine had assured me that a pharmaceuticals company was going to start operations in France and, immediately afterward, in America. He himself invested more than twenty million euros."

"And how much did you invest?"

"Seven million euros."

Babi is surprised. She hadn't imagined it would be such a large sum. How could her parents even have so much money to lose?

Claudio makes it all clear. "We put a second mortgage on the beach house, but also on this apartment, and all the land and the other real estate, including the two little shops that were offering excellent returns."

Raffaella emphasizes the concept more clearly for her daughters. "We don't have a penny left."

"Well, we're not completely broke. We have fifty thousand euros in our bank account."

"No, we have forty-six thousand, five hundred euros." Raffaella's clarification makes it clear just how painful this situation is for her.

Babi shrugs. "Speaking honestly, it seems like you engaged in some really reckless behavior. But I'm glad that this turns out to be the problem, rather than a matter of health. Papà, you'll see, things will work out. Maybe the two of you will have to be a little more careful in your spending, start scrimping and saving, and at the financial services company that you manage, you're going to have to start watching your step…"

Raffaella gives a false smile. "Yes, certainly."

But Daniela is much more direct. "Yes, but why have you called us here?"

Claudio says nothing. Raffaella looks at him for a long interval, and then, seeing that he's unable to come out of his silence, she shakes her head in disappointment. "We need your help. We've done our accounting. If we hope to stay in this apartment, it's going to cost us about eight hundred thousand euros. Of course, we've already thought of a repayment plan. We'd be able to pay a monthly installment of fourteen hundred euros. Maybe a little more." Raffaella looks at Babi. "For your husband, that would be a trifle."

Then she turns to Daniela. "Same thing for Sebastiano. We thought it could be six hundred thousand euros from Lorenzo and two hundred thousand from Sebastiano. The monthly installment could be split in two, with half going to each of them. But that's something you might have some choice on. You can give us the instructions that you think best."

Babi smiles. "Mamma, I'm so sorry, but I really can't help you at all."

"Excuse me, but just let Lorenzo decide. Maybe he's happy to do it. It might make him feel important, like a great gentleman."

"Give me a break, Mamma. You know that we're getting a divorce. I don't know whether or not it's going to be amicable, but no matter how well it goes, I certainly can't go to him for a loan of six hundred thousand euros for my parents."

Raffaella turns to look at Daniela. "What about you? What do you think of it?"

"Mamma, I know how much you helped me when I was a single mother, and I'll always be grateful to you for it. I'm happy I finally have a job, and that at last I can do without your money. Sebastiano has chosen to recognize Vasco as his own son, and he helps us enormously, but I absolutely wouldn't dream of making him think that I sought him out because of his money. I *only* want him to be Vasco's papa, and not Mr. Moneybags. He's got to give Vasco his love, his time, and his attention, in part because these things are worth much, much more than anything else, and even the wealthiest among us are often lacking in those very things."

Raffaella smiles. Then she looks at Babi and goes on smiling. Then, all at once, she entirely changes her expression, turning serious, harsh, and angry, the way her daughters have so often seen her.

"So now the two of you are teaching me a lesson, explaining to me what comes first in the priority of values. In fact, you're making me understand how lucky I've been, thinking that I never understood any of this. Isn't that right?"

Babi, big sister that she is, is the first to weigh in, doing her best to calm her down. "Mamma, don't take it that way. We're not trying to teach anyone any lessons. We're just explaining to you what our situation is, what we can do with our resources and our assets. If you need money, as far as we are able to help you, we'll give you whatever we can, I imagine…" And she looks at Daniela.

"Yes, certainly. If you have to give up this place, for instance, we'd be happy to take you in as guests in our house."

Babi nods. "Absolutely."

Raffaella smiles. "Good. Now excuse me, but I want to go to my room and think things over." And she stands up.

Babi follows suit. "Mamma, it's not so tragic. Just think, you're not sick. Nothing's wrong with you. You've been prosperous your whole life long. Now you'll just have to live a slightly more restrained lifestyle, and that's all. If you want to, let me repeat, my house is open to you. I have a guest bedroom, and I feel sure you wouldn't be all that uncomfortable there."

"You're both far too kind, thanks. Now I hope you'll excuse me." And her mother walks away, walking stiffly and proudly. She calmly and quietly shuts her bedroom door behind her.

Claudio looks at Babi and Daniela. "You're both right, and you've been very kind and helpful. Thank you, from the heart. This is just a bad moment. It's just that your mother never knows how to deal with change…"

And he smiles with the same lighthearted nonchalance with which he's just lost seven million euros.

Chapter 47

Hey, you came home late last night. I woke up at three in the morning, and you still weren't home." Gin smiles at Step over breakfast.

"Yes, it must have been about four when I got in."

"I wish I could have gone with you. I haven't been out dancing in years."

"The music was fantastic."

Gin gets up from her stool with considerable effort. "But how am I going to go anywhere with this belly?"

"Well, it is nice and round, I'll give you that."

"Come on, we're almost there. I went to the doctor's yesterday to make an appointment for an ultrasound, but from his preliminary examination, he told me that Aurora is doing just fine, and she's head down, ready to come out. I'm so happy."

Gin manages to pass her state of mind off as one of complete serenity. In reality, the doctor insisted on examining the progress of her lymphoma, but just as in all her previous visits, she has remained firm in her decision.

"Doctor, please don't insist. I don't want to worry any more than I have to. Whatever stage this monster has reached, I'm not

going to take action, so why should I just feel worse about it?"
Gin had asked.

"Well, your reasoning is impeccable. It's just that I'm seeing
you in this moment of such great beauty and happiness that
I wish I could help you to go on in the greatest calm and
tranquility."

Gin sat there, momentarily silent. What if that's not how
it turns out? How would Aurora survive without me?
My baby girl hasn't even come into the world, and I'm
already on my way out of it. *And a veil of sadness settled*
over her eyes.

The doctor must have noticed. "Ginevra, you need to remain in
your current state of absolute positivity, cheerfulness, and sunni-
ness. You need to keep thinking that everything's going to turn out
fine. Just like you told me. But wait, what are you doing now?
First you convince me, and then you change your mind?"

Gin laughed. "You're right!"

"Oh, there, that's the way I like to see you." And the doctor
walked her to the door.

⌒

Gin takes another sip of her soy milk decaf cappuccino and
then, suddenly, asks me, "Step, is everything okay?"

I'm knocked back on my heels. "Yes, certainly. Everything's perfect. Why do you ask?"

"I don't know, but sometimes I just get a strange feeling. Lately, you haven't been around much and when you
were there, you seemed different somehow. It's true that
I'm tired all the time. Actually, you men ought to try it
sometime, get the feeling of what it means to have a little

creature inside you, growing and stretching you out of shape, making you vomit, draining your strength, making you have strange cravings...No, not like that!"

"I know. The last time you made me leave the house at night, it was because you wanted the 'chill' of a watermelon. That was something all right! So how is this baby girl going to turn out? Will she have a watermelon birthmark or lots and lots of seeds?"

"Silly. You shouldn't throw these weaknesses in my face."

"You're right."

Then she throws her arms wide with a smile. "Will you give me a hug?"

She's obviously yearning for a dose of love, security, and calm. She just wants to be able to take shelter in me, to let go. So I step closer and gently embrace her. She rests her head on my chest, and I see her shut her eyes. I watch as she breathes gently, her respiration slightly moving that lock of dark hair hanging in front of her mouth. Who knows what she's thinking. I ought to be her happy island, a shelter that can withstand any and all sorts of foul weather. I ought to be her reinforced concrete bunker, solid, capable of protecting her against anything, even an atom bomb. Instead I'm none of all that. I'm just a soul adrift in the stream, steered by a heart that was taken prisoner so many years ago.

Then Gin pulls away from me. "Thanks, I really needed that." For a moment, she stares up into my eyes, and sees that they're glistening. Then she smiles at me. "There, that's the nicest thing about you. You get worked up even about simple ordinary moments like this. Well, I love you."

Chapter 48

Hello, Babi, have you already left?" Step asks.

"No, I was just getting started."

"I can't come. I'm sorry."

"What happened? Do you have a meeting you forgot about? Or are you going to lunch with another woman?" Babi laughs. "With your lover's lover! Listen, I warned you. If I catch you, I won't forgive you…"

"The baby is being born. I have to go be with them in the hospital."

And suddenly her tone changes. "Ah, forgive me."

"Why 'forgive me'? What does that have to do with anything? You couldn't have known, but it's not a serious situation… At least, I hope it isn't."

And so Babi resumes her cheerful tone. "Of course not! You're right. What do I know? I just thought I might have said something inappropriate. Go, go, my love. And congratulations. But text me. Let me know that everything's okay."

Babi ends the phone call. Unable to control herself, she starts crying. Then she looks at herself in the mirror and feels ridiculous, and so she starts laughing at herself.

There, look at yourself, you're just awful, sobbing like an idiot. How long has it been since you last cried? A lifetime! But instead you ought to be happy for him. These ought to be tears of joy. You don't actually know how to love. Shouldn't his interests come first? That's the way it ought to be.

Now he has a son of his own. Or, actually, he has two children now.

Chapter 49

When I get there, San Pietro Hospital strikes me as very different. I'd been there before, after a motorcycle crash, waiting hours outside of the emergency room because I'd sprained an elbow. Another time, it was for a dislocated ankle after a soccer game, and one night after a brawl at the Piper nightclub. Pollo and I came here together, both of us swollen and black and blue.

We'd both sat down, side by side, in the emergency room waiting room, but then, seeing everyone who came in ushered in ahead of us because they were in worse shape, we just decided to go out to the bar on Corso Francia. We had them give us some ice, and we just sat down outside at a little café table, using dirty rags from our motorcycle to hold the ice cubes in place. We did our best to make sure the swelling went down so we'd be presentable before going back home. We'd run through our own amateur live coverage of the brawl, remembering more or less all of the most dramatic moments, exaggerating some and shamelessly making up others, but no two ways about it, it had gone better for us than it did for the other guys, that was the important thing. I was just a kid, with all that rage and all that violence pent up inside me, with my friend Pollo and all his lies. Those were different days.

Now I'm here because I'm changing my status in the city hall of records from husband to father. And in spite of everything that's happened in the last little while, I'm deeply moved.

I follow the arrows. I climb up to the third floor, and at the end of the hallway, I see Francesca with Gabriele.

"Ciao. How is Gin?"

Her father smiles and nods, but he doesn't say a word.

Francesca is much more relaxed. "It's all good. She's in the maternity OR. It won't be long because the doctor said dilation is complete. Go on in if you like, if you're not scared..."

I smile at her, and she, as if to apologize, adds, "Lots of men want to but then they can't handle it. With me, Gabriele couldn't bring himself to go in. Today it's just a miracle that he made it this far. When he goes into a hospital, he feels ill. Sometimes he even faints."

Gabriele laughs and finally seems to regain the ability to speak. "There now, you're exaggerating! I did so well this time. If I feel bad now, it's all your fault."

I leave them there, arguing lovingly, and I push the big door open. There I am, in a perfectly sterilized room, colder than the hallway.

A nurse appears immediately. "Who are you?"

"I'm Ginevra Biro's husband. She's a patient of Dr. Flamini."

"Yes, they're both inside. Do you want to watch? She's about to give birth..."

"Already?"

"Aren't you happy? Did you want to spend the whole day here?"

"No, no."

"All right then. Put these on." And she hands me a set of dark green garments contained in a small, transparent plastic bag. I open it and see that it's a light smock, a sort of cap, and a pair of shoe coverings. I quickly put everything on and head in the direction I last saw the nurse heading.

I enter a large room. There she is. In one bed, I see Gin, overheated, braced on her elbows with a sheet covering her all the way down to her bent knees.

The doctor is in front of her legs. "Come on. Keep going. That's it, that's it, perfect, push...Okay, that's enough. Now breathe. We'll start again in a minute."

Then the doctor sees me. "Hello. You can go over there by the head of the bed, behind Ginevra."

"My love, you're here."

"Yes." And I say nothing more to keep from ruining everything, to avoid any mistakes.

Gin smiles at me and extends her hand, and I take it and stand there, a little dazed, not quite sure about what to do, and then I feel her squeezing it tight.

"Here she comes now. I see her head. Keep going, that's it, push, Now breathe, now harder, push, push!"

Gin takes short breaths, one after another, arches her back, clenches her teeth, shuts her eyes almost all the way, and then crushes my hand until she brings Aurora out into the world. And we see this tiny creature, still attached to a long string of flesh, all smeared with muck and hanging upside down until the baby suddenly bursts into tears, taking her very first breath.

The doctor takes a pair of surgical shears and hands them to me. "Do you want to cut it?"

"Yes."

I always keep saying "Yes," but nothing else because I continue not to know what else to say.

So the doctor shows me the exact spot. "Right here."

I open those shears wide, cut decisively, and for the first time, Aurora is an independent life-form. The doctor hands the baby girl to the nurse, who immediately rinses her under a delicate spray of water, cleaning her all over with rapid movements, before drying her off and dabbing some sort of cream on her eyes. Then another doctor comes over and examines her, marking off something on a sort of report card. When she's done, she covers the baby up and carries her over to Gin. "Do you want her near you? Hold her there, on your chest."

And Gin accepts, hesitantly. And then she takes Aurora, gently, slowly, in her hands. She says nothing though and settles the baby girl on her chest. Aurora slowly moves her head, Gin looks at her with fascination, then turns to look at me, as if asking confirmation. *So, wait, did we really create this baby, you and I? That can't be. Isn't she the most beautiful thing in the world? Isn't this why we were put here on this earth? And isn't it for her that we met in the first place?*

Aurora moves her head again, and suddenly I'm on the verge of tears. In fact, I realize that my cheeks are drenched. I can't stop weeping, I can't do anything, nothing, nothing at all. I'm sobbing, sobbing for joy. If

Aurora hadn't arrived, I'd be somewhere else by now, with Babi, the way I've done for all the past few months, while instead I ought to have been by Gin's side.

And I'm ashamed of myself, ashamed of all my stolen happiness. I feel as if I've stolen it from someone else, someone who would have deserved more than I ever did, like that guy Nicola, for instance, or any of the thousands of other men who would have been happy and proud to be here in my place.

"My darling, what's wrong? Why are you crying like that? Everything's turned out well. She's beautiful, she's your daughter, she's Aurora. Take her, take her in your arms."

And I shake my head and continue to weep. I say, "No, no, I can't." But then I see that Gin pulls away a little as if she is trying to focus on the scene, as if she is trying to see me better, as if she can't quite figure it out.

Then I smile at her. I nod my head, and I step close to her. She calms down, a smile appears on her face, and slowly she hands me that delicate little bundle. I take her with both hands, worried that I might drop her, like the most fine and delicate crystal glass ever created, but at the same time, the most precious sweetheart in this world.

And when I hold her close, I see that perfect little face, those eyes shut in sleep, those tiny, thin lips, those tender little hands, so small that they're minuscule, practically translucent. Aurora. And I imagine her heart, as it pumps the blood that lets her move her tiny legs, the tiny hands that every now and then, as if in slow motion, open and close. That tiny heart that I would never, never ever, in all my life, ever want to cause any pain or suffering.

Chapter 50

W hen I leave Gin's room, I'm still in a state of complete shock, and I don't notice all the people who have arrived. The hallway is full of family and friends.

"Ciao, Stefano. Congratulations! Best wishes! How wonderful! When can we see them?"

Among the people I see are Simona, Gabriella, Angela, Ilaria, and several other of Gin's girlfriends whose names I can't remember. And of course, I see Luke, her brother, with his girlfriend, Carolina.

He hugs me. "I'm so happy. How is Gin?"

"She's fine, she's fine. If you two want to go in, you can in a little while. Maybe I'll let her know. She's recovering. But you can only say a quick hello, and not all of you at the same time. Otherwise she'll be overwhelmed…And you can say hello to Aurora too."

"What's she like?"

"She's gorgeous."

"But who does she resemble?"

"How am I supposed to know? You tell me who she resembles. I don't understand a thing anymore!"

Francesca starts laughing. "Leave him be. You're going to deprive him of oxygen, the lot of you!"

"Yes, help me, I need saving."

And then Gabriele arrives, bringing me a big cup of coffee in a proper mug, not a plastic demitasse.

"Where did you find this?"

"I bribed the floor manager. I know there's always a Moka Express pot hidden somewhere." And he grips my arm, slaps me on the back, smiles at me, and says in a low voice, "I'm a grandfather. Shhh."

As if everybody didn't already know. I nod. "Of course."

Then he starts laughing when he must realize that he's just not thinking straight. "What a dope I am!" Then he hugs me hard and almost makes me spill my coffee on myself. "This is the one thing I wanted most of all. Thanks, Stefano. You've made me so very happy."

I see Francesca looking at us. She's followed the whole scene, and she calls out to him. "Gabriele, come over here, leave that poor boy alone. You seem like an overactive toddler."

He goes over to her, and they embrace, and he plants a kiss on her forehead. Then the two of them start talking in low voices, and after that, I don't hear them anymore, but I can see them laugh. They're happy, they're a pair of young grandparents, they still love each other, and neither of the two of them seems to have so much as the shadow of a doubt, not a hint, much less another person on their minds.

They turn around, they look at me, and they smile. I give them a faint smile back. I don't even want to think about what would happen if I left Gin for another woman, how they'd look back on this scene. They'd see it in a very different light, how disappointed they would be.

"Wasn't it enough when Aurora arrived? Couldn't she have filled his days and his heart?"

"What about me? I'm the one who got them back together! It's all my fault. Gin didn't want to hear of it, and instead, one way or another, I convinced her to renew her belief in him. I got everything backwards. My poor daughter. I'll never be able to forgive myself for it."

I imagine these might be their words. Perhaps Gabriele might be even tougher. He wouldn't be afraid of me. He'd feel justified by the pain and grief he's experiencing. Maybe he'd insult me, safe in the knowledge that I'd never lift a hand to him. And he'd be right. They'd all be right. I could never find it in myself to forgive myself, first and foremost.

In the afternoon, my father arrives with Kyra. They've brought flowers. Actually, to be exact, an oversized plant.

"You can put it outside on the terrace or you can keep it in the house. I can't remember which is better. But it'll grow along with Aurora."

Then Paolo arrives. He came with Fabiola, and together they give me a giftwrapped present.

"Hold on. Come inside and say hello to Gin."

They've moved her to room 102. When we arrive at the door, I knock. "Can we come in?"

I cautiously open the door, and inside I see her aunt and uncle.

"Ciao, Stefano. Come in, come in. After all, we're just leaving." So they file out, and Paolo and Fabiola go in.

Gin smiles as she looks up at them, clearly a little

tired, but also on the mend. "Thanks for coming. Come on in!"

Fabiola takes the package out of Paolo's hands and gives it to her. "We brought you this. You'll see, it'll save you."

Gin starts to unwrap it. She puts the wrapping paper on the bed, and I take it. I crumple it up and throw it in the trash can crammed full of wrapping paper from other gifts.

Gin looks at the gift with a big smile. "How nice!"

Fabiola puts her arm around Paolo's and pulls him close.

"It's a music box, a moon that turns around and projects pictures on the wall." Fabiola is clearly proud of this gift of hers. "Trust me, this is a godsend! I don't know what Aurora is going to be like, but when Fabio was born, he just wouldn't stop crying. I was exhausted and hysterical, and Paolo was even worse off than I was. But this music box was the only thing that could get Fabio to relax, the only way to get him to sleep. Practically speaking, this turning moon saved us as a couple."

Happily, she turns and plants a kiss on Paolo's lips, and he smiles. A few other relatives show up. Aurora has been taken to the nursery, so I accompany them to look at her from behind a sheet of glass.

"There she is, that one there." And I show them who I mean.

A short distance away, a newly created parent is doing the same. A papa argues with a relative who's uncertain about which one is actually his son, unable to get a clear view of the number on the bracelet wrapped around the baby's wrist.

"It's this one..."

"No, I'm telling you, it's that other one, farther down. He's longer..."

So I leave them to their bickering and go back to Gin. "Can I come in?"

She's finally alone. "Yes, my love, I'm glad you came back. I was afraid you'd left..."

"Are you kidding? Here, I brought you something." I hand her a package, and she unwraps it.

"Oh, it's lovely." It's a little necklace charm made of white gold, in the shape of a baby girl, with a diamond and a fine chain. On the back is engraved the name Aurora. "Thanks. Should I put it around my neck?"

I step close and delicately manage to slip it under her hair and fasten it.

She places a hand on her heart. "I'm so happy."

"So am I."

"It all went well."

"Yes, you were so brave."

"You held my hand, and you bolstered my courage. When I felt you close to me, I stopped being afraid. With you, nothing bad can happen to me."

She smiles at me as I say nothing and smile back.

Then she seems almost sorry. "Lately, I haven't been very close to you. I haven't come to plenty of important events for your work, even the final wrap party for your first program. Can you forgive me?"

I don't know what to say. I have a knot in my throat.

She continues to smile at me. "I assure you that now I'm going to go back to being the Gin I've always been. I'll stay by your side, stronger than ever, and Aurora will be with us, and I won't be a scared or incompetent mother. I'll give it my all. And she'll give us even more light. She won't take anything away from us. We'll be perfect, the way you've always wanted." And for an instant, she seems indecisive to me, as if a thought had run through her mind, but then she turns calm again, once again outwardly certain of everything she's just said. And I wish I could be every bit as certain as she is.

"Darling, you couldn't have done anything any differently. Now, just worry about getting some rest so you can get better soon, and then we'll be able to go home. The most important thing is that Aurora was born, she's well, and she's beautiful." I kiss her delicately. "I'm going home. I'm going to take a shower, and then I'll bring my things back to sleep here."

"Oh, no, just stay at home. It all went great. It's not a problem. I'll call you if I need anything, but I really hope I won't have to."

I insist and eventually I manage to bring her around. Then I leave the room. I go upstairs where Aurora is being cared for. When I get there, there are no parents or relatives rubbernecking in the hallway. I step close to the glass. There's a nurse checking on the newborns. When she sees me, she recognizes me and very kindly wheels out the little cradle with Aurora in it and brings it closer, almost right up against the glass. I thank her and she walks away.

Aurora is awake. She moves her little hands, and every now and then tries to open her eyes, but she can't do it yet. Then she makes a series of strange grimaces, as if she is trying to cry or as if something is bothering her, but it's

over in the blink of an eye. She relaxes again and peacefully moves her lips as if suckling. She's so beautiful.

⌒

Someone knocks at the door of room 102. "Can I come in?"

"Yes, come in."

Dr. Flamini enters Gin's room. "Well, how are you feeling? Everything all right? The baby is wonderful and has
no problems of any kind. We did all the possible exams
and analyses, not even the faintest hint of jaundice."

"Yes, I'm happy. Thanks for everything, doctor."

"But I'm afraid we can't say the same for the mother."

Gin smiles at him. "It's not like it might all have
vanished by some strange miracle?"

"Yes, that would be wonderful, but we can't count
on miracles. We have medicines, and we need to make
the best use of them that we know how to do. We're
very advanced in our knowledge, and the techniques have
become increasingly refined. So I respected your decision
and I listened to you, but now we seriously need to get
busy treating your lymphoma. You didn't want me to
stress you out and so I told you nothing, but the latest
tests and sonogram we did tell us that it's mid-stage. It's
grown, not as fast as I feared, luckily, but we can't just
treat it with benign neglect. This is the time to attack it,
good and hard, with chemo and radiation therapy.

"If you're in agreement, I'd start the first treatment
tomorrow. I'll have a colleague in charge of it, Dr. Dario
Milani. I'm confident that if we get started right away,
we'll be able to beat the cancer in a short time."

Gin shuts her eyes for a moment and tries to gather her strength. "Yes, but does that mean that I won't be able to nurse Aurora?"

"No, you wouldn't be able to. But it's better to give her formula than wait any longer. I understand the choice you've made, but you absolutely should no longer underestimate the danger you're running. You're in a very critical situation. You need to do this for Aurora's sake."

Slowly, tears start pouring out of Gin's eyes. The doctor notices and hands her a box of tissues from the counter nearby.

"I know, it isn't easy, but you need to stay positive. Now, you get some rest. You're tired. If you need anything, call me."

Chapter 51

The days that follow are very strange. Gin and the little one are at home. Aurora's room fills the whole apartment with the sweet scent of a baby. Everywhere you look, there's something bespeaking the new arrival. Bottle sterilizers, jars of powdered milk, pacifiers of every size and description, baby bottles, a little scale to weigh her food, Gin says that will be important for weaning her, and a bigger scale to monitor her growth.

"Why don't you give her your own milk?"

"Because I don't have enough."

"You looked like you did."

Gin starts laughing. "Appearances can be deceiving. Aren't you happy that she sleeps regularly and wakes up at the right time to nurse with a bottle? She's much more precise, and you're only giving her the six o'clock bottle!"

"I'd be glad to make a sacrifice for a few more nursing sessions, if you like."

"No, I don't trust you. You're too distractable. You

have to be super precise with these things. Leave it to me."

"You look tired though."

"Don't worry, I'm getting used to it. You'll see, I'll recover."

Chapter 52

My love? I'm back!" I enter the living room and shut the door.

"I'm in the bedroom."

I join Gin. She's changing Aurora, who's lying on the bed. I embrace her from behind and give her a kiss.

She turns and smiles at me. "We missed you."

"And I missed the both of you. Look what I brought you." I put a package at the foot of the bed.

Gin finishes fastening up Aurora's onesie and then opens my gift.

"They're lovely, thanks so much!" Two light-blue T-shirts, identical but different sizes, with MATADOR written on them and a black picture of a bull. "I'm putting mine on right away." She puts it on, and then she smiles at me in delight. "How does it look on me?"

"Beautiful, *mi guapa*..." Then I realize that her face is white as a sheet. "Are you all right?"

"Yes, why?"

"You're a little pale."

"Aurora had colic all night. I didn't get a wink of sleep. Lucky you to have missed it! How did it go in Spain?"

"Really well. We locked up a three-year contract. Now I'm going to take a shower and go to the office. We have a very important day. We're trying to see if we can nail down a production deal for another drama series for next year."

"The one you let me read, *At the Bottom of My Heart?* The story of two young people in love even though they belong to two families that hate each other?"

"Yes, a modern-day *Romeo and Juliet.* It's nothing revolutionary or new, but it's well done, and lots of things happen."

"Yes, I agree. I liked it. Well, fingers crossed."

I go into the bathroom and take my clothes off. Then I realize there are lots of medicine bottles on the sink. I reach out for one, but Gin walks in. "What are these?"

"Nothing, just supplements. My iron levels are low. I need to build back up. That's partly why I look so pale."

"Tell me if there's anything I can do to help."

"No, darling, don't worry. You're back, that's the important thing. Maybe tonight, if I'm too tired, maybe you can give her a bottle or two."

"Sure, I'll set my alarm. It's no problem. Later on you can give me thorough instructions."

And I step into the hot shower.

Chapter 53

Gin is changing Aurora, talking to her in amusement, as if the baby could actually understand her. "How much poop are you capable of producing? Are you doing this intentionally? It's been since this morning that I have to change you every fifteen minutes! You're trying to keep me on my toes, aren't you?"

Then the cell phone that she left on the bed starts ringing, and without even glancing at the display, she answers. "Hello?"

"Gin, it's me, Giorgio Renzi. I'm sorry, but I need to let you know. Step is at Santo Spirito hospital. He's been in a crash."

"Oh my God. What? How is he? What happened?"

"I don't know anything. I just heard the news myself, and I'm on my way to the hospital."

"I'll see you there." Gin quickly finishes dressing Aurora and immediately calls her parents' house. "Mamma, I'm so glad that you are there."

"Yes, I'm here. What's wrong?"

"Step had a crash. I'm going to the hospital, I'm bringing Aurora over now."

"Yes, of course. Is Step all right?"

"I don't know anything. I'm on my way to you."

"Okay, but take your time."

⌒

Gin arrives in a rush at the ER, hurries down the hallway, and meets Renzi, who's been waiting for her.

"How is he?"

"It was a bad accident. He broke his arm, and I'm afraid he hit his head pretty hard. He's under observation. He has a hematoma, but luckily it's at the top of his head, the least dangerous location. They say they don't yet know how serious it is. They can't be sure yet. You know what doctors are like, they're always cautious."

"So what happened?"

"I don't know. He had an appointment for work, and apparently because we were running late, he decided to take his motorcycle to get there quicker. But I don't know exactly how the accident happened. He's here, in intensive care, but maybe we can see him."

They talk for a long time with the nurses and a doctor, and in the end, they're allowed through. Step is in a bed, surrounded by various monitors and an IV stand. His left arm is in a brace, there are stitches in his right eyebrow, and there's a large swelling to the left, and then there's a bump on his head. In short, it doesn't look as worrisome as they feared at first.

Renzi smiles at her. "He's not in such bad shape."

"There were times, when he liked boxing, that I've seen worse..."

"He's got a powerful physique. You'll see, he'll get better."

"Let's hope so…"

"Do you want to go home?"

"No, I'll stay here. Maybe we can take shifts. I took Aurora to my mother's place. I'm not worried about her."

"Well then, I'll go get something to eat, and then I'll come back to see you."

"Thanks."

"Should we alert his family?"

"Let's wait until we learn more. It doesn't do any good just to worry them."

"They've given him a sedative. They said that it's not very strong, though, and he might wake up any second now. Do you have my number?"

"Yes."

"If you need anything, call me."

"All right. Thanks."

Renzi turns and leaves. Gin walks around to the other side of the bed, pulls up a chair, and sits down next to her husband. Then she takes his hand and holds it tight in her own. *I can't believe it, now that I'm so weak, now of all times, when we need you so badly, especially Aurora, now is not the time to play tricks on me.*

She pulls out her cell phone and calls her mother, who answers immediately.

"Well, how is he?"

"He's okay. He doesn't seem all that bad off to me, after all. He's resting, and he broke his arm. The only real problem is that he hit his head, and there's still no way of knowing what the outcome is there. But they're monitoring him. How is Aurora?"

"She's just fine. She's fast asleep, like the little angel that she is. We put her in your bed, surrounded by cushions and pillows. She's fine."

"Did you give her thirty grams of powdered milk dissolved in water?"

"Yes, Gin. I did everything, just the way you told me. So many years have passed, but I still remember a thing or two. In about four hours, as soon as she wakes up, I'll give her something more to eat."

"Thanks Mamma. If you need anything, don't hesitate to call me."

"Yes, don't worry. Keep your chin up and keep me informed."

Gin ends the call, puts her phone on vibrate, and relaxes a little. She's so tired that she feels like crying. This chemo treatment that she's undergoing is seriously debilitating, and now the last thing she needed was this accident, just to make things worse. What she needs now is her strength. She needs to feel beautiful and not to have these continuous bouts of nausea. She'd managed to avoid them while pregnant, and she has to go through them now, now of all times, now that this has happened. She can't help but smile. The doctor said that I need to think positive—this too shall pass—and Step will get better, and everything will go back to the way that it was. No, even better than the way it used to be. And with that last thought, clinging tight to his hand, tired like she's never been before, she falls asleep.

She has troubled, agitated dreams. She's on a beach,

it's hot out, but there's no shade, not even so much as a beach umbrella, and absurdly enough, for some reason, it's impossible to go into the water. Apparently you're not allowed near the water's edge. There are even barriers to keep people out. She wants some water to drink, something refreshing, or at least some way to shelter from the hot sun, but none of that seems to be possible.

Not far away, in a bare cradle, without so much as a blanket, lies Aurora. So Gin walks over to the cradle and tries to block the sun by shielding the baby with her own body. She tries to cast at least a little shadow, but it's so hot that she feels like she's about to faint. She doesn't know how much longer she can hold out.

Then there's a sudden noise, and Gin wakes up. Her hand slipped and fell. She must have released Step's hand, which she'd been holding, and her wrist slammed against the side of her chair. Then she stands up brusquely, worried about what might have happened. Instead she is filled with a sudden surge of happiness as she sees Step slowly opening his eyes, looking around until he spots her, and then smiling.

"There you are. Don't you play tricks on me, don't even try. You're a father, and you can't afford it, understand?" And she gently strokes his hand while a few tears roll silently down her cheek. "I love you, so much. Don't you ever scare me like this again."

Chapter 54

Gin is waiting for Renzi to arrive so she can leave the hospital. The doctors have reassured her. The subdural hematoma has partly subsided. Step will be in a great deal of pain and will probably experience some difficulty getting around in the next few days. He'll also need a lengthy convalescence with plenty of rest before he's fully back in shape, but there should be no permanent damage.

Gin climbs into the car with a smile on her face. That's a relief; a complication like this would have ruined her at a time like this. She drives toward home. *I'm tired, low in energy, it's six in the morning, and it hardly seems necessary to awaken Mother—she and the baby ought both to be fast asleep by now. I'll go home, take a shower, get a nice sound sleep, and when I wake up, I'll go pick up Aurora.*

But when she reaches her building, she realizes that she has her ID but not her keys. She looks everywhere, but she must have left them at the hospital. The only thing to do now is go to Step's office, where they keep a copy of the house keys.

It's easy to find parking at this time of the morning because there's no one out and about. Gin exits the car and greets the doorman, who's sweeping the sidewalk right in front of the open street door. She climbs up to the third floor and enters the code on the keypad. Then she walks in and goes to Step's office. She walks to the wall safe and punches in the combination. It's the same as for the wall safe at home, their two birth dates. A click and the safe door swings open.

She rummages through in search of the keys and finally finds them. She grabs the set, but just as she's about to close the safe door, she realizes that these aren't their house keys. Curiously, she examines the keychain. It consists of a large letter *S*. Then there must be another one, a twin in the pair. She pulls out all the documents to see if the keys might have been pushed to the back of the safe. She stacks all the papers on the floor and finally finds the set of house keys.

But as she's putting back the documents, she notices one in particular. A lease to an apartment. A rental agreement. She goes on reading. It's a contract between Stefano Mancini and a certain Mariolina Canneti for a penthouse at Borgo Pio, no. 14. Gin continues reading, stunned and bewildered. *A rented apartment? And he never said a word to me about it?* She takes pictures of the contract with her phone, puts everything back into the safe, and then leaves the office with the two sets of keys.

The city is just waking up. There are very few cars on the streets, and there are just a few people, shivering with the cold, waiting at the bus stops. Gin drives slowly, but her heart is racing, filled with anxiety. Why on earth would there be a rental agreement for another apartment?

She desperately tries to come up with something that could concern her, something nice.

And then suddenly she smiles. *Maybe Step has decided to move us to a new apartment. He knows how much I love that part of town... And a penthouse, just think, maybe it could be bigger, and full of light.*

She accelerates ever so slightly because she's jumping out of her skin with curiosity. When she arrives at Via del Mascherino, she parks the car and gets out. She starts walking up Borgo Pio, looking for the street number. Then a doubt surfaces in her mind. She leafs back through her photo gallery in search of the pictures she's taken, opens one, and checks the date on the contract. He first rented this apartment six full months ago. *Then why hasn't he ever mentioned it to me?* Even so, in the end, her mind comes up with a tiny gap of credibility, a narrow possibility that still lets her believe that this apartment is going to be for the three of them, for her, Step, and Aurora. Maybe he's renovating the place, and the work isn't finished yet, but he's just finishing it now, and he wants it to be a big surprise!

And so, with that optimistic hope in her heart, she arrives at number 14. She fishes out the key and opens the street door. She goes in and lets it swing shut behind her. The heavy door booms against the doorframe, echoing in the silence of the building. That echo follows her for a few seconds.

The lobby is cool, thanks to those thick walls. A marble staircase stands alongside an iron elevator rising through the center of the stairwell. Gin pushes the button to summon the cab, and a moment later, the elevator arrives at the ground floor. She opens the door, then two glass-windowed inner doors and, shutting everything behind her, pushes the number 5.

When the elevator stops at the top floor, she steps out and shuts the doors behind her carefully. There's just one door in front of her, so there's no doubt about which apartment it might be. So she inserts the long key into the keyhole and hesitantly tries turning it in the lock. She hears the lock click: this must be the place.

Then Gin slowly pushes the door open, as if fearful of what she's about to discover, maybe someone else lives there, maybe the occupants might take her for a thief and shoot her. "New Mother Killed While Trying to Burglarize a Penthouse Apartment at No. 14, Borgo Pio." She smiles, but given her doubts, she decides she runs the slightest risk of that fanciful headline becoming reality.

"Is anyone here?" She raises her voice a little louder: "Is anyone here?"

Then, not hearing an answer, she enters the apartment and quietly shuts the door behind her. She turns on the light. The apartment is lovely, fully furnished and decorated with bright colors.

Someone lives here. There are books, lamps, carpets, sofa, a plasma-screen television set, and a framed photograph on the wall. And so, curious, Gin steps closer to see who the couple in the photograph might be.

And when she focuses on their faces, she feels like she's about to faint. It's Step and Babi sitting on a low wall, smiling at each other. It's a photograph from many years ago, that's true, but what on earth is a photograph like this one even doing in this apartment in the first place? Who lives here? What does all this mean?

And seized by an unexpected wave of anxiety, she continues searching. She frantically opens cabinets, cupboards, and clothes closets. Gin rummages through the bathroom, but she finds nothing that can provide her with any useful information, not a time or an action that can shed light on all this strange mystery.

Then she arrives in the last room. She opens the door. There's a neatly made bed with dark silk sheets and nothing in the bookshelves but two photo albums. She takes them down, lays them on the bed, and opens the first one. In it are photographs of a little boy, a handsome little boy who grows from year to year, and beneath each picture is a handwritten note indicating what's happening in the photograph. *Massimo turns one year old. Massimo celebrates his birthday at school with his friends. Here we're at the amusement park. This is his first game of soccer.*

Gin quickly leafs through the album. There is nothing but notations concerning a broad array of different moments in that little boy's life. They say nothing more, nothing, until that last photograph. There is a large crowd of people and the little boy is at the center of the photograph. *This is his first recital, the only one who wasn't there was you!*

Gin's head is spinning at this point. What is that phrase supposed to mean? You, but why "you"? Then, practically certain that she will learn the truth in that second album, she picks it up, pulls it closer, and opens it. One after another, she continues, glimpsing photographs of the present day. Step and Babi in a great number of different candid moments, in this apartment, in the kitchen, sitting on the sofa, a series of more or less causal selfies stolen from their life together in the last several months.

Gin's eyes are welling over with tears, but she goes on turning the pages, and as she does so, she continues sobbing, harder and harder, until she practically dies of the pain of glimpsing them in bed together.

But how could this even be possible? *You're the father of my daughter. You're Aurora's father, you're my husband. You didn't die a short time ago in that crash, but you sure are dead to me now. Why did you do all this to me at all? Why have you chosen to punish me like this?* And she goes on turning the last pages of that album, sobbing, blinded by her tears and her sorrow. Until that last page with the photograph of the three of them together, Babi, Step, and that little boy. And then the words underneath: *Remember that your son and I will always love you. Even if we can't be with you, you'll be in our hearts every single day.*

Your son? That little boy is Step's son? Gin can't handle it anymore. She feels as if she's about to faint. She feels the gorge rise in her throat, and she runs to the bathroom, lifts the lid, and bends over the toilet, screaming and vomiting at the same time.

Chapter 55

Several days have passed. I've returned home from the hospital. I'm still pretty sore, but really, it's Gin who appears to be doing worse from almost every point of view.

"Do you need anything?" Gin asks. "I'm going out."

"No, thanks. Is everything okay?"

"Why do you ask?"

"You seem kind of strange," I say.

"I'm just a little tired. And this accident has really been terribly stressful."

"I wasn't trying to make it happen. I did everything I could to avoid it." I start laughing, doing my best to make that laughter infectious, but it doesn't work.

"Try and look in on Aurora every now and then. Even if Mara's here, it's a good thing if you check in."

"Yes, of course."

Then she steps forward and gives me a light, graceful kiss, as if she didn't want to linger too long, and hurries away.

I'm choosing Gin, and it makes me happy. Even if I miss Babi terribly. Not a moment goes by that I don't think of her. I see her every time I close my eyes, when I relax, when I'm about to fall asleep, and it's as if she were trying to occupy my mind, as if by some higher, prior right.

I haven't approached Gin since. I can't bring myself to do it. It would almost seem as if I were betraying Babi, but I know that I won't be able to go on acting like this. I'm going to have to succeed in forgetting her, and in fact, I thought that I had done it, but it's as if the time that we've spent together has made it clear to me, and I have accepted once and for all, that this will never happen.

"By now, you're all mine," Babi told me once. "I never confessed this fact to you, but I'm actually a witch."

"Seriously?"

"Yes, I've had you three times, and now you'll never escape my clutches. You're three times mine."

"Bewitched by Babi..."

And now, more than ever before, she's with me. In my silences, in my dreams, in my smiles, in my pain at having lost her again.

Gin is fantastic. She's sweet, she's beautiful, she's adorable, she's my wife, she's Aurora's mother, she's loving, she's intelligent, and she's fun. But... There's a "but." But she's not *her.*

There's nothing else to say, there's no other way to think about it. It would be wonderful to be able to fall in love on command. I'd be happy with Gin. Everything would be perfect.

And this is all killing me. It negates the decision that I just made with such determination to be with Gin. Why am I so helpless in the face of this love for Babi?

Gin is waiting, seated all alone in the waiting room, when the assistant arrives.

"Come this way. The doctor will see you now."

She follows the woman down a hallway and then reaches a door. The assistant opens it, and Gin walks into the office of Dr. Milani, who stands up as he sees her come in.

"Come right in. Please, be seated." Then he notices that she's alone. "Didn't anyone come with you?"

"No."

The doctor must be less than pleased, but he conceals the fact. He picks up the test results but then he sets them right back down on his desk. "We should have started the therapy much, much sooner."

Gin says nothing for a moment. She decides to be courteous. "I know that. I made a conscious choice."

"We started from stage two, and now we're at stage three, even though you seem to be tolerating these cycles perfectly. You show no signs of the impact."

"Oh, but I can feel them inside." *And you can't imagine how badly, doctor*, she's tempted to add. *It's painful, so painful and devastating, and we're not talking about the pain you're thinking of.*

"You shouldn't be carrying this whole burden all on your own. Have you talked to your husband about it?"

"No."

"Then talk to a girlfriend, talk to your mother, a family member, someone who can be close to you in this difficult moment. You can't just keep everything pent up inside, I know that you have a little girl, but she can't be the only person in your life. You need to find the peace of mind and tranquility to face up to this moment with the right state of mind, with the right head space, with the same serenity every time you look at... What is your daughter's name?"

"Aurora."

"Okay. Well, we need to bring about a miracle, for Aurora's sake."

~

Gin is sitting at the Due Pini café, at a small table outside in the open air. She's been fortunate because the sun has come out from behind the clouds. She looks up at it with something approaching envy, and a sense of total resignation suddenly pervades her. *How long will it be until I can no longer experience this pleasant warmth?* And the thing that hurts her the worst is that she won't live to hear Aurora speak her first words.

Gin is about to start crying, but then it's as if she's found the inner strength to stanch those tears, to rediscover a sense of equilibrium. *You can't give up now of all times, Gin, you're halfway through, nothing is certain at this point, and you're still here, on the face of the earth, clear-eyed, well aware, strong, more or less sure of yourself, but in any case, the way you've always been. You've only lost a few strands of hair, but no one even seems to have noticed.*

Then she sees Ele arrive. She smiles at Gin and waves hello from a distance. She locks her car and strides over with her incredibly fast step. Ele kisses her and then lets herself collapse into the chair facing Gin. "Oh, at last. I thought I'd been the maid of honor for a ghost. Damn, we've been playing phone tag and just tag in general all week long."

"You're right. I apologize. I haven't been feeling all that well. I've had a bit of a problem."

"What problem?"

"Step."

"Have you lost your mind? You told me all about it, you know that, right? The accident, but he's recuperating, isn't he?"

"Yes, of course. But I'm the one who feels like she's been run over by a freight train. I've just discovered that he's renting a penthouse apartment on Borgo Pio with Babi."

"Say *what*?" Ele's eyes bug out. "But maybe you're making a mistake. How can you be so sure?"

So Gin explains how she's discovered the whole situation. "So, as you can see, there's really no room for any confusion here. I'm afraid I'm one hundred percent certain. I wish I could think I was wrong. I really do."

Ele, too, looks wrecked by this news. She shakes her head, clearly grief-stricken. "Damn. That's the last thing you needed. I'm really sorry."

"How do you think I feel? I'm literally destroyed."

"Okay, but you've also told me that they've broken up, that you found this album that clearly documents the fact."

"I understand that, but he never said a word to me. He has a son with another woman, and he never thought to mention that fact to me? Then he starts seeing her again after he swore to me that he'd never speak to her again as long as he lived. And it's not like he meets up with her over an espresso in a public café...He rents an apartment for her! That's not asking her out for an espresso. That's guzzling down all the coffee in Colombia, that asshole!"

Ele starts laughing. "Gin, you're completely crazy! The things you say! This is a tragedy, and you peel off wisecracks?"

"It's life itself that I think must not take me seriously. Otherwise, it wouldn't have played this trick on me. I mean, come on, he gets in a crash, and while I'm miserable, worried that he might be seriously injured, I find out all this...It's just not right."

"But you love him?"

"Sure, I love him a lot, but I hate him too. I'd love to punch him in the face."

"Take advantage of the fact that he has his arm in a sling!"

"Listen, I'd do it, for real..."

"What should we order?"

They decide on a couple of espressos and go on talking.

"So he never said a word to you about any of this?"

"No."

"Still, can I tell you something? If you love him so much, anyway, and if he dumped her..."

"Yes, but I don't know why it ended, who decided. I don't know anything."

"Okay, but whether it was him or her, what do you care? The main thing is that it's over, right?"

"Yes, definitely."

"Well, in that case, just forget about it. Go on ahead as if nothing happened. You two have a daughter, maybe nothing more will ever happen, with her or with anyone else. She was his only weakness, and you always knew it, right?"

"Yes, but he swore an oath to me."

"Think about Aurora. Make it clear to him that he didn't make a mistake, that he made the right choice, that you're so much better than she is…"

"But I *am* so much better than she is!"

"Then don't let him forget it. Don't throw this mistake in his face. Forget about her and just think about all the time the two of you can spend together, just you and him, and Aurora…"

"Right, except there's another problem there…"

"Another problem?"

"I'm afraid so. I don't know how much time I'll have after all."

Ele looks at her, bewildered.

"I've just come from a visit with my oncologist. I'm afraid I have a tumor."

Ele breaks into tears. She looks at Gin and weeps in silence, unable to say a thing, not a word, and then, in the end, once she's recovered a little, she whispers, "Forgive me…"

"Oh, don't be silly." Gin smiles at her. "Just think that the doctor told me to talk about it with someone, to choose a person among those closest and dearest to me so that I wouldn't have to carry this burden all by myself, and I chose you. Looks to me like I made the wrong choice though."

And Ele starts laughing, or a mix really, laughing and crying at the same time. She picks up a paper napkin and blows her nose into it. "Oh, damn it to hell, I never should have started crying. I'm just no good at this. And here I was, ready to tell you my wonderful news, Marcantonio asked me to marry him, but as usual, you come along and steal my spotlight."

This time it's Gin who laughs. "Come on. I'm just too damn happy right now. I hope I will be there that day too."

"Oh God, don't even talk like that. I'll just run out of tears. Maybe it's not so serious after all, right?"

"Well, I couldn't really say for sure, but I'm afraid that it really is. The doctor is talking about needing a miracle."

Chapter 56

Gin has been awake for about an hour now, and she has given Aurora her milk. She's holding the baby in her arms and is bouncing her lightly, waiting for the tiny burp that finally comes. I see them profiled in the living room window, illuminated by the morning's first light.

"How was dinner?" I ask.

Gin turns around in surprise. Then she smiles at me. "Not as good as I'd hoped. But it's probably better that way." She walks past me and goes to set Aurora down in her bassinet. Then she goes into the bathroom and washes her hands. She puts on her dressing gown and walks into the kitchen. "Do you want an espresso?"

"Yes, please."

A short while later, she comes back into the living room and brings me a demitasse.

"I added some soy milk, but just a little."

"Good, that's how I like it. Thanks."

I sip a little hot coffee. Outside the window, the sky is slowly turning shades of blue, losing the bright indigo and veering toward lighter shades. Now it's a pale blue, and there's not a cloud in sight.

"It's going to be a beautiful day." Gin looks in my direction.

I look at her. I say nothing for a moment but then I make up my mind to tell her the truth. "I think there's something that you need to know."

"Well, I do know something…"

"Maybe, but I want you to know everything. Otherwise, we'll really never be able to start over again. I'd always feel like a liar at your side so I think this is the only way. Then, if you want, you can send me away, but in the meantime, I need you to listen to me. I had an affair with Babi. I was seeing her for about six months. I rented an apartment where we met almost every day, but when Aurora was born, I was just too ashamed. I've always thought that, anything that happened to me in my life, any harm that might be done to me, I'd be able to overcome. I'd never stop in the face of anything. But I can't put the blame on anyone else. The real problem is me. I don't like myself anymore."

I look at Gin, and I see tears rolling down her cheeks, but I can't stop myself. "I've discovered that Babi's son is my son. There, that's it. I'd never known a thing about this latest development until this year. I was tempted to tell you, but I found it out the very same day that you told me you were expecting Aurora. It would have simply ruined everything."

Gin smiles. "Don't worry, you managed to do it anyway."

I try to smile back, but I know how badly I must have hurt her. "I don't know what came over me, Gin. I'd made you a promise. I didn't want to disappoint you again, I didn't want to make you suffer. I tried, I really gave it my all, but that's just the way it went."

Now she gets angry. "Don't even try it." She gets up from the sofa and walks toward me, pinching the fingers of her right hand as if they were a bird's beak and taps them against my chest. "Don't you try to pull the wool over my eyes. You're the man who does a *thousand* push-ups, a man driven by rage and sheer willpower. You never even felt pain when you made up your mind to go all the way. Your determination has always been stronger than your head and your heart. You could have kept all this from happening. You weren't drunk, you weren't high on drugs, you knew what was happening. Don't tell me that's just the way it went. You're the one who made sure it went that way."

"You're right."

"That's not enough. I know that I'm right. But I wanted to be your first choice. Instead I feel like I'm plan B, nothing more than a spare tire. You make me feel as if, unable to have *her*, you chose me in an attempt to settle for second best and be happy with it. But that's no way to find happiness."

"No, that's not true. I want to be happy, and I want to be happy with you."

"Right, just think that you even made a promise to the Lord. You were supposed to live with me, you were supposed to have me and hold me, honor me and treasure me. Be at my side in sorrow and in joy, in the good times and the bad, and love and cherish me always, in poverty and wealth, in sickness and in health. But all you had to do was see her once, and you forget about everything."

"I'm not the man you wanted. I was wrong, and I'm sorry. But let's start over from today. I'm begging you. Look at that, look at how beautiful..." And I point out the window, directing her attention to the sunbeams piercing a collection of distant clouds. They seem like the rays of a crown, making that sky unique, special, almost sacred. "Please, my love, forgive me. Let's not throw it all away. I told you everything. I think that I've done a lot of wonderful things for you and just one that was wrong. That *is* something I did, and it *was* wrong, that's true, but it was just *one* thing."

"But don't you think that this is something you can never get past? This love that you still feel for her, isn't it something you'll never be able to put behind you? All of this is something that goes beyond my ability to understand..."

Gin looks tired to me, as if defeated. She shakes her head, and her shoulders droop, but she clearly wants to say something more. "Maybe it's what you want, but you can't do anything about it. It's always going to be like this. You'll never be entirely, completely mine. Can't you see that that's something I can never accept?"

I remain silent for a moment. "I wish I could be a better man."

Then she puts her hand on my face. "I know that, but you can't be a better man with me when your heart belongs to another woman."

"It's not like that, Gin. Please don't obsess about

this. Just think of Aurora. We have our whole lives ahead of us."

"Ah, about that, there's another problem there, I'm afraid. And seeing how things have gone, I don't think there are going to be any miracles awaiting us."

Chapter 57

It's Sunday morning, not even nine o'clock yet. The sun is warm, and Gin and I, along with Aurora in her baby carriage, are out enjoying a nice walk at Villa Glori. You can catch a whiff of the smell of the horses emanating from the stables farther along, but you can also smell the scent of the rain that fell overnight. We stop at a little café and order cappuccinos.

"Nothing to eat for you?"

"No, thanks. I'm not hungry."

"I'll have a whole-wheat pastry."

We collect our order and go on walking, and Gin turns to look at me, and she smiles.

I notice that there's a film of cappuccino on her upper lip. "You have a milk mustache. Hold on." And I delicately run my forefinger over her lips.

She holds my hand, shuts her eyes, and kisses it. Then she holds it tight against her cheek and then, once again, pulls it back to her mouth, opens her eyes, smiles at me, and releases it. "I've forgiven you, you know that?"

I walk along close beside her. I know that, in this case, anything I could say would be wrong. To say "thank you" would just be awful. So I say nothing.

But she continues. "You've given me the most beautiful thing in the world, the thing I most dearly desired. You gave me the finest gift there could be, and having it from you makes it even more special."

"Gin, I…"

"Shh." She raises her hand and shuts her eyes for a moment. Then she starts pushing the baby carriage again, doing it slowly, perhaps to keep from awakening Aurora. "Let me say a few more things. You have your whole life ahead of you to say plenty of things. Now let me talk, and you just listen…" Then she smiles at me. "Well, okay, every now and then, you can still say something, but don't argue with me. If you do, you're just going to wear me out if I have to come up with answers to your points…"

We continue strolling along the inner road in the park. Every so often, a young person jogs past, an older woman goes speed-walking by, or on a bench we see a gentleman reading the newspaper, while just a short distance farther on, at the water fountain, a woman is letting her little Jack Russell terrier have a drink before she opens a bottle to fill it with cool water.

We continue along the road in the park that leads to the little piazza atop the hill. Here we no longer encounter anyone else, and the sunshine is dazzlingly beautiful.

And then, suddenly, perhaps filled with inspiration from all this tranquility, Gin starts talking again. "I want her to learn to be a boxer. I want her to be strong but still feminine, elegant but also athletic, intelligent and amusing. I want her to resemble me..." Then she thinks better of that last one. "I want her to be like me in some ways, to have something that makes you think of me, every now and then, maybe when you're all alone, something that makes you smile and appreciate my finer qualities, through her."

"But I've always appreciated them."

"Yes, that's true. In that case, let's just say that she needs to have them in any case, okay?" And she starts laughing. "I want to know that you'll always be there for her, that she'll never have to wonder where you are, that you never miss her birthday, that when you scold her, you do so lovingly, that you always make her feel capable and important, even when she's making her first, beginner's mistakes. That whoever she has beside her, you will trust that person one hundred percent. I want you to be like Mel Gibson in that film we saw together, *What Women Want*, do you remember it?"

"Yes. It was summer, and they were showing a festival of Mel Gibson films at the Cinema Tiziano."

"He could read women's minds. And he helped his daughter, who didn't really know what she was doing, in preparing for the prom, and he helps her when she's about to go to bed with a guy for the first time."

"I don't remember that part!"

"Liar. Or else you just need to see it again. You need to be present at those moments too. You'll have to think about her love, guide her, but never force her. Give her advice, but always leave her free to make her own choices...That's how."

So now we're at the top of the little piazza. Gin stops beside the bench and looks down into the baby carriage. Aurora is still asleep. She delicately slips her hand under the sheet and carefully tucks her in.

I look at her too. Both arms are thrown wide, up near her face, as if someone had seen her unexpectedly and cried out, "Put your hands up." And Aurora lies there, obediently, and goes on sleeping peacefully. Her cheeks are pink, her tiny mouth is ever so slightly open, and she's so, so beautiful.

Then Gin climbs onto the bench and sits on the back-rest, making herself a little taller than a normal person sitting up. She brushes back her hair. "How do I look?"

"Very nice."

She shakes her head. "And to think that I continue to trust you..." Then she reaches into her purse and gets out her iPhone, readies it, and hands it to me. "Someday in the future, when she asks about me, I want you to show her this video we're about to make..."

"But..."

"No ifs, ands, or buts. I know that this isn't original, but I'm not in a competition to see who did what first. I just want her to know something about me, that she be able to get to know me at least a little, that she not have to just look at still pictures that wouldn't tell her a thing. I want her to hear my voice, see my laughter, be able to imagine what her mother was like. Tell me the truth now, how do I look?"

"I told you, you look great. You're beautiful as ever.

You're just a little tired, but when I frame you, it's nothing you'd notice."

"Okay, well that's already a much more perfectly acceptable lie."

Then she takes a series of deep breaths, pushing the air in and out of her lungs, like a free diver preparing to go under for what he hopes will be a longstanding world record. "Are you ready?" she asks.

I nod my head.

"All right, then. Start recording."

And then, after a brief moment, Gin starts talking. "Ciao. Here I am, I'm your mother. I so wish I could have been there for you every single day, be at your side, but in some sense, I really am, a little distant perhaps, but I'm still there with you. I held you in my arms all the time I was able, and I never pulled away from you. I gave you all of my love, and I prayed every day that you would be exactly as you are, as I'm imagining you, as I wish I could have lived to see you every instant of your life.

"Now, you may have seen a few pictures of me, but I want to tell you something more about me, something that perhaps you might not have known. I was very shy when I was small, and in spite of the fact that everyone told me I was pretty, I didn't feel like I was at all. But after all, beauty isn't all that important. Your father loved all my defects, and you'll need to find a young man who will be able to love all of yours.

"But above all, try always to be happy. Sometimes you don't have time enough to savor your happiness, and when that's the case, we're never happy enough."

Then she tells a few stories about high school, a few

of her boyfriends that even I had never heard of, and how strange her first kiss turned out to be, and in so doing, she even manages to coax a few laughs out of me.

And she continues talking with great tranquility until she gets up from the bench and walks over to the stroller. I never stop filming her even as she bends over and delicately picks Aurora up and holds her in her arms. "Here I am, my darling love. This is what you are right now . . . And we're together." And she shows Aurora to the cell phone camera and gives her a tiny peck on the cheek. "You're sleeping, and I am awakening you as I always will in every instant of your life."

Then she hugs the baby close to her face, shuts her eyes, and breathes her in. "I can smell you and feel you. We're close as close can be, the way I always would have wanted our lives to be. Promise me that you'll be happy. I love you so very much."

I see that she's nodding her head, as if to say that she's finished, so I stop recording.

Gin delicately sets Aurora down in the baby carriage. She covers her up with the sheet and then turns to look at me. "Thanks."

I say nothing. I feel like weeping, but I choke back the tears. In the end, I manage to speak. "She'll be happy."

"Yes, I'm happy I did it." Then she locks arms with me and leans her head on my shoulder. "Will you push the baby carriage for a while?"

"Certainly."

And so we start walking toward the long path that leads down to the Villa Glori exit. Then Gin caresses my hand. "I've loved you so very much. We could have been a very nice couple. Too bad there wasn't more time. Now let's go to my parents' place. We can drop Aurora off with them."

"Yes, all right."

"And then you can take me to the hospital."

Chapter 58

I've managed to get a room at the Quisisana Clinic, the finest there is, a small suite with the option of having Aurora in the adjoining room.

At first, Gin was very anxious. "What am I going to do about the baby bottle and the milk? Will we have enough? We're going to have to make sure that we get the right kind. I've seen that other brands bother her. And then later on, when it comes time to wean her, we'll need to use vegetable broth, baby foods, tapioca flour and rice flour. We'll need to ask her pediatrician which ones to use..."

"My love, I've brought everything. Don't worry about it. Little by little, we'll get it all organized."

"I won't be there, I won't be there."

And she bursts into tears, and I embrace her and hold her tight, and I really don't know what to say to her. I feel so helpless, so inept.

Then Gin calms down. "Forgive me. This isn't right. I want to leave you with a pretty picture of me, and now I won't be able to."

"Whatever else you do, it won't matter. Be yourself,

be whatever you feel like, do what you've always done. It's what I've always liked so much about you. Don't go changing."

Then she smiles at me and takes the key. "Let's go into the bedroom."

Over the next few days, everyone comes to visit Gin, taking turns in an orderly fashion. Her father, her mother, Eleonora, Ilaria, her brother, Luke, with Carolina, her other best girlfriends—Angela, and Simona—her grandmother Clelia, Adelmo, her cousin, Uncle Ardisio's son, and also Maria Linda, her colleague from the university.

Dr. Milani stops by twice a day, always with an elegant and dutiful attitude, but sadly he knows that he can't tell us anything different from what we already know all too well.

On Monday morning, the doctor comes to see me. "We've had to increase the dosage of her morphine. She'll experience less pain that way. It seems awful to make her suffer."

I can't think of anything to say but "Yes."

In the afternoon, Don Andrea stops by. "How are you doing, Stefano?" But I can't bring myself to answer the question, I just bow my head a little, and I sit there, staring at the floor.

Then he lays a hand on my arm. "I'm so sorry. Apparently, the Lord has other plans for her."

"Yes."

And I'm reminded of my mother. I've already

experienced all this once before, but only at the end. I didn't know that there, too, I was dealing with such an extreme situation. "It's a pity, though, that He can't surprise anymore with some miracle or other..."

Don Andrea looks at me, but he says nothing. Then he shrugs. "Well, I'm going to go see her." And all alone he walks into Gin's room and remains in there for more than forty minutes.

When he emerges, I can see that he's less tense than before. In fact, he actually smiles. Then he walks over to me and gives me a hug. "Gin is stronger than any of us. She's surprised me in the past, but now she's completely astonished me. She's extraordinary. I have to go. If there's anything you need, reach out. And then...you'll let me know what you want to do." He leaves.

How long are we talking about when we say "And then..."?

⌣

I wake up early, and after feeding Aurora her bottle, I enter Gin's room. She's already awake, and she's eating breakfast in bed.

"Good morning. Did you sleep all right?" I ask.

"Like a dream."

The doctor had said that she'd do much better thanks to the morphine.

"Good, I'm glad to hear it. Unfortunately, this morning I'm going to have to go into the office. Renzi had set an appointment to meet with the new director of scripted television. We were going to have a work session at the office and then a luncheon, but then what do you think happened? That he, of all people, the precise Signor Renzi, had another thing going on, and he'd forgotten all about it."

"Well, I guess that means he's not really all that 'precise.' So much the better, right? You'd said that there were times when he seemed like a space alien, and that you found it vaguely unsettling."

"Very true. Oh well, I'd better get going. If you need anything, call me. I told the nurses to help you with Aurora if you need it. There's Claudia, the nurse in charge of this floor. She has two small kids, she's young, and she's happy to help out."

"Is she attractive?"

"No, Gin, she's not attractive in the slightest. But she seems to know what she's doing, and what's more, I've paid her extra to help out and be competent too."

I step toward her and give her a kiss.

"I'll see you later today."

"Yes."

Softly, I shut the door. That burst of jealousy made me smile. It was a spontaneous moment. I only wish it was all a little simpler, but how can it be?

⌒

Gin is alone now. She sends a text message from her cell phone containing all the necessary instructions. Then she goes over to look at Aurora. The baby girl is sleeping calmly and peacefully, the warmth in her bedroom is just perfect. Accommodations and comforts in this clinic are ideal.

She walks over to the big picture window and looks down. Behind the building is a tree-lined boulevard. There are hedges and a garden that's not especially large but with a small patch of roses. Everything has been tended to, right down to the smallest details. The nurses do their best to make you feel at ease here, making sure there are no problems, that there is no noise. Maybe that's why Aurora sleeps so well.

Then Gin goes back to her suite and into the bathroom, where she undresses, takes a shower, and gets dressed. She does her best to be elegant with what she has. She puts on her makeup in front of the mirror. She's happy that not all of her hair has fallen out, even though it is definitely thinner than it used to be.

Ten minutes later, someone's knocking at the door. "Can I come in?"

"Yes, come in." Gin smiles at Giorgio Renzi.

"I got here as fast as I could. When you texted me that Stefano had left the clinic I was actually already on the road, but I ran into a little traffic at Piazza Euclide. Now then, tell me, what can I do for you?"

"Listen, it's very simple." Gin starts explaining what she needs, which is what she believes is the best solution.

Renzi is speechless. "If you're convinced this is the thing to do, I'll do it. But I'm going to need some time."

Gin shakes her head. "Yeah, so would I, more than you know...Unfortunately, there's no more time left." She hands him a sheet of paper. "Here you'll find everything you need to do things faster."

Renzi takes it and reads it while Gin explains how she did it.

"Do you need anything else?" he asks.

"No, thanks. You're very kind to take care of this. I'll expect you back here. But don't take too long."

"What if I can't get it done?"

Gin smiles at him. "I turned to you because you've succeeded in doing much more complicated things than this. You'll get it done."

Chapter 59

Y ou're Babi, aren't you?"

Who is that man who stops her like that, outside her front door? Today Babi left home a little later than usual to head to the office, but she didn't have any appointments, and she wasn't expecting any messengers either. She'd completed and handed in all her most important projects. This is a relaxed period, or at least it had been until just a moment ago.

"I'm Giorgio Renzi. Pleased to meet you." He extends his hand, but Babi doesn't move.

"I don't know you. I don't recall ever having met you before."

"Yes, we did meet once, at the Goa Café, but there were lots of people there. It's only normal you wouldn't remember…" Renzi smiles at her. "In any case, I've heard so much about you. I work with Stefano Mancini."

Babi stiffens.

Renzi goes on, "Step…"

"Has something happened to him?"

"No, he's fine. But the situation is pretty complicated. His wife, Gin, is very sick."

"I'm sorry to hear that, but I don't know what you want from me."

Babi wonders what this Renzi knows about her, what on earth Step could have told him, but especially why Step might have sent him to see her. She's about to ask him when Renzi beats her to the punch.

"It's Gin who sent me to see you. She'd like to meet with you."

Babi suddenly feels the blood drain from her face. What, meet with her? What could have happened? What did Step tell her?

"This is the paper that she gave me this morning."

Babi takes it. On it, she sees a printed photograph of her along with a list of her scheduled appointments and all her likely routes, including when she goes to pick up Massimo. Now Babi grows defensive. "What do you want from me, sir? What did she say to you? Why does she want to see me? I don't like having her know about all of my personal matters, to say nothing of my son. With this sheet of paper, I could report you to the police."

"I don't think she wants an argument. She just wants to talk to you. She doesn't have the strength for an argument. She's dying."

Then Babi tries to calm down and hands him back the sheet of paper.

Renzi folds it up and puts it back in his pocket. "If you're unwilling to accept, I can certainly understand. Finding yourself face-to-face with sorrow is unsettling. Not long ago, it was for me. But now, being here with you, trying to convince you, doing something to help Gin—well, it makes me feel better. So my line of reasoning is purely selfish. If you did come to see her, it would be an act of love toward everyone involved...Sometimes, doing good helps us to erase a little bit of our worst sense of guilt. At least, that's the way it works with me." Then he smiles at her. "But I'm going to have to do a lot more good, that's for sure."

Gin has Aurora in her arms when she hears a knock at the door. "Come in."

Renzi walks into the room and shuts the door behind him. "I'm back."

"Well? How did it go?"

"Fine."

Gin smiles at him. "I was sure you'd succeed. Let her come in and then make sure I'm not disturbed for any reason whatsoever. But let me know if you hear that Step is about to arrive."

"No, don't worry. He's very busy."

"Great. Can you wait until I'm done? It won't take me long."

"Okay. Can I show her in now?"

"Yes."

Gin puts Aurora back in the crib, sits down in the easy chair, adjusts her robe around her, and shuts her eyes for a moment. Then she hears someone knocking on the door again. "Come in."

And Babi walks in. And so, for the first time, the two women come face-to-face. Gin had seen her often, but only from a distance. Babi, on the other hand, has only seen Gin in pictures. They remain motionless for a moment, eyeing each other.

Then Babi extends her hand. "Ciao. I'm Babi. I'm so sorry to have to meet you in this kind of situation."

Gin looks at her hand extended in midair in her direction. Then she looks Babi right in the eyes and, in the end, takes her hand. "Can I offer you anything to drink or eat?"

"No, thanks."

"This is my daughter, Aurora."

Babi walks over to the crib. "She's beautiful."

"Thanks. I know that you have a little boy too. Massimo. In fact, to tell the truth, I've seen a picture of him, and I know all about him."

Babi is about to come up with a reply, but Gin stops her. "I don't want to argue. I've thought it all over, at considerable length. It's only natural to think that I'd be angry at the two of you, and at you in particular, but in reality, when things like this happen, the people involved can't see themselves from outside. But I did my best to get that perspective, and I realized that I was at fault, terribly and grievously at fault, because I wanted a person who wasn't really mine."

Babi looks at her but says nothing.

Gin throws both arms wide. "You see, I understood this one fundamental thing. Whatever else happens, even if you don't love him anymore, even if he'll never be with you, he's going to be yours for all time. This is the feeling that I envy so badly, but I know that there's nothing I can do about it. It's not even a defeat. It's really just the most beautiful nature of things, it's what I really yearned for, it's love."

Babi tears up and turns away to try and conceal it.

Gin continues. "I know that's how it is. There's nothing wrong. You're not to blame. Absurd as it is, you even tried to prevent it, both of you..."

"Yes."

"But now there's something important that I want you to do for me."

Babi turns and looks at her in surprise.

"I want you to make sure that Step is happy, I want you to fill his life with love in a way that I've been unable to do. I'd like to be able to think of the two of you together, like a happy family, without shadows or problems. But if that proves to be impossible, if you can't do it, then don't waste his time. There, that's really all I wanted to tell you." Then Gin sits down in her armchair. "Forgive me, but I'm a little tired. Why don't you sit down too? If you feel like it."

Babi sits down on the sofa, facing her.

Gin takes the glass sitting on the table and sips some water from it. "I don't know if you're thirsty. I'd pour you a glass but I don't have the strength. Please forgive me."

"I'm happy to do it. Don't worry. It's not a problem." Babi takes another glass nearby and fills it up.

"I'm happy you could come by. You could just as easily have refused to meet with me."

Babi drinks some water and then sets the glass down on the low table. "Yes, I could have been a coward. But that's not the way I am."

Gin smiles at her. "There are surely some who might think that it's easy to say the kind of things I've been saying when a person knows they're on the verge of death.

But it's not. I really think it. I love Step so much, and that has nothing to do with my own state of health. It would have been selfish to make him stay with me in any case. If you really love a person, what do you want for them more than anything else?"

"For them to be happy."

"That's it. Exactly. And with you, he can be happy."

They sit in silence for a while. Gin looks out the window. It's a lovely day, and she can feel the sun warming her legs.

Babi finally says, "We would have been good friends, you and I."

Gin turns to look at her. "No. We would have been 'frenemies,' I'm afraid, just like in the movies."

"Gin, I'm so sorry to have to finally meet you this way, and I'm sorry about everything that's happened. Forgive me. I would never be able to act as you have. You're a much better person than I am."

Gin smiles. "Maybe, but not all that much better. Still, it is what it is. Now I need to get some rest."

Babi stands up and walks toward the door.

"Ciao. Thanks for dropping by. And don't forget what you promised: make him happy."

Chapter 60

When I return to the Quisisana Clinic in the afternoon, a pleasant surprise is awaiting me. I knock at the door. "Can I come in?"

"Of course!"

Gin is dressed and has put on makeup, and she's playing on the bed with Aurora. "Ciao, my love. How are you?"

"Much better. I'm not feeling any discomfort."

Unfortunately, it's entirely due to the morphine. That morning, when we crossed paths in the hallway, the doctor made matters all too clear to me.

Gin is brushing the scanty hair on the back of Aurora's head. She looks at me with great satisfaction. "Do you see how lovely she is?"

"Yes."

"If you ask me, she resembles you very much."

"That's not true. I see a great deal of you in her."

"Yes, the shape of the eyes, but the shape of the face and the mouth are completely you."

"Maybe so."

"Every so often, when you look into her eyes, will you think of me?"

"I'll think of you even when she's not with me." Then I gently caress her hand, lying on the blanket on the bed.

She smiles at me. "I'd like to go outside. I've seen that the garden in the back is very lovely. Do you feel like taking me there?"

And so we go out onto the avenue. The air is filled with silence, and the traffic noises are distant. We hear a few birds singing, and the sun is low by now. Aurora is sleeping in her baby carriage. We arrive at a small rose bush, and we stop. The walls of the buildings all around us are glowing orange. Somewhere in Rome, the sun is already setting, but we can't see it from here.

"You can see the most beautiful sunsets on Corso Francia." She had the same thought as I did. "How many times have I seen them from behind you on that motorcycle?" Then she tucks Aurora's blanket in a little. "With her, I've finally experienced happiness, the strongest emotions, and all of this is thanks to you."

"Don't say that. I've made lots of mistakes."

"Yes, I know that, but then you changed your mind all on your own, didn't you?"

"Yes."

Gin walks over to the rose bush, delicately takes a flower in her hand, and pulls it close to her nose. She shuts her eyes and breathes in. "Every time, the smell of the roses surprises me. It's so unique. I really love it. I want Aurora to smell of roses."

"She will."

"And when she turns eighteen, I want her to have a cherry-red dress, and on that day, I want a gorgeous bouquet of roses to be delivered to her, and a beautiful

piece of jewelry with both our names engraved on it..."
Then, all at once, she stops. "There are so many things I'd
like. Right now I'm only just starting to appreciate every
tiniest detail of life, and yet it was all right there before
my eyes every single day."

"My love, but you've never been distracted. You might
have been in a hurry, yes, possibly, but you always savored
everything."

"Yes, especially when we went out to dinner!" Gin
laughs, sincerely amused, with the lightness that she's
displayed so many times during the happiest, finest
moments we ever lived together.

"It's true. It was always wonderful to watch you eat.
You eat better and with more gusto than anyone else in
the world."

"Thanks! This time I believe you, and I'm willing to
accept the compliment."

Then we sit down on the nearby bench and remain
silent for a while.

"I saw Babi today."

I'm stunned. It even occurs to me that she might be
joking. "You saw her? How do you mean?"

"She came to see me."

"But I haven't talked to her or seen her. I had nothing
to do with that."

"I know. I invited her myself. Renzi persuaded her to
come meet with me."

I sit in silence and wonder why. What did she want
to know? Why would she want to put herself through so
much pain? But Gin seems calm and unruffled, and in the
end, she takes my hand and caresses it.

"I thought it would only be right for us to get to know each other. After all, we both love the same man, and maybe that same man loves us both, though in a different way for each. Do you like that solution?"

I say nothing.

"Anyway, I liked it. A lot. Usually when a woman meets another woman who has had interactions with her man, she can't figure out what it is that he could have seen in her. She deprecates her own qualities or she thinks, absurdly, *But why did he choose me if he likes a woman like her?* I never thought anything of the sort about her. All things considered, when the two of you were an item, I'm the one who busted into the middle of your love story by falling in love with you. Even if you didn't know it yet." Gin laughs. "I really wanted you. I was crazy with desire, and then, in the end, I got you. And I had a daughter with you.

"Now I just have this to ask you. Maybe you'll get back together with Babi or else you'll have some other young woman. That's your decision, but still, I want you to be the one who raises Aurora, your love for her must come first, before your love for anyone else, because inside you there will still be my own love, and so you'll have to love her for the both of us. And if you know that a woman won't love Aurora as if she were her own daughter, then I beg you, don't let her make our daughter suffer. You're perfectly capable of understanding all this, and you have to do it for me."

"Yes, you're right. I'll make sure it's that way."

"Promise me. And I'm sure that you won't make any mistakes about it."

"Thanks. I promise you, Gin."

Then we hug and sit in silence on that bench, and I'm pretty sure that she doesn't notice that I'm crying. But I'm wrong about that, as it turns out.

Gin pulls away from me and gives me a delicate kiss on the lips and uses her fingertips to dry my eyes. "You'll need to be strong. I'll always be there, at your side, whatever you do."

"Yes."

"Do you really think that I need to bolster Step's morale?"

And I burst out laughing, but in my laughter, the echo of a sob and deep grief can be heard.

"Now please take me to my room."

So we lie there, side by side, in the bed the whole night through. Aurora sleeps in the baby carriage beside us. And when I wake up at dawn to feed her, she's already wide-awake, lying there with her eyes open.

But her mother is gone.

Chapter 61

Don Andrea is putting away the last few items after celebrating the morning Mass. Then he notices the white roses in the corner and is inevitably reminded of Gin and that chat they'd had the last time he'd gone to visit her in the hospital.

"Don Andrea! What a lovely surprise…"

The room was full of light and very welcoming. He smiled at her as he walked in. "I just wanted to say hello."

He saw Aurora's crib, and he peeked inside. The baby girl was sleeping. Then he pulled a chair up beside Gin's bed and sat down, taking her hand. "I'm here to listen, anything you might want to tell me. Or else we can just sit here in silence, whatever you prefer…If you like we can pray."

Gin looked out the window. "Have you seen what a nice garden they have downstairs? The roses are just gorgeous."

"Yes. And it's a beautiful day today."

"I was just thinking about that book The Little Prince. *Have you ever read it?"*

"Yes, it's a wonderful story."

"Do you remember when he meets the fox and she tells

him that it's the time he spent on his rose that made that rose so important, that he'll always be responsible for anything he's domesticated, and that he's therefore responsible for that rose of his?"

Don Andrea squeezed her hand a little tighter.

"Well, you see, I've been lucky. In my life, I've had two roses, Step and Aurora. I've dedicated myself to them, and they've made me happy. But that's exactly why I'm responsible for their lives."

Gin turned and looked into Don Andrea's eyes. *"So I'll watch over them every second of every day. And you can help me."*

"How?"

"By making sure that, in their lives, they always do everything to make sure they're truly happy. By trying to watch over them, even if it's from a distance. And if you realize that something's not right, then maybe you can speak to them, the way you did with us that evening before our wedding."

Don Andrea remained sitting in silence.

"Will you promise me?"

"Yes, I promise."

"And if it seems to you that Step is having a hard time after my death, you tell him that he's my rose and that he needs to put his heart at rest because I'll always be with him. Just like I'll always be with my little Aurora." Then Gin turned once again to look toward the window. *"One time I read him a beautiful line from a book. Life is like a bicycle, to keep your balance you must keep moving and pedaling as hard as you can. Einstein said it. So, that's how I want it, Don Andrea. If you see them looking sad, share that quote with them."*

The priest was deeply moved, but he did his best to smile. *"Do you feel like saying confession now?"*

"*All right.*"

And so Don Andrea listened to Gin's confession, and after a few minutes, they both crossed themselves.

"*Now I'm going to have to ask you to excuse me, but I'm feeling tired.*"

"*Certainly, don't worry about it.*"

Gin shut her eyes. Don Andrea remained there, looking at her. In silence, he raised his right hand and blessed her. Then he stood up, put the chair back where it belonged, carefully to avoid making any noise, took one last look at Aurora, and left the room.

There, that's clear, Lord, such a beautiful and generous young woman. You certainly introduced me to her to teach me something. Right now, though, the only thing I know for sure is that I miss her.

⌒

Eleonora takes the large photo album bound in ivory leather off the bookshelf in the living room. Then she calls out to Marcantonio. "Are you ready?"

"Yes." Marcantonio arrives with a tray. On it are two herbal teapots, cane sugar, and a plate of cookies. "All set."

They both sit down on the large white sofa. And Ele starts leafing through the photo album. One after another, the pictures of their wedding go turning past. The church, the ceremony, the priest, and the hail of rice and tiny scraps of paper with famous quotes about love written on them. Then the park of the villa for the official photographs and, once more, the swimming pool with all the guests in bathing suits in the water. Their wedding reception was just like that, a big informal party where you could go swimming and just relax and float. In one photo, they see Step raising a glass of champagne toward the lens. But he's not smiling. After that, the dinner, the buffet, the musicians, and the bomboniere, fragrant-smelling party favors given out at Italian weddings.

"It was nice, wasn't it?"

"Just beautiful."

"She's the only one who isn't there..."

"Just because there are no pictures of her. But you know, she was there, and she's still with us."

"Yes."

Marcantonio embraces Ele. "Shall we drink our herbal tea?"

"Yes, let's."

"You know something? We're going to have to get another photo album."

"Why? Are we going to get remarried?"

"No, you dummy! You know the kind I mean, the ones with teddy bears or little flowers on the cover. I don't know which."

Marcantonio takes a sip of tea. Then he looks at her more closely.

Ele makes a funny face. "Do you or don't you want to take lots of pictures of your child?"

He stops drinking, sets his cup down on the living room table, and stares at her again. "Really?"

"Yes!"

And they kiss, joyously, happily, and incredulously.

Eleonora pulls back and holds up a hand to calm him down. "But there's one thing you have to promise me, something very important."

"What?"

"If it's a girl, we're naming her Ginevra."

Chapter 62

It's been many months since Gin passed away. She's always in my thoughts. This time I'll keep my promise.

The sea is nice and smooth today. The notary and the former owner have left. I walk through the house. I examine the small fixes that are going to need to be done, the furnishings left behind, some beautiful leather sofas, paintings of all shapes and sizes, generally thematically related to the sea outside or the boats sailing across it. Some of them are very nice, others are depressingly bad.

I wonder how many different things this house has seen, how many generations, how many nights of love, licit and illicit, just like ours. There's a bowl full of rocks, all of them different, some round, others brightly colored, and there's even pieces of glass from broken bottles that the sea has rubbed so smooth that they can pass as rocks and live undisturbed among their rocky neighbors. I wonder who put this collection together. Maybe it was a woman.

Not far away, there's an old clock hanging on the wall. It hasn't been wound, and the hands stand stock-still at 12:15 of who knows what date. There are light-colored armchairs covered with sky-blue sheets. At the center of the living room stands a large table. I sit down at it. Facing me is a large picture window overlooking the sea. On the right, I can see the entire length of Feniglia; at the center but farther away, I see Porto Ercole. Then the view opens out farther, onto the endless sea. Way out there, I can just glimpse the islands of Giglio and Giannutri and who knows how many others. I'd never have believed that I could afford a villa like this one, much less be able to buy this one in particular.

Then I hear a car horn honk, two quick taps, and immediately thereafter, the doorbell rings. I go into the kitchen. Right by the door, on the right, is a large plasma television screen with the picture split up into nine panels. In the first panel, on the bottom left, Babi stands. She's here. I lift the receiver of the intercom and push a button. I did it instinctively, but it was the right button.

I see the gate swing open. I see her get into the car and then wait until the gate is fully open before driving through. I stand there, watching the car roll up the length of the driveway, following it as it's handed off from one video camera to another, one panel on the TV screen after another, until it pulls up in the parking area in front of the house.

Then I walk through the living room and out the front door. "Ciao."

Babi gets out and smiles at me.

"You won't believe it, but just listen!" She leans in the car window and turns up the sound on the song they're playing over the radio.

You again. But weren't we supposed to stop seeing each other? And how are you doing, what a pointless question. You're just the same as me... Then she lowers the volume. "Can you believe it? It's a sign from above. This is really absurd."

"Yes, I thought you were playing it by choice!"

"Not at all. I don't even know what station the radio's tuned to." Then she looks around. "It's gorgeous. I didn't remember it being so beautiful."

"Come with me." I take her by the hand. Together we trace the same path we took so many years earlier, when we were younger, when we were unmarried, when we had no children but we were deeply in love all the same. We arrive at that little terrace overlooking the sea.

"No, but seriously, you really bought the place?"

"Yes. I wanted to break the window again, but then I would have had to fix the damage anyway, so I had a set of keys made."

Babi starts laughing. Her face is relaxed, untroubled, and the glints of sunlight play in her hair. I didn't want anyone other than her in my life. I'd have given up everything just as long as I never lost her. I'd tried desperately to forget her, to fall in love again with someone else, but enough's enough, I have to set my pride aside. I'm forced to accept that this love is stronger than anything else, than my own willpower, stronger even than the destiny that had decided otherwise for the two of us.

"Babi, Babi, Babi."

"Yes indeed, that is certainly me." And she starts laughing.

"I repeat it three times because I want to make sure I'm not dreaming. Each one is a chance, so I have three chances with you."

"Yes, and I love you three times more than when we

were together for the very first time, here, in this house," Babi says. "I thought you never wanted to see me again. I wrote you when Gin died, and you replied with nothing more than a curt 'Thanks.'"

"I was feeling awful."

"I'm sorry about all of that. Can you believe that she insisted on meeting me?"

"I know, you told me that, but you never told me anything about your meeting."

"Gin astonished me. I don't think I would have had that strength in her place. She was better than me. I would have just been mean. But she wasn't, not a bit. I expected all sorts of things, but instead she asked me something wonderful that I really hope I'll be able to do for her."

"What did she ask?"

"She asked me to make you happy."

At this point, I start to lose it. I'm reminded of how beautiful Ginevra really was, how big and generous her heart was, and how much she must have loved me to be able to say something like that.

"I needed this time. Forgive me."

"It doesn't matter." And she kisses me delicately, she hugs me tight, and she speaks the words to me that I've awaited for such a long time. "I love you, Stefano Mancini."

And I can't really bring myself to believe that I'm back together with her again.

"I love you too."

And we remain wrapped in an embrace, caressed by the sun, our eyes shut, breathing in silence, setting aside all useless thoughts, savoring this moment that life has chosen to give us once again.

Then we go back inside and start fantasizing.

"Right here, I'd like to put a great big television set. Here, if you ask me, a very long sofa would be nice, and another one facing it for when we have friends over."

"My friends or your friends?"

"Our friends."

And we decide on the color of the curtains, the sad paintings we're going to get rid of, and how we're going to spend the summer here, with our children, and how deeply Babi will love Aurora.

"She'll be our baby girl. I'll help you with everything, and I'm sure that Gin will be proud of her daughter and of her borrowed mother."

And Babi has changed. She's still herself but even better now, and so we go on imagining small and large changes, the dishes in the kitchen, the towels for the bathroom, the flowers in the garden. And we walk through the living room, hand in hand, knowing that we will never lose each other again.

About the Author

Federico Moccia is one of Italy's publishing phenomenons, and his emotional stories have been compared to the works of Nicholas Sparks and John Green. The first two Babi and Step books were blockbuster bestsellers in Italy, spending three full consecutive years on the Nielsen bestseller list. His books have been published in fifteen languages worldwide and have sold over ten million copies, and there are feature films in Italian and Spanish based on the first two books in the trilogy.

Learn more at: FedericoMoccia.es
Twitter @FedericoMoccia
Facebook.com/FedericoMocciaOfficial

ABOUT THE TRANSLATOR

Antony Shugaar is a translator and writer who lived for many years in Italy, France, and Spain. He has received two translation fellowships from the National Endowment for the Arts. He has translated close to forty books for Europa Editions and has worked for many of the most prestigious publishers, trade and academic, in the US and the UK. He has translated extensively for the *New York Review of Books* and has written for the *New York Times*, the *Times of London*, and many other publications.